A New Year *in the* Keys

≈ A COCONUT KEY NOVEL ≈

Book 8

HOPE HOLLOWAY

A New Year in the Keys

Coconut Key Book 8

Copyright © 2024 Hope Holloway

This novel is a work of fiction. Any references to historical events, real people, or real locales are used fictitiously. Other names, characters, places, and incidents are the product of the author's imagination, and any resemblance to actual events or locales or persons, living or dead, is coincidental. All rights to reproduction of this work are reserved. No part of this publication may be reproduced, stored in or introduced into a retrieval system, or transmitted, in any form, or by any means (electronic, mechanical, photocopying, recording, or otherwise) without prior written permission from the copyright owner. Thank you for respecting the copyright. For permission or information on foreign, audio, or other rights, contact the author, hopehollowayauthor@gmail.com.

Cover designed by Kim Killion

If you're longing for an escape to paradise, step on to the gorgeous, sun-kissed sands of Coconut Key. With a cast of unforgettable characters and stories that touch every woman's heart, these delightful novels will make you laugh out loud, fall in love, and stand up and cheer...and then you'll want the next one *right this minute*.

A Secret in the Keys – Book 1
A Reunion in the Keys – Book 2
A Season in the Keys – Book 3
A Haven in the Keys – Book 4
A Return to the Keys – Book 5
A Wedding in the Keys – Book 6
A Promise in the Keys – Book 7
A New Year in the Keys - Book 8

For release dates, excerpts, news, and more, sign up to receive Hope Holloway's newsletter! Or visit www.hopeholloway.com or follow Hope on Instagram, Facebook, or BookBub!

CHAPTER ONE
BECK

"Happy New Year's Eve...Eve!" Lovely's voice echoed through the main floor of Coquina House, suitably soft for seven in the morning, but with enough joy that Beck stepped out of her owner's suite with a smile on her face.

"Good morning! You didn't have to come over so early." She walked toward her mother, arms outstretched for a hug. "You should have slept in. And you're all dressed and ready to roll, looking beautiful, I might add."

After a quick embrace, Lovely swept a hand over her flowered maxi dress, a staple from her always elegant wardrobe of beachwear.

"Sleep in when we have guests arriving? A B&B to run? A dream job alongside my darling daughter? Beckie! Coquina House is open and that means your partner has made the hundred-yard commute—barefoot in the sand, as one does—to do my share."

Beck gave her mother another impulsive hug, the enthusiasm she showered on their co-venture always better than coffee on mornings when they had new arrivals at Coquina House.

Although, right now, coffee sounded pretty good, too.

"I know we said we'd keep the place closed this week between Christmas and New Year's, but..." Beck put an arm around her mother's narrow shoulders and guided her toward the kitchen and the aroma that called like a siren to her senses.

"Oh, let me guess," Lovely teased as they walked through a spacious living area warmed by morning sun pouring over shiplapped walls and pale blue sofas. "Someone called to make a reservation, and they were so nice and heard so many good things about Coconut Key's newest and greatest B&B and there wasn't another place to stay this week in all of the Keys, so..." She took a breath. "You folded like a baby palm tree in a hurricane."

"Basically." Beck shrugged, not ashamed that she put her guests first. "Would you turn down a woman named Melody with a sister named Jazz coming all the way from California for a special vacation with their elderly father, Eddie?"

"Turn them down? Not for love or money," Lovely joked, using one of their favorite expressions as she rounded the island to her favorite seat at the end. There, she often commented, she could soak up an unobstructed view of the Atlantic Ocean through French doors and still watch over the kitchen activities.

"I don't know about love." Beck pulled their favorite mugs from the cabinet. "But the money? Whoa, this lady did not flinch when I quoted the 'seasonal-and-we're-supposed-to-be-closed-this-week' rate. She was absolutely relentless in her determination to stay here for two weeks."

"Which rooms?" Lovely asked.

"The sisters will take the whole third floor and apparently Elderly Eddie can still do stairs, so I put him in the Royal, since it has the best view on the second floor. All at a premium rate." She tapped the cups together. "Cheers, Momma. January's quota is made."

"Not surprised, Beckie." Lovely gave a happy sigh, looking like she belonged in the cheery, expansive kitchen. She'd certainly played a large part in the remodel they'd done last year, helping Beck transform their family-owned and somewhat dilapidated beach house into a cozy, coastal oasis for discerning guests. "As my darling great-granddaughter, Ava, would say, we have *slayed* the B&B world."

Smiling, Beck turned from the coffee pot to respond, but the sight of her mother seated in the sunshine brought her to a standstill. Good heavens, Beck loved the woman.

Despite finally admitting that she'd hit the milestone of seventy-five, Lovely Ames was still aptly named, beautiful from her braided silver hair right down to pink-tipped toes gracing bare feet.

Her only flaws—if they could be called that—were some laugh lines and crow's feet, and a few faded scars from a car accident that nearly took her life.

But that accident had given Lovely a fresh outlook on life, and subsequently gave Beck a whole *new* life. Spurred by what Lovely insisted had been a "near-death experience," she'd sought out her long-estranged "niece" and invited Beck to Coconut Key.

As their friendship developed, Beck had ultimately discovered that she was not Lovely's niece, but her daughter. Young and unexpectedly pregnant back in the sixties, Lovely had agreed to give up her baby to be raised by her older sister, Olivia, who was married but couldn't conceive.

Olivia had passed away seven years ago, taking the secret with her to the grave. She'd made it her life's mission to keep Beck from ever seeing her "Aunt" Lovely—especially since Beck looked so much like her biological mother.

But once the truth was out, nothing could stop the mother-daughter duo from forming a lasting bond. They'd been inseparable for nearly two years now, deepening their friendship, and building a life together in Coconut Key.

The highlight of that life was that they'd reimagined Lovely's waterfront childhood home into a B&B with five guest suites and some of the most stunning views in the Lower Keys.

And the icing on the cake? Two of Beck's daughters had relocated here, and her third, a law student at NYU, was currently home for the break.

"I know we have guests coming, but hasn't it just been a perfect holiday season so far?" Beck stepped to the oversized fridge to get the heavy cream they both loved. "Christmas Day was sheer perfection, with little Dylan so excited about Santa. And Peyton and Savannah both pregnant at the same time—who'd have guessed that? And Callie home from law school? I've loved every minute."

"It was dreamy," Lovely agreed. "You looked so happy surrounded by your three girls and your main squeeze."

Beck laughed softly at the term, since they always joked about calling Oliver her "boyfriend."

"And speaking of," Lovely added. "Josh seemed quite happy with Julie. I think they're serious."

"I agree and I'm delighted for him," Beck said, and meant it. She'd dated Josh, her childhood friend's brother, for quite a while, but they couldn't manage to take their friendship to the next level.

However, it sure hadn't taken her long to get there with Oliver Bradshaw. They'd just passed six months together and she was well and truly in love.

Lovely sighed, pulling Beck back to the conversation. "Peyton looks like she'll never make that January twenty-first due date. I half expected her to go into labor during Christmas dinner."

Beck smoothed her white jeans as she sat next to her mother to savor the first sip of coffee. "Doctor says she's already dilated, too. My firstborn is having her firstborn—and a girl!" She gave a playful shiver. "I just love that."

"And your second daughter is having her second child," Lovely added with a happy smile.

"She sure is carrying this one differently," Beck said, thinking of Savannah in a body-hugging red sweater dress that really showed her five-month baby bump. "Must be a girl, even though she refuses to let the doctor tell her."

Lovely nodded. "Also, it's different because she was on bed rest with Dylan."

"Now she's on *no rest* with seventeen-month-old Dylan," Beck joked, absently checking her watch. "I do hope these folks aren't too late this morning. It takes time to greet the new guests and get them acclimated and settled. Heather and the kids are back from Charleston, and I promised her we'd meet at the café after the breakfast rush to help her finalize some wedding plans. Can you join us?"

"Absolutely," Lovely said. "I can't believe Heather and Kenny want to get married at the end of the month and don't have a single thing planned yet."

"Second weddings for a widow and widower in their forties? They want to keep it small, just close family and friends, with a party at the Coquina Café after a church ceremony," Beck said. "Not a whole lot to plan, but we should help her nail down a few details. With the holidays, the babies, and her trip back to Charleston, I think their nuptials have gotten lost."

"We cannot let that happen," Lovely said. "Those two are a match made in heaven—literally, if you hear them together—and we need to honor and celebrate them. How can we move things along quickly here? I can change beds, place fresh flowers, and prepare the welcome tray."

"All done but the tray," Beck said. "And we have about forty-five minutes until their ETA. Let's enjoy this coffee."

"Everything's done? Already?"

She smiled. "Oliver helped me last night."

"Oh, that man. Doing my job and being perfect at it."

Beck laughed, unable to hide her contentment when it came to her amazing Aussie. A sixty-two-year-old widower with a toe-curling accent, Oliver had come last year to see his son, Nick, marry Beck's daughter, Savannah.

Beck and Oliver's connection and chemistry had been instant and unstoppable. He'd returned to Sydney, but before long, he'd come back...and, except for a week here and there over the last six months, he hadn't left.

In fact, he'd rented a small canal-front home, took to fishing like he was born for it, and organically folded into life in Coconut Key.

Beck couldn't help but get hopeful that he would make this island his permanent residence. He still owned a home in Sydney, though he'd put it on the market, and a small beach house in a place called Wollongong that he couldn't bear to part with.

Recently, he'd talked a lot about splitting his time between the U.S. and Sydney, leaving Beck to wonder where that left them exactly.

"You know," Lovely said as she rubbed her thumb along the mug handle. "You're talking about a part-time cook? What if we considered a full-time housekeeper? Or a manager onsite?"

Beck drew back, jaw loose. "You want to replace me, partner?"

"I want to *free* you," she said.

"I'm not a prisoner, and if I am?" She gestured toward the sunny surroundings. "I do not mind my cell."

"But you can't ever leave."

"Of course I can."

"Not for any length of time," Lovely countered. "You think I can't do the heavy lifting because I'm seventy-five years old."

That was true, but Beck didn't like to remind Lovely of her age, since she'd always been a bit cagey about it. Probably because she'd so young when Beck was born. Plus, she didn't look, act, or think like she was a day over sixty.

"I don't *want* you to do the heavy lifting," Beck said. "You gave me this beautiful home and business when I was reeling from an awful divorce and a mid-life kick in the teeth. I'll do the hard work."

"You financed the remodel," Lovely reminded her.

"Actually, the awful divorce did. Lovely…" She gave her mother a suspicious side-eye. "What exactly are you getting at?"

She angled her head and made a face. "I'm…doing a favor for Oliver."

"A favor? What kind of favor?"

"He asked me if I could urge you to take that trip to Australia with him. He's aching to take you there. He wants to show you his country and introduce you to the friends he left behind." Lovely tsked. "I know you won't go and leave me to handle this place alone, even if I *could* do it in my sleep."

She couldn't change five beds in a morning, Beck thought, or haul loads of laundry up the stairs. She couldn't hustle down to Coquina Café at dawn for scones and pastries. But Lovely's heart was in the right place and Beck loved her for it.

"I told him we'll go next summer, when the season dies down."

"There's no season in the Keys," Lovely said. "We could be as busy in July as we are in October. Even busier."

"And he recruited you to get me to go?" Beck laughed, shaking her head. "I told him I can't leave this place now, Lovely. Not only because of this business, but Peyton's baby is coming any day, then Savannah's four months later. I don't want to leave now, and I sure don't want to dump full responsibility for this place on you. Oh, there's my phone."

Happy to change the subject, she pushed off the stool and gestured to the counter where she'd left her cell. "Could be the musical sisters and Elderly Eddie. Or Peyton's water broke."

"Oh, true," Lovely agreed. "How old does one have to be to qualify for elderly, anyway? Please tell me it's ninety or above."

Beck bit back a laugh at that, turning her phone over to read the text message.

"Yep, it's Melody Davidson. They just passed Little Torch Key and they're coming to the bridge into Coconut Key. ETA is fifteen minutes."

"Okay, let's get that tray done." Lovely slid off the stool. "What about the fruit bowl? And is it too early for Welcome Mimosas?"

"For what they're paying?" Beck lifted a brow. "We should break out the Veuve."

Lovely laughed. "You run a great business, Beckie."

"*We* run it, Lovely," Beck reminded her. "You get the fruit—it's all cut in the fridge—and I'll pour the orange juice and make the tray."

"On it like a bonnet," Lovely sang, taking one final sip before diving into her role. "It's time for *The Beck and Lovely Show*, morning edition."

Beck smiled at her mother, a swelling of contentment in her heart for their partnership and business. Yes, she loved Oliver, but right now, there was nothing else she'd rather be doing and no one else she'd want to do it with.

CHAPTER TWO
LOVELY

Oh, my. Eddie was certainly not...*elderly*.

He might be in the same seventh decade as Lovely, yes. But based on the graceful way he climbed out of the compact SUV, sporting a surprisingly thick white ponytail hanging between his shoulder blades, and a fitted T-shirt and jeans that could have been on a younger man? Elderly Eddie was winning the war against Father Time.

Staying back in the shade of the veranda, Lovely stood next to their signature welcome tray, filled with orange juice flutes, an open bottle of champagne, and fruit kebabs garnished with bright pink hibiscus blooms.

Beck walked down the three steps to the recently paved circular drive to greet the new arrivals. Her wheat-toned hair fluttered over her shoulders in the breeze, her shoulders square with pride and confidence.

"Welcome to Coquina House," she called to her guests, her voice, as always, exuding joy for the role as proprietress of this one-of-a-kind establishment.

Instantly, three heads whipped around to look at Beck. For a few beats, they were perfectly silent, staring at her, maybe not even seeing Lovely in the porch shadows.

"Hello," Beck said. "It's so nice to have you here."

For a good five seconds, they still didn't say a word, taking Lovely's attention from her daughter to the strangers.

Did they speak English? Were they at the right place? Why were they looking at Beck like she was an alien?

Lovely's gaze moved from the silver-haired man to the two women. One looked a little younger than Beck, maybe fifty or so, with a gorgeous mane of dark hair that had matching white streaks dramatically framing her face. Her eyes were midnight dark with an almond shape that, along with her flowered dress, made Lovely think of Hawaiian sunsets and luaus.

The other looked to be in her early forties, if that, with a sleek blond bob and sparkling blue eyes. She was sharp, slender, and dressed in a crisp white top and white jeans that looked like they had never met a speck of dirt.

Sisters? They didn't even look remotely alike. But they did appear...shellshocked.

"Is one of you Melody?" Beck finally asked with an uncomfortable chuckle, obviously noticing the awkward silence as well. "Or have you come to the wrong place?"

"Oh, gosh! I'm so sorry." The dark-haired woman came closer, extending her hand. "I...I just...yes, I'm Melody Davidson and you...must be Rebecca."

She cooed the name with a subtle sense of amazement, no doubt because Beck had been so kind in opening the B&B to them this week.

"Not very many people call me that," Beck said. "It's Beck. Beck Foster." She shook the woman's hand. "Welcome to Coquina House," she said again.

"Thank you... I..." She appeared to be speechless again, when the other woman stepped in.

"Beck, hello. I'm Jasmine Sylvester, Melody's sister. Please call me Jazz. And this..." She shook Beck's hand, then gestured toward the man who stood on the other side of the small vehicle.

He slowly raised his sunglasses and, even from this far away, Lovely could see light blue eyes pinned on Beck.

"Eddie Sylvester," he said. "I'm the, uh, father."

Very slowly, he came around the front of the car to greet her, staring at her like he'd never actually met a woman who owned a B&B before.

What a strange crew, Lovely thought, hanging back to watch the scene unfold.

"Beck," he said. "It's...wonderful."

What was? The house? The weather? All of Coconut Key?

"Hello, Eddie," Beck said, offering her hand in greeting.

He took it, held it for a second, then drew her in for a very light, quick, but unexpected hug.

"Oh!" Beck laughed. "So nice to—"

He inched back, looking just a little sheepish. "Sorry. I'm a hugger."

"It's fine," Beck assured him. "Most people don't hug when they arrive, but they always do when they leave Coquina House. You're just getting a jump on things."

She gracefully stepped back and swept a hand toward the three-story Key West-style bed-and-breakfast. "Coquina House will be your home during your stay in Coconut Key," she announced, the well-practiced words easily covering the awkward exchange.

To help her, Lovely stepped forward to be introduced.

"This is my mother and partner—"

They all gasped and looked up at her.

"Your *mother*?" Melody said, her voice rising in disbelief.

"I know, she doesn't look old enough for that," Beck said easily, the picture of class in front of these admittedly odd people. "But she brings the history and knows everything you ever want to know about Coconut Key. She grew up right here in Coquina House and now lives in a beach cottage you passed on the way down Coquina Court."

As Lovely came down the top stair into the morning sun, she caught a look passing between the two sisters, rich with a silent message she couldn't begin to decipher.

"All true," she said lightly. "My parents built this house, and I lived here with my sister, Olivia—"

"Who is dead, right?" the blond sister asked.

Lovely blinked in shock. "Why, yes. Seven years now. How did you..."

"We've researched the house," Melody said quickly. "I wanted to know where we would be staying and there's quite a bit about your family on file. We thought we read that, um, Olivia was Rebecca's mother. So, that's not you?"

Beck drew back, clearly as mystified by the grilling as Lovely. They'd never been asked about any of this before. With few exceptions, they kept the complex and private story of how and why Beck grew up thinking Lovely was her aunt entirely to themselves.

"Olivia raised me," Beck said, obviously making one of those exceptions now. "But Lovely is my mother. I'm not sure why that—"

"You're Lovely!" Melody and Jazz exclaimed in perfect unison.

"Lovely?" Eddie nearly croaked the word. "That's your name?"

"Yes, it is," she replied, having had just about enough of

this interrogation. "I am Lovely Ames, co-owner of Coquina House, lifelong resident of Coconut Key, and mother to this beautiful lady right here."

Was *that* enough to satisfy their curiosity?

"Dad," Jazz muttered to her father. "Her name is Lovely."

"Tell her, Dad," Melody said, jabbing him with her elbow. "Go ahead. Tell her."

Somebody needed to tell her *something*, Lovely decided. This line of questioning had gone beyond awkward, past rude, and into intrusive.

For a few seconds, Eddie stared at her, his summer sky blue gaze locked on her.

"I have a tattoo that says…" he finally whispered, lifting up the sleeve of his T-shirt. "Look."

Despite his tanned skin, Lovely could see the softest flush on his rugged cheeks as he angled his arm so she could read the words *Her Name Was Lovely* with a single musical note next to it.

She blinked, a melody suddenly playing in her head. "Like the song?" she asked. "Electric Breeze?"

His jaw loosened. "You *know* that?"

"I loved the song, for obvious reasons," she admitted. "I guess you did, too."

"He wrote it," Melody said. "And was the lead singer of Electric Breeze. Eddie Sly."

"Oh, wow." Lovely felt a huge smile pull, resentment fading in the face of someone who'd given her hours of pleasure. "I didn't know the names of the band members because…"

His eyes twinkled with warmth as her voice trailed off.

"Because we had one hit and one hit only," he said with a humble laugh. "But so few people know the song, so that's cool."

"I want to say...1968?" she guessed.

"And you'd be right."

"Oh, I think you were three, Beckie," she said, turning to her. "I sang that song to you a lot."

"You still do," Beck joked. "She's got it on all her oldies playlists, too."

"Thank you," he said, still smiling at Lovely. "Thank you so much."

"Me?" Lovely scoffed. "I count *Her Name Was Lovely* as one of my top five. Don't make me sing it because I know every word."

Eddie laughed at that, his eyes crinkling, so maybe he did look older than he had at first glance. "That's amazing. Really."

"It's an honor to have you here," Beck said. "All of you. But let's get out of the sun and comfortable, shall we? I can give you the tour and get you all settled. We have juice and fruit and, for the adventurous, champagne."

"You ladies go in," Eddie said, taking a step back. "I'll get the bags and...get the bags. Yeah. And, uh, Mel and Jazz?"

They turned to look at him.

"That's enough about my past, okay? We're just here for a couple of weeks of relaxation and vacation. Don't bombard these ladies with any more questions." He tipped his head in apology. "I'm afraid my daughters are very protective of me and my fleeting brush with fame. They like to make sure they know all the players when we travel somewhere new, so they end up with just enough information to be dangerous. We didn't mean to pry."

"It's fine," Beck assured him as she led the other two women upstairs. "We're honored you cared enough to look it all up."

Still, Lovely thought, it did seem like a lot of digging for a man who had just one hit song in his life, even if that tune was near and dear to her.

Eddie studied her for a moment as he walked to the back of the SUV, a curious look on his face as he passed.

"I can't believe you know that song," he said, lifting up the hatchback.

"Sometimes strangers sing it to me," she admitted on a laugh. "There's a guy in the Publix deli who belts out the chorus every time I buy roast beef."

Eddie snorted a laugh. "I'll have to go do a duet with him while I'm here."

"Oh, old Deli Dave would love that."

"Maybe you can take me to meet him sometime," he said, hoisting out a bag. "If you're, you know, not busy."

Was the man asking her out? Well, to the Publix deli. Not exactly a dinner date.

"I'd be happy to," she said. "I, uh, better get inside. Are you good with the bags? I can take something, if you like."

"No, no, please. You..." He looked hard at her again, his blue eyes warm and undeniably penetrating. "You fit your name, Lovely."

"Oh." She felt a flush rise. "Thank you."

With another smile, she headed up the stairs, her cheeks warm and her smile wide. Had Eddie of the Electric Breeze just flirted with her? That was...interesting.

As she got to the top stair, she turned to see him standing behind the gaping hatchback, his head back, his eyes closed, and both hands clasped over his chest.

Saying a prayer? Thanking God that someone remembered his one big hit? Or...

She didn't know. But there was something very peculiar about the man that tweaked her spirit. Peculiar and...vaguely familiar.

Well, she'd probably listened to *Her Name Was Lovely* a million times in her life, pretending it had been written for her. Maybe she'd seen his picture somewhere...close to sixty years ago.

Beck was right—she did have the song included in the "Sixties and Seventies" playlist that her great-granddaughter had made her and taught her to use on her phone.

She loved the music from that era, and that song always struck her as a bit out of touch with its time, a bubblegum ballad in the era of angsty folk and protest music.

Maybe that was why the Electric Breeze never had another hit.

Now that she'd thought about it, the earworm hummed in her head...taking her back.

Stars in the sky, stars in her eyes...girl in my arms, moon on the rise.

A secret kiss, I was never the same...I can't forget her beautiful name.

That always reminded her of—

"Lovely?" Beck called, waiting for Lovely to reach her in the entryway. "Help with the tour? You add such color and glimpses into the past."

"Of course, Beckie." She slid her arm around her precious daughter.

The song always reminded her of the night she made a big mistake that turned out to be an even bigger blessing.

She gave Beck a spontaneous kiss on the cheek.

"I know," Beck whispered, out of earshot of the two women who'd gone into the kitchen. "Nosy as all get out, aren't they? They just asked me about my three daughters!"

Lovely drew back. "What did they do, hire a private investigator?"

"Apparently, Eddie was a big record producer and owns a label. Famous people can be weird, I guess."

"Nick's famous," Lovely said, referring to Savannah's husband, who might be a retired actor, but qualified as a household name. "He doesn't do a Google search every time they stay at a hotel."

"Maybe he does," Beck said, tugging her closer. "Let's move this along and get these people checked in, give them a list of local activities and a lock code. I want to skedaddle before they start talking about my divorce next."

Lovely agreed, but something deep inside felt unsettled by their arrival, and she couldn't quite shake the feeling.

CHAPTER THREE
EDDIE

"Dad!" Melody practically exploded into his room, with Jazz hot on her heels.

"Close the door," he insisted, looking behind them for signs of the mother-daughter duo who'd rocked his entire world.

"I thought you were going to tell her!" Melody exclaimed.

"Tell her?" he sputtered. "You two practically grilled the women on their family tree and attacked poor Lovely for the sin of still being alive!"

"Well, we thought Rebecca's mother was dead. We read her obituary. Olivia Mitchell. Dead as a doornail." Melody turned to Jazz. "You said Lovely could be a nickname for Olivia."

"Could be, but isn't." Jazz dropped into a chair in a corner sitting area. "Cool it and think, you two. There is definitely some confusion in the facts. Are you sure you read all that Ancestry.com stuff correctly, Mel?"

"Every word, and then Lark dug through every database and newspaper and real estate record, and my daughter is nothing if not thorough," she said. "So Lovely is alive. It doesn't really change anything, does it?"

"Oh, but it does." Eddie walked toward the sliding glass doors that led to a small second-floor balcony, his gaze locked on the blue water beyond but only seeing a face...from his far and distant past. Two faces, actually.

Those of the women connected to him inexorably by a one-night stand he hadn't thought about in decades...until his granddaughter, Lark, showed up at his door, waving her phone, and announcing he had another daughter named Rebecca.

"I think it changes everything," he said.

"How?" Melody asked. "We came here to meet Rebecca Foster, a woman we believe is our half-sister and your daughter, based on the fact that my daughter found a perfect match to our paternal DNA on Ancestry.com. The mother was supposed to be dead but—"

"But now she's alive," he said, turning to her. "And who knows what she told her daughter about her conception? She might have married and claimed her husband was Beck's father."

"She might have," Jazz conceded. "But in this day and age, with all the DNA testing available and the databases giving access to customers? Those things don't stay secret. My firm funded a start-up dedicated to this very thing and I know the statistics. There are biological reunions going on all over the world as we speak. Hundreds of babies from the same sperm donor, twins separated at birth, and babies given up for adoption finding siblings online. It's very common."

"Common, maybe, but not easy," Eddie replied. "All those babies have stories, all those siblings have lives, and all the parents have reputations to protect."

"And you're protecting hers, aren't you, Dad?" Melody guessed.

Of course he was. "Look, when I thought Lovely was dead, I was prepared to meet Rebecca Foster. My plan was to determine what she'd been told, if anything, about her conception. I'd either keep that story out of respect for Lovely, or share the truth if it seemed appropriate. If the door was open to get to know her, great. But I didn't plan to blow in here and wreck Lovely's life. Or Rebecca's, for that matter."

"That's sweet, Dad, but her conception is ancient history," Mel said. "Honestly, no one cares that two strangers met at a rock festival and hooked up in a tent fifty-seven years ago. The shock value is zero nowadays."

"Please, Mel." He shot her a harsh look. "I do not want to march downstairs and announce I'm Beck's biological father."

"Why not?" Mel demanded.

Of course, he understood she believed in the truth at all costs...but the cost *might* be too high for Lovely to pay.

Even nearly six decades later, he instinctively sensed a few things about the girl named Lovely who'd inspired his one big hit. She'd been a young, reckless virgin who'd sneaked off to a concert, gone too far too fast with a boy who'd shared a little pot. She'd run off early the next morning without saying goodbye or telling him her last name.

He suspected she'd gone way out of her comfort zone that night, and disappeared so she didn't have to face the shame—or him.

Except they'd conceived a child. So her life had probably been turned inside-out by a pregnancy he hadn't even known about. She'd lived with the consequences of the night, and he'd paid none. And she deserved far more than raised eyebrows or crass jokes about "hooking up" in a tent while The Dave Clark Five crooned *Catch Us If You Can* at the other end of a parking lot in Key West.

And now she was very much alive—vibrant, in fact—and still had an angel's smile and unforgettable eyes, just like he'd written in that song.

"So, what do you want to do, Dad?" Jazz asked, studying him carefully.

"I don't know," he admitted. "I know what I *don't* want to do, though. I won't drag that beautiful woman through the mud of her past, publicly or privately. Not yet. I have no desire to cause whitewater or heartbreak. I wanted to meet my third daughter but not open old wounds with her mother."

"Your third daughter who doesn't look anything like you but is a carbon copy of Lovely," Mel noted, leaning back on the bed, braced on her elbows. "What is it about your DNA that always takes a backseat?"

His eyes shuttered as he refused to answer the question, even though it wasn't that far from the truth.

Melody, ruled by her feelings for every one of her fifty years, was so like her mother, whose passionate Hawaiian roots made her spontaneous, emotional, and willing to risk anything for someone or something she loved.

And Jasmine, now forty-three—but she'd acted that age since she was a toddler—was a study in rationality and common sense, like *her* mother, a scientist with a crazy high IQ.

"The way I see it?" Jazz looked from one to the other.

"We already provided a logical reason for our interrogation about their family and covered our initial shock."

"Sort of," Eddie said, having clearly seen the dismay on Lovely's face.

"What's your point?" Mel pressed her sister.

"My point is we don't have to tell them anything. We could actually let the whole thing go. No harm, no—"

"No!" Melody shot up. "She's our *sister*, Jazz! We have to tell her! I will not leave without the truth on the table. And she has daughters who are our nieces. And at least one grandchild! So many people who share our blood!"

"Mel, this is not your call," Eddie said softly, used to refereeing between his polar-opposite daughters. "I agreed to come with you two on this mission with one caveat—I make the decisions. If and when we drop this bomb on these ladies, it will be in the most gracious and kind way possible and after we've determined that Lovely wants the story to come out."

"But we came here with the explicit purpose of telling Rebecca Foster that the online DNA sites confirmed that we are her half-sisters," Melody said.

"The DNA could be wrong," he said.

"Not a chance," Jazz said. "It never is. Plus, based on her birthday, Rebecca Mitchell, married name Foster, was conceived around the third week of March, which, in 1965, was the date of a certain music festival in Key West. Not to mention there's a perfect paternal DNA match. And remember, they could find that information as easily as we did. But whoever submitted their tests never even opened the message I sent."

"So you can't be sure Beck is—"

"Yes, we're sure." Jazz tapped her phone, reading a screen. "Her name was listed and then it was just a matter of finding her, which took a little digging, but we did it. Rebecca Mitchell Foster turned fifty-seven on May twentieth. Her mother—at least legally—was Olivia Ames Mitchell, a widow who remarried twenty years after her first husband's death, then divorced him less than five years later. Rebecca spent most of her life in the Atlanta area, has three daughters, divorced a year or so ago, moved here and opened Coquina House."

He huffed out a breath. "People's lives are an open book—er, phone—now."

"Welcome to the twenty-first century, Pops," Jazz said, her favorite nickname for him taking some of the bite out of all the information she was dumping on him. "So, what are we going to do? Drop the bomb, play it cool, or just have a nice vacay in the Keys with some sunshine and sleep? God knows I need both."

He didn't answer, but unlatched the sliding glass door and inched it open, stepping outside. Instantly, he was assaulted by balmy air that seemed absolutely dense compared to the dry breezes of northern California.

Mel joined him, putting a gentle hand on his arm. "You're reeling, aren't you?"

He smiled down at her. Yes, she was right-brained to a fault, but that made this beautiful woman deeply empathetic and wildly good-hearted.

"Spinning like I could fall off this balcony," he said.

"Well, don't. If you want to keep the past buried, then I'll respect that. But Beck is about to have me as a friend, whether she wants me or not. Because she is my big sister, and I've never had one of those."

Smiling, he put his arm around her and gave a squeeze. "I get that. Let's just give it some time, okay? No more probing questions but we'll get to know these ladies."

Jazz joined them, stepping to Eddie's other side. "Honestly? You have the truth inked on your arm, Dad. How many women named Lovely are there?"

"You'd be surprised," he said on a dry laugh, thinking of how many he'd met over the years. None of them made him take notice...until today.

Because *this* Lovely? She was the one he'd written about.

"She might put two and two together," Melody said. "Most people know Ned is a nickname for Edward. And maybe she saw pictures of you when your song became famous and said, 'Look, there's my tent guy.'"

He cringed at the thought of being her "tent guy."

"You know as well as anyone that despite my hotshot agent changing my name from Ned Sylvester to Eddie Sly, I never made the cover of *Tiger Beat*," he reminded her. "The Electric Breeze broke up a year after that song came out, and there would be no reason for me to ever be on her radar."

Until now.

"And the more I think about Olivia raising her?" Jazz added. "It makes sense if you consider when this happened. Yes, the world was changing in the decade of free love, but this is a small community. Lovely was, what? Eighteen?"

"I hope," he muttered.

"Well, it was 1965 and teenage pregnancy was considered a scandal. I bet Lovely's sister raised the baby as her own, saving Lovely's—and probably the whole family's—reputation. Somehow, sometime, the truth came out and now

Lovely and Beck don't try to hide it." She shrugged. "Makes total sense to me."

"We don't know any of that," Eddie said, uncertainty wrapping his chest in a vise. "But here's what I'd like to do, girls."

They shared a smile, as they always did when he called them that.

"There's no rush," he said. "We're here for two weeks. I'd like to get to know them both and when the time is right, it won't have to be an explosion that destroys their world. Until the time is right, there will be no...whisper of truth."

"Ooh. *Whisper of Truth*." Mel's dark brows rose. "Sounds like an Eddie Sly tune. Write it, Dad."

For a split second, he almost said yes to that. But he just blew out a breath. It had been a long time since he'd been able to get past the first line of a song, even with a title that good.

"I'm retired," he volleyed back. She rolled her eyes, knowing better than anyone that it was just an excuse for his writer's block.

"So, is that our plan?" Jazz asked after a beat. "We go down and surreptitiously interview them? Get them to reveal everything without knowing who we are? I can do that."

Mel nodded slowly. "It's kind of subterfuge-y, but I'm okay with that. Lark would love it," she added, smiling at the thought of her twenty-six-year-old daughter, who'd set this whole earthquake in motion.

"We won't *interview* these ladies," Eddie said. "We will talk. We'll build bridges. We connect and then...we'll see."

"We're not doing any bridge-building today," Jazz reminded them. "They left."

"What?" Mel's jaw dropped. "They just ditched us?"

Jazz laughed. "We're not guests in their home waiting to be entertained," she said. "They own the B&B. They check us in, show us our rooms, ply us with mimosas and coffee and those delicious baked things. They said they'd be gone with family for the day."

Mel groaned. "More family we *have* to meet."

"They gave us a list of things to do and see, told us where to rent bikes, and showed us the beach." Jazz pointed to the water. "Let's go there now, shall we? I don't get a lot of vacations, and I want to do *whatever* people do when they vacate their offices."

"But Rebecca *lives* here," Mel insisted, ignoring their conversation. "She should be around for us to...not interview."

"Beck," Eddie corrected. "She specifically asked to be called Beck."

"You're already defending her." Mel grinned at him. "Father of the Year, I tell you."

He just shook his head, smiling at her.

"Then let's ride bikes or go to the beach," Jazz said. "We are in the Florida Keys. First time for all of us, right?"

Eddie gave her a look. "Not me," he reminded her. "I was at a rock festival in Key West in March of 1965."

They laughed at that, and Mel slid her arm around his waist. "I've got an idea, Dad. Let's go to Key West. It's fifteen minutes down the road and a tourist mecca. We can see Beck and Lovely when we get home."

He nodded, searching her face and seeing—as always—the memory of Kailani Kahue, his first true love. But Lani was gone now, ashes fluttered into the Pacific, mixed with his tears. Her spirit lived on in Melody, and his grandchildren, Lark and Kai.

"Thanks, Mel. You're the best."

"What am I?" Jazz cracked. "Chopped liver?"

He turned to her and reached out a hand, and like he had with his other daughter, he only saw her mother, Victoria Swann, still one of his best friends, even though their marriage ended years ago.

"You, my dear, are the brains of the operation."

"I'm the heart," Mel chimed in.

"That leaves you as our soul, Pops." Jazz pointed at him. "And we'll follow your lead. Until you say so, we won't utter one...what did you call it? Whisper of truth."

He squeezed each of his daughter's hands in his. Ooh, it *was* a good song title.

"You know, I might have written a lot of songs over the years, but my two greatest works of art are right here."

"And Beck," Jazz said softly.

"And somehow we're not supposed to tell her she's our sister." Melody groaned. "It's impossible, Dad."

"Nothing's impossible, Mel. You will not tell her. You will not imply the truth to her. You will not."

She curled her lip. "Fine. I'll do my best."

Eddie knew that keeping a secret wasn't impulsive Melody's strong suit. So he'd have to move quickly to breathe his *whisper of truth*.

When the girls left, he changed for the beach, and couldn't help himself. He pulled out his notebook, stared at the page, and grabbed a pen.

Green eyes...how they glint.
Could I ever...give a hint.

"Oh, please," he muttered, ripping out the page and balling up the dreck.

But he could imagine how Lovely's eyes would flash if he would...whisper the truth.

Part of him was terrified. The other part? Could not wait.

CHAPTER FOUR
BECK

Beck walked out to the shaded terrace of the Coquina Café, barely noticing the turquoise and navy water that stretched from the sea oats to the horizon. Instead, her attention went right to the only people out there—her two older daughters, standing side by side against the white railing, deep in a lively conversation.

Normally, this in-demand seating area of the Coquina Café was packed with locals and tourists enjoying the diner delights made by Beck's closest childhood friend, Jessie Donovan. But today, Jessie had closed off the whole section for privacy to plan a wedding.

If all went according to that plan, Heather, Jessie's younger half-sister—also her assistant manager and pastry chef—would marry Beck's son.

"Are you discussing names?" Beck guessed, smiling from one very pregnant daughter to one who was getting rounder by the day.

"I'm trying to get her to sit before her water breaks." Savannah nudged her older sister toward a chair. "Are you sure you're not having twins? Maybe they missed one hiding in the uterus shadows."

Peyton looked across the table at Beck, making a face. "Permission to kill her?"

Beck laughed, comfortable in the knowledge that any animosity that had kept these sisters from being close as they grew up had melted in the Keys sunshine over the past two years.

"You'll have your revenge in four months, Peyton," Beck said. "She'll be wide and waddling and you'll be bouncing sweet baby Sanchez."

"Baby Sanchez!" Savannah grunted, dropping her head back. "Pick a name for this girl already. I can't decide on a girl's name until I know you haven't taken Danielle."

"Danielle?"

"After Dad," she said dryly.

Peyton snorted at the very idea, both of them having forgiven but not forgotten what their father put the family through when he left Beck for his law partner. Today, Dan was single, buying fancy cars, and barely speaking to his daughters. Beck, on the other hand, was living her best life in Coconut Key, with these two in her life on a daily basis.

Sometimes revenge really was sweet.

"You won't call her by the right name anyway," Peyton said. "You'll hang a handle on her like Baldy McFatFace and that's what she'll be forever, just like Dylan, AKA French Frye."

"Huh. Baldy McFatFace." Savannah nodded. "That has a ring to it."

"Please, Mom?" Peyton fake whined. "Make her stop."

Savannah laughed and gave her a sisterly hug before dropping down in the seat between them.

"I'll take it easy on account of your hormones, Peyote. And as far as li'l Frenchie, I didn't make that up. I honestly think it was Ava. Speaking of..." She looked around. "Is the teen contingent coming? After all, it's Ava's father and Maddie's mother who are getting married. And those two girls are joined at the hip—unlike their parents, who haven't joined anything because...the Bible."

She didn't roll her eyes, though, which Beck appreciated. Their love for their older brother, Kenny, and his fiancée, Heather, included an abiding respect for the couple's faith.

"I think the girls are on their way," Beck said.

As the sliding door opened, they all turned to see Callie, Beck's youngest daughter, coming out to join them.

"Hello, fam." She gave Beck a hug, blew kisses to her sisters, and pulled out a chair.

As she sat down, she tossed back some of the silky black hair that always reminded Beck that her youngest daughter—surprising them a full ten years after Savannah—favored Dan both physically and in her relentless dedication to her future law career.

But Callie had chosen to come to Coconut Key, not Atlanta, for her law school winter break, which Beck considered yet another win.

"Mom, Lovely says you have new guests," Callie said. "See why I wanted to stay in Savannah's guest house? I knew you'd take some stragglers in at the B&B and I'd never have the quiet I need to get a head start on reading my Con Law text book before next semester."

Now Savannah rolled her eyes. "So glad 'ridiculous overachiever' isn't a generational curse we all have."

"They're not exactly stragglers," Beck said. "But they are very, uh, interesting."

"Ooh, do tell," Peyton requested, absently rubbing her giant baby bump with one hand.

"Well, *he* is none other than Eddie Sly, the lead singer for Electric Breeze."

She got three blank stares in response.

"The band that recorded the song *Her Name Was Lovely*," Beck explained. "And with him are his extremely inquisitive and too-well-informed grown daughters, named Melody and Jazz."

Savannah almost choked on a sip of water. "I don't know where to start with that one. Melody and Jazz? And Dad's a singer in some lame band?"

"Wait. Are you talking about that 'Lovely' song that Lovely has on every playlist?" Peyton asked, incredulous.

"He sang it and wrote it," Beck said. "And get this—they got out of the car and were shocked to find out Lovely was alive, confused because they thought my mother was named Olivia, and that she'd died. Oh, and they knew I had three daughters."

Callie drew back. "How? Is it on your website or in your marketing materials?"

"No. They claimed they couldn't be too careful, with the famous father and all, and had to know the backgrounds of the B&B owners."

"I call foul," Callie said, pulling out her phone.

"I don't know if it was foul," Beck said, "but it was a first. Does Nick do background checks when he stays somewhere, Savannah? He's a genuine celebrity and this guy is an admitted one-hit wonder."

Savannah shook her head. "He sometimes checks in under a fake name—or he did when his career was thriving. But these days, his star status is diminished, since he's a stay-at-home dad whose current claim to fame is directing the high school play for the second year in a row."

"It doesn't make sense," Peyton said. "What does finding

out if someone's mother is dead or alive tell you about the management at a B&B? Why would they care?"

"Because they're scam artists," Callie said with a shocking amount of authority as she looked at her phone.

Beck gasped. "What?"

"They could be stealing your identity or casing the B&B to rob you blind or planning not to pay their bill," Callie said, rattling off the awful-sounding options like she was reading a menu. "The possibilities for fraud are endless."

"Fraud..." Beck felt her heart climb into her throat. "What do you mean? They're alone at Coquina House now. Should I be worried?"

"I doubt they're cleaning out the silver," Savannah said, turning to Callie, who was already madly tapping her phone screen. "Looking up case law on B&B scams?"

"No. Doing our own background check." Callie tapped her screen. "Eddie Sly, you said? And..." She shuddered. "Electric Breeze? Seriously?"

"It was the sixties," Beck said, as if that explained everything.

"Okay, okay, I got something here." She swiped up. "His real name is Edward Sylvester. He's seventy-six years old. This your guy?"

They all leaned in to see a picture of the same man Beck had just met, wearing a tux on a red carpet. Hair pulled back, giant smile, and the camera caught those distinctly blue eyes.

"That's him. He really doesn't look seventy-six."

"He's kind of handsome, in that silver fox way," Peyton mused.

"Save us from Harrison Ford with a ponytail," Savannah murmured, sitting back to let Callie continue reading.

"He founded, and is currently chairman emeritus of, a pop label called Sly Records, based in San Francisco. He retired from day-to-day responsibilities six years ago, handed over the reins to his oldest daughter, Melody Ono Davidson—"

"Like Yoko?" Savannah asked.

"Do you mind?" Callie shot her a death glare. "Melody is fifty years old, the daughter from his first marriage to Kailani Kahue."

"Yes, she looked Hawaiian," Beck said.

"Kailani passed away in 1975," she read.

Peyton made a face. "Aw, sad."

"He rebounded," Callie told them. "He married ice cream heiress Victoria Swann in 1977—"

"Mmm." Savannah leaned into Peyton. "Ice cream."

Callie's eyes shuttered as she powered on in the face of their jokes. "He had a daughter, Jasmine Swann Sylvester, in 1980, and then divorced. He co-owns a small winery near Napa with his ex, and lives on a ranch outside of San Francisco recently valued at—*whoa*—seven million smackeroos."

"Sounds like *Lifestyles of the Rich and Famous*," Peyton said.

"*Real Housewives of Northern California*," Savannah added.

But Beck was amazed. "How did you *get* all that, Callie?"

"Legal database from when I worked for Dad. I saved the login and use it all the time." She held up the phone. "But only the free basic service. For twenty-five bucks, we can find out where he banks, who his doctors are, and what kind of cars he drives. Level Two will give us the legal filings on his divorce, how much he owes on his credit cards, and what he ordered from Amazon last year."

"Good grief," Savannah said. "What's Level Three? Account passwords and underwear preferences?"

Callie lifted a brow. "Close. But it costs a fortune."

Beck swept her hand, uncomfortable with the conversation. "He's just a very careful and successful record executive."

"Wait, wait." Peyton tapped the table in front of Callie. "Mom said two daughters. Tell us about the one named Jazz."

Callie clicked the phone with lightning speed, her dark eyes narrowed in focus. "I got a little on both of them. Melody is married to Gideon Davidson, the chief operating officer of Sly Records. She has two kids, Lark and Kai, both also employed at the label. This Mel?"

She showed them an image, and Beck nodded, instantly recognizing the beautiful woman.

"I liked her," she said, studying her dark eyes and the eye-catching silver streaks. "She had a lot of personality and spunk. The other one was a little cooler."

"Jazz Sylvester," Callie said, back to reading. "Forty-three years old, a partner at Sullivan Mease Venture Capital." Her brows shot up. "Nice. She's a UCLA undergrad, has an MBA *and* a law degree from Stanford, and was a software engineer at Modesto Technologies."

"Smarty-pants," Savannah muttered.

"And she's taken no less than a dozen companies public in the last three years." Callie let out a whistle. "I might be in love."

Savannah laughed. "You're so easily impressed, Cal."

"These people are impressive," Beck said. "Too rich and successful to be scam artists. And it explains why no one flinched at my astronomical holiday rates."

"You should have booked a Level One investigation and doubled the cost," Savannah cracked.

"I would never do that," Beck said. "The research or the price gouging. In fact, I don't like this conversation. So they did some checking on us. That's how they roll and that's fine."

"But they were confounded by the fact that Lovely was alive," Peyton insisted. "Why would they know that or care?"

"Whose name is on the tax rolls as the owner of Coquina House?" Callie asked. "Lovely or Olivia?"

"Mine, now," Beck said. "But Granny Sue left it to both Olivia and Lovely. Olivia just let Lovely have it, maybe as... as..."

"A consolation prize for getting to raise you?" Savannah guessed.

"Something like that," Beck said, purposely vague as she always was when this subject came up. Mostly because she wanted to protect Lovely, but also because this was ancient history and Olivia—the grandmother these girls called "Grandie"—was long gone. "Where are you going with the tax roll question, Callie?"

"Maybe they knew Grandie?" Callie suggested. "Maybe they—"

"Wait a second." Savannah smacked both hands on the table. "Maybe it wasn't *Olivia* they knew...maybe it was *Lovely*. Or *you*, Mom."

They all looked at Savannah, curious.

"Well, you said this guy sang the song about a girl named Lovely back in the sixties, right?"

"Sang it, wrote it, and has it tattooed on his..." Beck's voice faded out as the blood drained from her head as she read the very clear expression in Savannah's coppery-green eyes. "What...are...you..."

The girls all shared a look, silent, but did they have to say it?

"You think he's..." Beck tried to swallow, but nearly choked.

Peyton sucked in a soft breath and Callie put down her phone, the four of them dead silent as the real and shocking possibility of who the man with the *Lovely* tattoo might be.

"How?" Beck croaked the question. "Lovely didn't know his last name. How could he know hers?"

Savannah grimaced. "Might be me," she said. "Nick and I did one of those DNA things a while back, when his mother showed up and then we met his biological father. Who is now your boyfriend," she added, pointing at Beck. "I had to find out the gene pool, Momma. And Nick wanted to know if their story was legit. So we spit in the bag, mailed it in, and kind of forgot about it. But once your info is in the database..."

"They can just find you?" Beck asked.

"Kenny found you," Callie said, referring to the son Beck had given up for adoption...whose wedding they were on this balcony to plan.

"His mother had my name and gave it to Ava, remember? No DNA." Beck shook her head. "Wait a second. Wait a darn second. Are you saying this Eddie guy is...my *father*?"

"Hang on. That's a huge leap," Callie said, holding out

her hands to rein in her sisters, who looked like they might hoist their pregnant bodies over the railing and run down the beach to the B&B. "We have no evidence whatsoever."

"Got it, counselor, but we're talking about our biological *grandfather*," Savannah said.

"Let's just ask him," Peyton suggested.

"No, no, *no*." Beck used her strongest mother tone, looking from one daughter to the next. "This is Lovely's *life* we're talking about."

"And your *father*," Savannah reminded her.

Beck shivered. Was that long-haired tattooed man her—

She wiped the thought away and looked at Callie, who appeared to be the most reasonable. "What do you think?"

"I think..." She leaned back. "As a granddaughter, I want to know the guy right this minute. But, honestly, this is a pretty significant logic leap with no hard evidence except some strangers' curiosity and a tattoo."

"Exactly," Beck said. "Can't we do a little more digging with that website of Callie's or even look at the DNA information before dragging Lovely into something...embarrassing?"

"Embarrassing?" Peyton asked. "I'd think she'd be excited."

"It was a one-night stand," Beck said, aware that only she knew just how *one night* and *stand-y* it was.

Savannah snorted. "You really think I'm going to judge? Hello, Starbucks barista and the cute guy in the baseball cap. Whole latte-love that night."

"Oh, man." Callie groaned. "Does *any* woman in this family ever get pregnant *after* they're married?"

"Now *that's* our generational curse," Savannah quipped. "Be the one to break it, Cal."

Beck barely heard her daughters' banter, which blended into the sound of a gull and the splashing of waves beyond the balcony. Her head was thrumming with the possibility that Eddie Sly was Ned from the tent...and *her biological father*.

"Let me talk to him," she said, instantly knowing it was the right thing to do. "Don't say anything to Lovely yet. Let me find out what his game is and determine if there's a shred of truth to this. Then we'll tell Lovely, or he may want to do that himself. Remember, he came here thinking my mother had passed away."

"Which means he came here looking for *you*," Peyton said.

"It won't take Lovely long to put the puzzle together and come up with Sly Fox as her baby daddy," Savannah said. "I mean, the proof is written on his arm."

"That's not proof," Callie insisted. "He commemorated his one hit song, and she's certainly not the only woman to be named Lovely."

Peyton reached over the table and put her hand over Beck's. "You okay, Mom?"

Beck inhaled the briny air as she considered the question, looking from one beloved and beautiful face to the next, not surprised by how they handled this.

Savannah joked, Callie reasoned, and Peyton empathized. And Beck just wanted to protect her darling mother.

But still...only one thought echoed in her head.

"I never had a father," she said the words out loud on a soft whisper. "I never counted the man Olivia married briefly after I was an adult. For all but the last two years of my life, I thought my father was Lance Corporal David Joseph Mitchell, who died in Vietnam when my mother, Olivia Mitchell, was pregnant with me."

"Then you found out that Lovely was your mother," Peyton said. "And what has she told you about your father?"

"That he was a guy named Ned she met at an outdoor concert in Key West in 1965."

"Ned?" Callie asked. "That's short for Edward."

Beck dropped back against the chair just as the sliding door opened and Jessie, Heather, and Lovely came out, laughing and holding notebooks and pens.

"Time to plan a wedding, girls!" Jessie announced, pulling out chairs.

As Lovely looked around the table, she narrowed her eyes suspiciously. "Everything okay out here?"

Her daughters didn't say a word, but Beck managed a smile. "Yes, of course. Everything's great."

But she had a feeling Lovely's whole world was about to tilt sideways and all Beck could do was hope none of them fell off in the process.

CHAPTER FIVE
HEATHER

*I*t shouldn't be difficult. It shouldn't be a struggle. In fact, everything about planning her wedding should be joyous. Heather Monroe was marrying an amazing, faithful, loving, and kind single dad who'd changed her life and finally allowed her to truly appreciate the biblical concept of "equally yoked."

But the past week she'd spent in Charleston haunted her. Heather and her teenagers, Maddie and Marc, had spent Christmas with her late husband's family, seeing them for the first time since they'd moved to Coconut Key a little less than a year ago.

And that visit had turned out to be a very, very bad idea.

"Do you want to wait for Maddie and Ava?" Jessie asked, putting her hand on Heather's shoulder as if she somehow sensed her little sister was having a tough time. Heather hadn't been back very long, so she hadn't yet filled Jessie in on the details of her trip.

"Um, I don't know." She looked around the table at the six faces of women she loved—and who loved her. Should she pour her heart out and get advice? It was tempting, but she could end up in tears and more confused than ever.

Beck was Kenny's birth mother, and her advice was always maternal gold. Savannah, Peyton, and Callie already felt like blood relatives, even though they wouldn't officially be sisters-in-law until she married Kenny. And Lovely?

She was like a grandmother to Heather, trusted and beloved.

And, of course, Jessie, her much older half-sister and boss, was Heather's closest confidante other than Kenny.

The opinions of these women were a lot more valuable than... Oh. She shuddered at the thought of the woman who'd cornered her in the kitchen on Christmas Day and spit vitriol and accusations at her.

The echo of Blanche Henderson's angry words reverberated in her head, louder than the chatter of the women around her, the splash of the surf, and the occasional squawk of a gull that provided the soundtrack to this gathering.

What on God's green earth is wrong with you, Heather? How could you waltz off to the Keys five minutes after my brother died and shack up with some firefighter or construction worker or whatever he is! Did you just forget about Drew when you buried him? And what kind of life is that for your kids? Not to mention you're just leaving me alone to deal with my ailing, aging father?

Heather looked beyond the railing and the water, pinning her gaze on one puffy cloud that seemed lonely in the blue skies over the Keys, but the view didn't wipe out her sister-in-law's words.

Or her own silent defense, the one she'd been too timid to deliver to Blanche.

Where to begin with how wrong she was? Andy Monroe was not ailing or aging! Drew's father was barely seventy and went fishing in his outboard boat. And she hadn't *waltzed off* to the Keys or *shacked up* with anyone! She'd come for solace and a fresh start and met a wonderful man—a man she'd barely kissed and was about to marry. A man who, for the record, owned a successful and thriving construction business.

What kind of life for her kids? They loved it here! Kenny's daughter, Ava, was truly a sister and best friend to Maddie. Marc had made the baseball team at school as a transfer student, thanks to Kenny, who'd agreed to coach.

Blanche's impression of Heather's life and decisions could not be more wrong.

"Have you, Heather?"

Heather blinked at Lovely, pulled from her thoughts. "Have I…"

"Settled on a dress," she finished, a tiny frown pulling as if she, too, noticed something was off with Heather.

"I thought you were going with the pale pink tea-length," Peyton said. "The one we found in Miami."

"Um, yeah. I like that, but… I don't know…"

"Oh, you could wear white," Savannah said, misreading her uncertainty. "You're walking purity."

Purity? She was covered in guilt and shame and a whole lot of doubt.

"You'll find a dress," Callie said, leaning in and focusing on her. "The real question is, DJ or band?"

"And what kind of cake?"

"And how many people?"

"Have you picked the flowers?"

"And who will walk you down the aisle?"

The questions blended into chaos and cacophony, and she tried to answer.

"Um…chocolate. Hopefully not more than fifty or seventy-five people. Haven't thought about flowers and…

what else? The aisle. Yes. Well, he doesn't know yet, but I was thinking Marc could walk me down the aisle."

"Aww, sweet," Jessie said. "And what will your first dance be?"

She stared at her sister, blinking as tears sprang to her eyes.

"Heather!" Jessie had an arm around her instantly, then the others seemed to lunge closer. Well, not Peyton. She didn't lunge with that soon-to-appear baby. But Heather could see the true concern on her friend's face.

"I'm sorry," she blubbered, swiping her cheeks. "I don't know why..." But she *did* know. She knew *exactly* why she was crying.

"Heather, honey, talk to us," Jessie whispered. "Unless you need privacy or..."

Heather held up one hand and took the napkin Callie offered with the other.

"I'm sorry," she repeated, dabbing under her eyes, though she knew her mascara was a lost cause. "I...I just...I don't know what to do."

Six women stared at her, silent.

Jessie inched closer. "To do...about what? We don't understand."

Heather didn't understand. How could they? Wiping her eyes again, she glanced at the door. She could tell this group of women anything. But not her daughter. "If Maddie comes..." She sniffed. "I don't want her to know any of this."

"Do you want me to go out front and watch for them?" Callie offered gently. "I can detain the girls, if you like."

Heather sighed and shook her head, taking Callie's hand.

"Thank you, sweetie. No. I'll tell you guys what's going on, but if they walk out here—"

"We'll wedding plan," Savannah said. "Dive right into flower arrangements the minute that door opens."

"If that's what you want," Jessie added.

"Of course it is, but..." She dug deep for composure, swallowing and knowing her tale of woe wouldn't take long.

"Don't worry." Beck lifted her phone. "Ava just texted me, Heather. They're still twenty minutes away. I believe there was a shopping detour, but they told us to start without them."

"Maddie is a fine and responsible maid of honor," Savannah said. "Knowing exactly when to be absent."

Heather managed a smile. "I gave her my credit card and told her to go shoe shopping."

"Whoa." Callie leaned back. "You *did* want to get rid of her for a while."

"I just needed time to think and talk." She looked at Jessie. "I guess, deep inside, I wanted to fill you in. All of you," she added quickly, taking a sip of the water that Jessie slid in front of her. "Okay. I will, now."

They all scooted a little closer, quiet while she gathered her thoughts, letting the tropical air and dear friends fill her with strength. Closing her eyes, she mentally prayed what Kenny called the "big three-worder"—*Help me, God.*

She needed strength and wisdom that she believed came from the Lord. To be honest, neither felt like they were in great supply after that trip to Charleston.

"It's about my sister-in-law, if I can still call her that, I mean, since Drew has passed. So, former sister-in-law, I guess."

"Doesn't matter what you call her," Jessie said. "I know Blanche. She's harsh. The woman doesn't mince words, and is a walking martyr who thinks the world owes her a favor."

"Not the world," Heather corrected. "Me. She thinks I need to get back up there, help her with her father, and end this...this 'childish rebellion' of 'dragging my kids to the Keys' and...and 'shacking up' with Kenny."

"Shacking up?" Savannah choked. "Have you ever slept under the same roof?"

"Childish rebellion?" Peyton's brows shot up.

"Dragging the kids?" Beck asked.

"What a bunch of unfiltered stupidity," Lovely finished the outpouring of support with a dose of her common sense, while Jessie just shook her head in disbelief.

"Thank you," Heather muttered, a little overwhelmed by the love. "Obviously, she's wrong about all that. Of course we've never spent the night together. I started my life over after being widowed, moving to finally live near my sister." She put a hand on Jessie's shoulder, the person she'd leaned on so many times since Drew died eighteen months ago, taking another breath before she continued.

"The fact is, if anyone dragged anyone, it was Maddie who begged to make this move—and in her senior year, too. But Blanche thinks I'm a monster for taking the kids out of their school, and a fool for selling my café up there, and a criminal for not mourning her brother for a decade before I so much as dated again, let alone marry."

She let that sink in, and turned to Jessie, whose slightly freckled face was pink with fury.

"How dare she?" Jessie ground out. "She didn't lift a finger to help you when Drew was sick! She was always too busy with her important pharma sales job, marching from doctor to doctor, but never so much as offering to pick up the kids or bring you dinner."

Heather waved off the criticism. "She loves her job, and she's very good at it, and believes in what she sells. And she's divorced and doesn't have kids, so I don't think she really understands my life. She's consumed with the responsibility of helping Andy."

"I didn't know your father-in-law was sick," Lovely said gently. "He's younger than I am, isn't he?"

"He's seventy," Heather said. "And he's not sick. He's had a few health issues—high blood pressure and some sciatica—since Grandma Winnie died, and that was before Drew passed. No surprise, he took Drew's death very hard. If anything, he's sad and lonely." She groaned and shuttered her eyes. "And that's why I feel so guilty. Grandpa Andy glommed onto Marc while we were up there this past week, and those two have always been close. He cried when they said goodbye and…" She grimaced. "So did Marc. He tried to be strong, but that boy has the softest heart."

"Maybe Andy could move here," Beck said. "He could be near his grandkids and there are enough of us to help you keep an eye on him if he needs it."

"I begged him to do that," Heather said. "I honestly made the most compelling argument. But he was born and raised in Charleston and lives out in the Lowcountry, where he loves it so much. He can't even seriously talk about leaving. And Blanche would have a cow!"

"Why?" Peyton asked. "She wants you to take care of him."

"She wants his beautiful waterfront property when he

dies," Heather said, then cringed. "I don't mean to gossip but I know what she wants and if he moved, he'd have to sell."

"If you won't gossip, I will," Jessie said. "That woman is awful. She's manipulative and deceptive and greedy."

"Tell us how you really feel, Jess," Savannah cracked.

Jessie sniffed, refusing to back down from an opinion Heather knew she'd held for years.

"Listen to me, Heather," Jessie insisted. "You grew up far away from me, a half-sister that Josh and I barely knew after Dad left us and married your mom. You deserve to be near family, and so do your kids. And we deserve to have you as much as anyone. And as far as Kenny? He's just—"

"She says it's too soon," Heather interjected. "And it's hard to argue with that. We've only been completely committed to each other for about seven months, so maybe we are rushing this."

A chorus of disagreement rose.

"You two were made for each other," Beck said, louder than the others. "From the moment you met, we could all see it. There's no reason to wait. Your kids love each other, you love each other, and both of you have prayed and are certain about this."

Heather couldn't disagree. "Blanche says we're just rushing it so, you know, we can be with each other physically."

She didn't want to repeat or even think of the ugly words Blanche had said, accusing Kenny of marrying Heather just to get a good Christian girl in bed with him.

"As far as the kids?" she continued. "I'm afraid Marc doesn't feel quite as gung-ho as Maddie and Ava do."

"Marc's happy here," Jessie said. "He's playing baseball and every time I see him with Kenny, he's laughing."

"He loves Kenny," Heather agreed. "But he spent five solid days with Grandpa Andy, who is a good man. It was clear Andy's depressed, and he told Marc openly that he wants us to come back. He took Marc fishing, and they spent hours out on the water, and every night Marc came home a little more blue. He's a compassionate boy, and he thinks we should all move back there. With Kenny, of course."

All of them seemed a little stunned by that.

"Is that a possibility?" Beck asked. "Have you talked to Kenny about it?"

"Briefly. You know Kenny—if I want to go, he'll pack." She laughed softly. "He's the definition of the man who'd get the moon for his woman."

"Do you?" Jessie asked softly. "Do you want to move back to Charleston?"

"No, but..." She swallowed. "I always want to do the right thing, you know. I always listen to what God's will is, and try to follow it. Andy is my late husband's father, and they loved each other. Marc adores him, and it's mutual. Maddie will be going to college in the fall, and...I don't know. There are more people's feelings involved than just mine right now. In fact..." She took a slow, deep breath. "I'm wondering if I should get married at all."

All six of them stared at her in complete shock.

"It feels fast and...scary," she said softly. "My husband died eighteen months ago. Is it right to do this so quickly?"

"Honey, you're the only person who can answer that." Jessie wrapped a loving arm around her. "Just know that we're here for you."

"Thanks." She swiped under her eyes and leaned back, taking in their surprised, worried, and broken expressions.

She didn't want to leave these people, but she did owe something—many things—to her late husband. She had absolutely no doubt what he'd want her to do. What he'd *insist* she do. Drew Monroe, for all his "seize the day" bluster, would be on Team Blanche and utterly furious if Heather didn't go back to Charleston.

That knowledge, and his memory, made her the most uncertain and uncomfortable.

Beck cleared her throat. "Maddie and Ava just texted that they are parking and will be up here in two minutes. What do you want to do, Heather?"

"Proceed...with caution." She smiled. "So, back to planning. Yes, I love the pink dress, but deep inside? Savannah's right. I do want to wear something white. Simple, clean, and maybe cream or eggshell. Unless that makes me a hypocrite."

"It makes you an angel," Jessie whispered, giving her a loving squeeze. "A dear angel that we all adore."

She sighed and dropped her head into her hands. "I don't know what I'd do without all of you."

And one thing she was certain about? She didn't want to find out. But she would if that's what God wanted her to do. He'd open doors to lead her where He wanted her to be. She just hoped it was the same doors she wanted to go through... but sometimes God's plan was far, far different than hers.

CHAPTER SIX
EDDIE

*J*ust when he thought the sun never stopped shining on this island, Eddie noticed that dusk was descending, turning the water outside his room spectacular shades of grape and tangerine.

Which reminded him—he was hungry.

He'd had a great outdoor lunch with Mel and Jazz in a Key West pub, walked around the colorful little town, and spent the day being a total tourist. As it grew later, though, his daughters wanted to go to Mallory Square and get a spot to watch the epic sunset with fifty-seven bazillion other people.

No, thanks. It wasn't just the sea of cargo-shorts and sunburns that put him off, or the fact that, at seventy-six, he didn't relish the idea of smashing next to strangers to watch something that happened every day.

It was…Mallory Square. Today, it was a paved paradise with vendors selling souvenirs, tropical drinks flowing, and street musicians strumming. But nearly sixty years ago, it had been a massive dirt-covered wharf with a makeshift stage and music-loving teenagers sleeping in tents.

Although some of them weren't *sleeping*.

Nope. Couldn't go there. Without having told Lovely why he was here, or coming clean to Beck, he wasn't ready for Mallory Square memories.

Not that he really had much of a *memory* of the night.

Just what threads of colors and sounds he'd managed to bring alive in that song, which had played in his head non-stop all day.

After sneaking in an afternoon nap that he'd deny he ever took, he stared out at the water, then stared down at a blank page, then stopped staring to go find food.

He made his way downstairs to the hushed quiet of an empty house. At the bottom step, he glanced toward the vestibule that Beck had said led to the owner's suite, but that door was closed tight. The living and dining rooms were washed in a late-afternoon glow streaming through plantation shutters.

The light fell on framed pictures perched on bookshelves and inviting groups of chairs for lounging and reading. The furniture was like old-school Victorian-meets-the beach, in muted colors and soft textures.

A throw blanket here, a small vase of flowers there, carved moldings around the windows, and wide-planked wood floors all made him feel like he was in a magazine...but also in a well-loved home.

Around the corner, he stepped into an oversized kitchen with sparkling white countertops and one whole wall of glass that looked out at the water. On the center island, he spotted a framed, handwritten message to guests, inviting them to help themselves to snacks in the pantry or drinks in the fridge and to feel free to enjoy the deck or head down to the water for a stroll.

For a few seconds, his gaze stayed locked on the words at the bottom of the note.

With love and gratitude to have you as our guests,
Beck and Lovely

Something about their togetherness, the oneness of these women, lifted his spirits. They were clearly quite close, with that special connection that he sometimes suspected God saved for women. That made him a weird mix of jealous and grateful.

He wasn't sure where that left him, a genetically connected outsider who could conceivably throw a grenade in the middle of their relationship.

Mulling that, he rounded the counter and headed to the fridge. Inside, he instantly zeroed in on a pitcher of lemonade, a bowl of blueberries, and a platter of chocolate-covered...somethings.

Yes, please, screamed the sweet tooth he tried to ignore.

He assembled himself a small plate of treats, impressed by how easy his hostesses made it for a guest to navigate the kitchen. He poured a giant glass of lemonade—massively better than iced tea, in his humble opinion—and took it to the deck.

There, he settled at a table to watch the east-facing water change colors as the sun set on the other side of the island, mostly thinking about how to handle his next conversation with either or both of the women.

Yes, he wanted to interview, investigate, and tiptoe his way through any landmines. But mostly, he really wanted the truth on the table. He wanted those cards or chips or whatever to fall—as long as it wasn't one of the nice ladies who did the falling.

He tipped his head back to the violet-tinged sky and closed his eyes, imagining just how he could and should tell his tale.

Fact was, Mel would do it for him if he didn't hurry.

That much he knew from her anticipation and impatience today. So, how much did he need to know before he shook up their worlds? Did he need to know everything about their history or who they imagined Beck's father was or—

At the sound of a car door, he sat up, listening. He heard footsteps coming up the stairs to the stilt home, waiting to see whose head would appear at the top of the stairs.

"Oh, hello."

It was Beck, wearing the same white jeans and pink top she'd had on this morning, but her smile appeared a little less bright than the last time he'd seen her. She didn't seem surprised to see him, but... cautious.

"Hello, Beck."

"Eddie." She took the last two steps to the top, glancing at the table. "I'm so glad you found the candies and lemonade. If you want something stronger, we have beer and wine and, of course, champagne."

"Never touch the stuff." He angled his head toward the other chair, following a gut that rarely let him down. "Wouldn't mind some company, though, if you're not busy."

She hesitated for a second, then nodded, eyeing him with curiosity and...suspicion? He couldn't tell, but the fact that she joined him felt like an open door. Well, at least it wasn't locked.

"So, where are your daughters?" she asked.

"A place called Mallory Square." He stood up as she pulled out the chair, catching her look of surprise as he made the gentlemanly gesture. "You familiar with it?"

She gave an easy laugh. "Of course. They stayed for sunset?"

"Along with all the tourists who ever were," he said,

gesturing toward the kitchen. "Can I bring you a glass of some of the finest lemonade I've ever had?"

"That's Lovely's lemonade," she told him, her smile growing. "She's famous for it. And I'm supposed to be waiting on you."

He held up a hand. "Allow me. You enjoy the view."

"Then I'll take a glass. Thank you."

Inside, he took his time filling a glass with ice and pouring her drink, using the brief distraction to plan what he could say.

Maybe this should be information gathering only. He supposed he needed to know some of their history—what Beck had been told, how Lovely had handled being a pregnant teenager...whatever.

Then, and only then, would he plan how he'd tell Lovely and let *her* break the news to Beck.

Satisfied with that strategy, he walked back outside and found Beck gazing out at the water. He slowed his step for a moment, studying her profile. Was that his mother's slightly upturned nose? Yes, she favored Lovely in her coloring and facial shape, but he chewed his lip just like that when he was concentrating.

Oh, staying quiet would be hard. This was *his daughter*. He nearly dropped the lemonade as the impact of that hit him.

She turned and smiled—now, *that* expression belonged to Lovely—making him shake off the thought and remember the job at hand.

"You look deep in thought," he said, placing the lemonade in front of her. "I'd say a penny for your thoughts, but it would date me and make me sound way too uncool."

"My mother says that all the time, and she's timeless and totally cool."

Smiling at the kind and considerate response, he sat down and lifted his drink. "Then I'll toast to Lovely, always a favorite name of mine."

She dinged his glass with hers. "That inspired the song."

Wait. Was that a question or a statement? And did she mean...the *name* or the *woman* that inspired the song?

"Yeah," he said, purposely vague. "What a coincidence, huh?"

She didn't answer, but took a sip and lowered the glass, holding his gaze with something of a challenge in her green eyes.

"She wasn't kidding when she said she loves the song. Just imagine...what a gift you gave her."

"I...oh, well, that's nice," he said, not sure how to interpret that. But the door felt like it had just cracked open another inch, so he headed in. "I admit, I was surprised by your comment that another woman had raised you," he said. "Too personal to ask why?"

She searched his face, considering the question. "A little personal, but that's fine. Lovely was a teenager when I was born, and the world was different. Her sister, Olivia, was twelve years older and childless at the time, after years of trying to have a baby. She and her husband were living at a military base. Lovely went to stay with them in Carlsbad and gave me up at birth to raise."

"Carlsbad, California?" He tried and maybe failed to keep the surprise from his voice.

"I was born there," she said. "But I only learned that about two years ago."

First, he mentally gave points to Jazz, who'd called that one on the nose. Then a bunch of new questions formed, but one rose to the top. "You only found out two years ago? You didn't know your whole life?"

"My mother—Olivia—was very controlling. And one of the things she controlled was how frequently I saw Lovely, which was pretty much never. My grandparents were sworn to secrecy and even my father didn't know because he thought I was conceived while he'd been home on leave."

"And Olivia never told him, either?" He wasn't sure if he respected the woman or wanted to strangle her.

Beck shook her head. "He died in Vietnam before I was born."

He sucked in a breath. "Viet— Oh, wow. I'm sorry, Beck." Sorry he'd used a draft deferment to pursue his musical career and stay the heck out of Hanoi. Shame punched him, making him lean back and feel it in the gut. "So you never met him. That's...wow. Did she, uh, remarry?"

For some reason, he hoped Beck had *someone* in the role that should have been his.

"Briefly." She swallowed and looked directly at him. "I was already an adult, and she divorced him a few years later. I've never really...had a father."

The words jabbed him right in the...tear ducts. Casting his gaze down toward the table, he dug for composure.

"After I was born, Olivia moved back here to Coconut Key," she told him, the words sounding a little rushed, as if she'd been holding them back. "We lived in this house, with my grandparents and Aunt *Lovey*, as I called her, until I was ten. Then Olivia took me away to Atlanta."

"Took you away?"

"I didn't want to leave, but I was a kid. And she would never come back. Not even for either of my grandparents' funerals. I...lost touch with Lovely. My mother guarded her secret and took it with her to the grave, knowing that if Lovely and I spent too much time together, I'd get suspicious. The genes are strong, and the resemblance is undeniable."

"How *did* you reconnect with her?" he asked.

"Lovely reached out to me," she said, looking back at the water for a moment. "She had a, uh, major change in her life."

"A death?" he asked gently, imagining that she'd lost a husband or a child.

"Hers."

"Excuse me?"

She took a deep and slow breath, turning from the water to face him straight on. "You may have noticed some scars on her face. She was in a terrible car accident and was pronounced dead at the scene."

"What?" He barely breathed the word as chills tiptoed up his spine, the story getting twistier and more shocking with each revelation.

"She was technically dead briefly—a few minutes, I think—but in that time, she had the classic near-death, walk through the light, go to the other side experience. Only hers ended with meeting Olivia, who'd died almost five years earlier."

More chills, but this time they marched. "You better explain that, Beck."

"In that, uh, heavenly encounter, Lovely believed her sister gave her permission to tell me the truth. So, she reached out and invited me here. I was in the throes of getting divorced and my oldest daughter, Peyton, came with me." She smiled, looking almost relieved to have shared all that. Did she tell most guests? Most strangers? Something told him the answer was no.

"Anyway, we never left," she finished. "I've lived here for almost two years."

"How did Lovely tell you?" he asked. "What did she say? And were you upset to have been lied to your whole life?" He held up a hand that he hoped she didn't notice was trembling. "I know I shouldn't pry but...I'm invested. In the story," he added quickly.

A glimmer of a smile pulled. "I appreciate your interest, Eddie. She didn't tell me right away, but the truth did come out and I was... Yes. I was upset."

And would she be upset again? When this new truth came out?

"I understand," he said. "Being lied to your whole life is upsetting."

"It was but, you know, Lovely is...lovely." Her voice grew thick as she spoke. "First, she'd made a written promise to her sister, signed and sworn on the Bible, and no one keeps her word like Lovely Ames."

Another admirable trait, he thought.

"Second," she continued, "that woman has more heart, soul, kindness, spirit, tenacity, strength, and love than ten mothers wrapped into one. I love her and am so grateful for these years we have. It was easy to forgive her for the decision to keep the truth from me, and we've gotten past it."

"Good, good," he said softly, wondering if he'd be

forgiven, too. But he still didn't know who Beck thought her father was.

For a moment, they didn't speak, the silence heavy between them. He had to know. He had no choice.

"And...your father?" he finally whispered. "I mean, the father...the man who...biological..." *Geez, get a grip, Sly.*

She gave a soft smile, as if she could hear his inner thoughts. "Lovely...um...well, this might be more information than I should share...so..."

"Please, Beck. Share it."

Even in the waning light, he could see her pale as she stared at him. "She never knew his last name, only his first."

His heart felt like it was folding in half, hammering and tight and achy and about to explode with one simple thought...

Tell her, tell her, break all your plans and rules and tell her!

"Does she want to know his name?" he asked, every word halting.

She tried to nod, but her eyes filled with tears, and he simply couldn't help himself. He reached over the table and put his hand on top of hers. "Do *you* want to know, Beck?"

"I think I already do...Ned."

The word shot like a bullet into his belly, stealing his breath. His head felt light, his heart heavy.

For what felt like eight measures of dead silence, they didn't move or speak, his hand over hers, their gazes locked.

"You're crying," he whispered.

"So are you."

He gave her a bittersweet smile. "Of course I am. Because...because..." Damn, the tears rolled. "Because..."

"Please." She used her free hand to swipe a tear. "I can't play games and dance around and ask you questions. It's not my style."

He felt a smile pull. "It's not mine, either."

"It must be hereditary." They said the words at exactly the same time, in the same tone, and punctuated them with the same shocked laugh.

In an instant, they both rose and came around the table. All they could do was hug, a father and daughter, holding each other tight for the first time in fifty-seven years.

He embraced her for a long time, unable to move, unable to breathe, unable to speak.

He had another daughter, as beautiful, brave, and spectacular as the other two and, right then, he'd never been happier.

CHAPTER SEVEN
BECK

*S*he liked him.

For some reason, that was a huge relief to Beck. She didn't think she could stand it if Eddie were arrogant or demanding or flippant about his liaison with Lovely.

He was, in fact, none of those things. Eddie Sylvester—Eddie Sly, as he was known to everyone—had an undercurrent of gentleness to him, a calm air of wisdom, and a deep sense of caring about others that just pleased Beck.

After the emotions settled and the moon rose, she listened while he explained how his granddaughter, Lark, had started the whole chain of events by doing some DNA testing at one of the big sites. One discovery led to another, and soon, Eddie and his two daughters had enough information about Beck to find her.

"When we found out you owned a B&B, we thought we'd be super crafty and meet you as guests, so I didn't have to knock on the door and go all *Star Wars* on you." He leaned across the table where they'd been for what seemed like an hour since their heartfelt hug. "'I am your father,' Beck," he said in his best Darth Vader voice.

She laughed. "My daughter figured it out," she told him. "I told them how you'd asked all these off-the-wall questions. My youngest, Callie, a lawyer-in-the-making, went straight to 'scam artists out to steal something from the B&B.' But

Savannah, the middle daughter, was the one who put two and two together."

"And the oldest?"

"Peyton? Her concern is always how I'm handling anything."

He beamed at her, wearing an expression she couldn't quite interpret until he sighed and said, "You realize you're telling me about my granddaughters."

"Oh." She gave a soft chuckle. "I guess I am. What would you like to know about them?"

"Every single thing," he said. "I mean, if you'll let me meet them."

"Of course! And Kenny, my son. Oh, you have a great-grandson, Dylan, and a teenaged great-granddaughter named Ava, who is Kenny's daughter. And Savannah and Peyton are pregnant right now. Peyton's having a girl sometime in the next few weeks."

He dropped back, clearly having a hard time taking it all in or keeping the names straight. "And...Lovely?" he asked. "What does she think?"

"She wasn't there when we figured it out," Beck told him. "I asked them not to say anything because I wanted to be sure first. And I thought you might want to tell her."

His eyes closed on a sigh. "God love you for that. Thank you. I...I don't really know how."

"You can be honest. She's strong and—"

He held up a hand. "I don't want to stir up bad feelings of shame or anger," he said. "What I did was unforgivable. I never even asked her last name and..." He shook his head. "I don't have a son, but I'd kill my grandson, Kai, if he behaved that way."

Beck considered that, again struck by what a good man he seemed to be. "Kids make mistakes," she said. "For instance, I had Kenny when I was young and unwed. I gave him up for adoption, but his daughter found me. Savannah says unmarried motherhood is our generational curse." She gave a humorless laugh. "I can't let you take all the blame."

A slow smile pulled as he searched her face, studying it for a long time. "You remind me of my mother," he finally said.

"Everyone says I'm a carbon copy of Lovely."

"You are, physically. But there's something steady about you that really makes me think of the late, great Willie Sylvester."

"Willie?"

"Wilhelmina Sylvester," he explained. "My dad died when I was young and she raised me alone, with my sister. She was a strong woman, fair and loving. She'd have adored you."

The compliment warmed her, bringing another smile just as they heard two car doors closing from the front.

"Uh, your sisters are here," Eddie said.

Beck put her hand to her lips. "Never had sisters, never had a father, never dreamed this could happen."

He stood slowly. "Should I go give them a heads-up? I can tell you now that Melody is going to pounce. With love, of course. And Jazz will...examine you for flaws. Not that she'll find any."

"She won't have to look hard. Please, if you want to warn them, you can. Otherwise..."

They heard the women's voices, with Melody's hearty laugh and Jazz hushing her.

Beck and Eddie shared a long look, then he shrugged. "Just...tell them."

Nodding, she stood and took a few steps to the top of the stairs, seeing the two women walking up in the soft light from a wall sconce. Catching sight of her on the top landing, they both paused halfway.

"Oh, hello, Beck," Melody said. "Everything okay?"

"Your father's up here," she said, gesturing them closer. "Or should I say...*our* father?"

Melody gasped noisily, practically leaping up the last two steps. "What? You know?"

Jazz joined her in a second. "How? Who? What?"

Beck just threw her head back and laughed, opening up her arms to the two of them for a group hug. "C'mere, sisters."

Melody squealed and did a little dance as she hugged Beck. Jazz's hug was less effusive but just as genuine, with lots of laughter, a few tears, and more hugs.

Eddie joined them as they both exclaimed, "What happened to waiting?" and, "I thought we were going to get to know them!"

After a few minutes, he got them all drinks and more snacks, and they huddled together to try and catch up on a lifetime of not even knowing this family existed.

Melody wanted to know everything about the people—Beck's daughters, her son, the grands, and Beck herself. She wanted to know what everyone was like, how they'd take this news, and all the history of how they'd come together on Coconut Key.

She was a laugher, a big talker, and oozed warmth.

Jazz was definitely the quieter of the two sisters, asking far more about facts than personalities—ages, jobs, how long married, how many kids. Melody teased her about it, and Jazz threatened to get a notebook, but Eddie informed Beck that with Jazz's IQ, they didn't need one.

Beck looked from one to the other, still blown away by the whole thing.

"You know, you two are my daughters' aunts," she said. "And I can see a little of them in both of you. Savannah and Melody—you'll be two peas in a pod. And Jazz? Callie's already looked up your resume and pronounced you her next hero. I can't wait for you to meet them."

"What's stopping us?" Melody asked, pushing back from the table. "It's not even nine o'clock. Let's have a family reunion!"

"Hold your horses, Miss Impulsive," Eddie said, patting her arm. "Lovely doesn't know."

Melody opened her mouth to reply, then closed it. "You want to tell her," she said, obviously knowing her father well. "Okay, we'll have to wait then."

"How, Dad?" Jazz asked. "What's the plan?"

"We were talking about that before you two showed up." Eddie turned to Beck, a question in his eyes. "You know her best, Beck. What approach do you think will be easiest on her?"

"Quiet, personal, and...sweet," she said, without giving it too much thought.

"Maybe a walk on the beach," Melody suggested.

"Or take her out to dinner," Jazz added.

"Or both," Beck said, getting all their attention. "For

special occasions, we set up dinner al fresco on the beach. A small table right down there on the walkway, lanterns to light the path, candles, tablecloth, champagne, the works. In fact..." She hesitated, thinking through the impulsive invitation. She'd planned to share that very beachfront dinner with Oliver tomorrow night for New Year's Eve. But would he mind if she gave the special "Beach Table" to Lovely and this man? Not Oliver. He'd love that gift, in fact. "You can have a Beach Table dinner tomorrow night, and when it gets dark, there will be fireworks all over the Keys."

"Oh, there'll be fireworks, all right!" Melody cracked.

"It sounds kind of romantic," Jazz said. "Won't that give the wrong impression?"

Eddie shook his head. "This dear woman deserves a little romance. Frankly, I'm fifty-seven years too late."

"I think the trick will be getting her to agree," Beck said, already knowing Lovely would give her a side-eye and a hoot at the idea of a New Year's Eve date with a guest. "I suppose I could figure out a reason that—"

"I'll handle it," Eddie said confidently. "I may be old, but I think I know how to ask a woman to dinner. Will she be here tomorrow?"

"At some point," Beck said. "She frequently walks her three dogs on the beach very early and heads over here for coffee."

He held up a hand. "I got this," he said. "And I promise I will break the news gently and do my best to earn her forgiveness and friendship. After that, we can meet the family."

Beck smiled at him, touched by his caring nature. "We can do that on New Year's Day," she said. "My daughter

Savannah is planning a beach party at her house for everyone. And I do mean *everyone*."

"Sounds like a baptism by fire," Jazz joked.

"Sounds like a dream," Melody countered.

They all looked at Eddie to see what he thought it sounded like, but he leaned closer to Beck and put a hand over hers.

"Thank you," he said softly. "I'm honored to call you my daughter."

"The honor is mine," she whispered, and meant every word.

A TEXT from Oliver forced Beck to end the lively gathering, as much as she didn't want to. It seemed they all had so much to share, but Oliver's note was brief and direct, enough that it really got her attention.

I need to see you. Can you come over?

It wasn't like him to ever ask her to leave the B&B in the evening, knowing she'd be getting ready for the next day of work and guests. So they all hugged goodnight, and she made sure they had what they needed, then made the short drive to Oliver's rental house, still on a high from the new "family" she'd discovered.

She fairly danced up the stairs to the main floor of the stilt house, seeing lights inside, but no sign of life on the wraparound patio that looked out over thick palms and a narrow canal.

She hadn't even knocked when the door opened to reveal the face of a man she fell a little more in love with every day.

As always, her heart swelled at the sight of his dark eyes, slightly tousled golden hair with a bit of silver in the temples, and a day's growth of beard over a strong jaw and handsome face. But it dropped when she saw something in his expression that looked...troubled.

"Is everything okay?" Beck asked as he invited her in.

A silent response flickered over his features as he angled his head as if to say...maybe not.

"Oliver?" she pressed.

He let out a sigh and wrapped her in a hug, the strong arms of a former semi-pro rugby player and a man who made regular trips to the gym. Sinking into the embrace that always warmed her, she bit her lip, waiting for him to tell her what was the matter.

Instead, he slid an arm around her and walked her through the small kitchen and living area to the bedroom side of the house, rounding the corner to the master and pointing at the bed.

Where a suitcase lay open and packed.

"Where are you going?" she asked.

"Sydney. Tomorrow."

"What?" She barely croaked the word. "Why?"

"The good news is I've sold my house for full asking and they want to close rather quickly."

She inched back, ready to agree that was, indeed, great news. "What's the bad news?"

He shrugged. "The agent said he could get a ten-day close, all cash, if I empty the house as quickly as possible. The bad news is I want you to go with me in the worst way and I'm not going to be happy if you say no. Only for a week, maybe ten days, Beck. I know the baby could be born any minute but..." His voice faded as he no doubt read her expression. "It's a no, isn't it?"

She heard the defeat in his voice and hated that she simply couldn't remove it.

"I'd love to, Oliver," she said, walking in and dropping on the edge of the bed next to the suitcase. "I really would. I might even take a chance of missing Peyton giving birth..." She made a face, knowing that probably wasn't true. "But there's a new wrinkle in my life. It seems I've got a father."

"Pardon?"

She smiled. "Tear you away from packing for a few minutes? I've got an unbelievable story."

"Only if I can have a beer. How about you?"

"Just water, but yes. Fortify. This one's a doozie."

A few minutes later, they were on the patio sofa with Beck's feet propped on his lap. Laying back on a pillowed armrest, she told him every detail she could remember, pausing while he reacted with expected shock and questions.

She finished with her idea for a "date" when Eddie could break the news to Lovely.

"So you were going to give our romantic New Year's Eve dinner away even before you knew I'd be on a plane over the Pacific?" He gave her bare toes a playful squeeze. "I'm crushed."

"I thought we'd be right here, still able to see the fireworks, but secure in the knowledge that we'd done a good deed for Lovely."

"Makes sense." He took a final sip of his beer and put the empty bottle on the table. "Well, I knew the baby's due date was working against me, but I can't take you away from a brand-new dad and two sisters who are only here for two weeks. Not a chance."

"I'm sorry, hon," she said, and meant it. "I want to go, I really do. But does this trip to Sydney mean you won't meet any of them?"

"If I get back before they leave. As far as tomorrow? The only decent flight I could get leaves at two from Miami, so I'd have to leave here by nine or so to make the drive and be at the international terminal on time." He leaned all the way over and kissed her lightly. "All alone, sadly."

"Did you really think I could pack and join you with that little notice?"

"A man could hope," he said. "But, honestly, no. I knew you'd look at the calendar and Peyton's belly and turn me down. I'll miss you." He kissed her again, a little less lightly. "But I will expect daily reports on the new crew, the baby arrival, and, of course, Lovely's romance."

"Romance?" She sputtered the word.

"Don't tell me you're not thinking about it," he teased. "Your biological parents, reunited fifty-seven years later, rediscovering a connection that might bring them together in their golden years?"

She laughed softly. "I wasn't thinking about that, but..." She lifted her brows. "Would that be so bad?"

"I think it would be wonderful," he said.

"Well, I don't believe that's going to happen, Oliver. At best, I'm hoping my mother can let go of some decades-old guilt from a wild one-night stand. I want her to be content in the knowledge that her moral compass may have been a bit off that night, but her instincts led her to a good man."

"Or she could fall flat on her face in love and be the next one dancing down the aisle in Coconut Key." He leaned close again and whispered, "Wouldn't it be hilarious if she beat us to it?"

Chills exploded from his voice and breath and the words he sometimes dangled to delight and excite her.

"Well, that would be the twist I never saw coming," Beck said on a laugh. "Not that it would be the worst thing that ever happened."

"Not at all. Unless…he wants to drag her off to California to live in his—what did you say? Seven-million-dollar ranch and a winery in Napa?"

Beck felt her eyes open in horror. "She wouldn't!"

He shrugged. "I've seen people change their life for love. You, my dear woman, are looking at a man selling a beloved home that he built and lived in for many years."

"Then if they fall in love, he can sell the ranch, take vacations at the winery, and settle himself in Coconut Key. Just like…" She walked her fingers up his arm, enjoying every inch of the muscle. "The man I love."

A slow smile curled his lips. "You love me, huh?"

"Not enough to go to Australia but enough to lose my entire day and drive you to the airport. It gives us three and a half extra hours, even if they are in the car."

"I'll take them and that is true love. Thank you."

For a long moment, he just looked at her, a strange, uninterpretable expression on his face. Wistful and sweet…but was there hesitation in his eyes? Was he second-guessing the decision to sell the house he'd built with his late wife? Uncertain about the move to Coconut Key? Unsure about Beck?

The momentary shadows lifted from his eyes as quickly

as they'd come as he slid an arm under her and lifted her to meet him this time.

"I'm going to miss you," he said on a rough whisper. "Very, very much."

"I'll miss you, too."

With one deep kiss, he erased all those flashes of doubt.

CHAPTER EIGHT
LOVELY

*L*ovely read Beck's text with an inexplicable thud of disappointment. Oliver was leaving for Australia... *today*? And Beck would be gone the entire day and into the evening because she was taking him to the airport in Miami and doing some shopping up there.

Beck assured her that the Coquina House guests were all settled and Lovely could have the day and night free. Free to do what?

It was New Year's Eve, for heaven's sake, and she suddenly felt very much alone. Tomorrow was a family party at Savannah's, but today stretched ahead—alone. That gave Lovely an empty sensation she didn't relish at all.

Not that she'd expected Beck to spend the evening with her—she and Oliver had the Beach Table dinner planned.

Oh, wait. Was that not happening now? Should Lovely cancel the caterer? Beck hadn't even mentioned it.

On a sigh, she dropped her head back on the sofa, the sting of unwelcome and unexpected tears behind her lids.

Why would she be weepy?

Since her family had blossomed over the last two years, the lonely blues, as she called them, had rarely plagued her. Before that, even with Jessie and her brother Josh living nearby, Lovely did get some bouts of solitude sadness, and sometimes spent days staring at the beach, trying to paint but mostly questioning her life's choices.

Then she had the accident, met her dead sister in the afterlife, and finally, finally contacted Beck.

Once the truth was out, sadness disappeared. Not only had the weight of keeping a lifelong and life-*changing* secret been lifted, a new light shone brighter than the Florida sun.

Her relationship with Beck bloomed, the family tree grew, and they created the B&B, giving Lovely's life purpose and non-stop laughter.

So, did one day without Beck mean she slipped right back into that hole of unhappiness? Of course not! She was too old to blame hormones, but something had been gnawing at her soul since...since...yesterday.

It definitely started yesterday, this low-grade hum of... something that made her sad.

With her eyes still closed, she could hear Pepper growling on the deck, a prelude to a bark. Basil shifted positions noisily from his bed as if he knew his break was over.

And on her lap, Sugar stirred and licked Lovely's hand.

Like they were all telling her she was never, ever alone in her cottage full of terriers.

Lovely stroked the precious Westie, who gazed up with soulful brown eyes full of comfort and love. Lifting up the dog for a nuzzle and a kiss, she whispered, "No, my darling pup, I have you and Pepper and Basil. I should—"

Pepper barked, one sharp noise, then a series of warnings —no doubt sending a message to a human who dared walk the beach that they mustn't come any closer. The bark grew more insistent, so Lovely stood to go out to the screened-in deck and bring her in before she annoyed the beachwalker.

This stretch of sand and sea oats on the Atlantic-facing side of Coconut Key wasn't a common place to find tourists, since the dead-end street that made up this little peninsula was secluded and off the beaten path.

But walkers did make their way out here, and Pepper had to let them know she didn't approve.

She rounded the sofa and Basil followed, the two of them stepping out the sliding glass door to the real gem of her stilt beachfront home—the screened-in deck that ran the length of the house and faced the water.

Instantly, she saw the focus of Pepper's attention—a man standing in the shallow water, letting the gentle waves lap his bare feet, his back to Lovely. And his silver ponytail falling just past his shoulders.

"Oh." She drew back, feeling her eyes widen. "If it isn't Eddie the Elderly."

Pepper's barking intensified, and Eddie turned, looking straight toward the cottage. Instantly, Lovely felt...something. What was it about that man?

Maybe she should find out.

"C'mon, doggies." She lowered Sugar to the deck. "Let's greet the man who made my name famous. He might need something, and Beck's not there."

But was that really why she felt compelled to talk to him?

The three dogs darted to the stairs that led to the beach, galloping ahead. Even with their tiny legs, they made it to the lower deck in a flash, then ran to the small piece of grass they used as their bathroom.

After a quick stop, they trotted to the sand, reaching the hard pack long before she did.

At the same time, Eddie strode toward her, laughing at the pack coming at him.

With each step, Lovely got a better look at him, noticing

that he wore a loose cotton shirt and simple, baggy bathing trunks. Once again, she noticed he was fit for his age, which had to be close to hers, and carried himself with square-shouldered confidence that she'd always found attractive in men.

Not that she was...attracted.

Good heavens, was *that* what these blues were about? Hadn't those hormones checked out twenty years ago? Could she...

No! Impossible. Otherwise... Oh, Savannah would *never* let her hear the end of it.

"Why is this woman smiling?" he called as they got closer.

Was she? "If you can't smile in Coconut Key," she said, "you can't smile at all."

"Catchy. Let's give that line a tune."

She laughed. "That's right, you're a songwriter. I hope you're inspired by the view."

He slowly lifted his sunglasses and propped them on his head, giving her a jolt at the sight of eyes the color of faded denim jeans—and just as welcoming.

"I'm utterly inspired, Lovely," he said.

Oh...*my*.

"And who are these fine little fellows?" he asked, looking down at the two dogs who were barking, sniffing, and circling him.

Sugar stayed close to Lovely, gazing up with a question on her dear face.

"The brown and white Jack Russell is Basil, who will obey any command, and I do mean *any*. The one glaring at you is my personal bodyguard, Pepper, and she will not let anyone near me who hasn't been properly sniffed and approved. And this is Sugar," she said, bending over to pick her up and give the dog yet another reassuring kiss. "Attached, insecure, and sweet as pie."

"I come in peace, Pepper." He let the dog smell his hand, then tousled her rough coat with a friendly stroke. Still bent over, he looked up at her, one brow lifted. "Am I trespassing? I didn't see a sign."

"It's not a private beach, just feels like one," she said, petting Sugar's head as she studied the man across from her. "Is everything okay at the B&B? My partner left for the day, so I'm here if you need anything."

As he straightened, he took a breath as if...no. He couldn't be *nervous*. But he did seem just a bit tentative before he spoke.

"I understand you're the Lemonade Lady."

"I've been called worse," she replied with a tip of her head.

"Then I confess I've cleaned your B&B plumb out of the stuff, and have come to offer whatever you like for more. Cash, credit, or my firstborn—though I warn she's a handful. Name your price. I appear to have a Lovely's Lemonade addiction."

She let out a laugh, delighted by the compliment.

"It's the mint and basil," she told him. "I soak some in with the lemon water, then strain out the leaves. Come on." She waved him closer. "I just made two batches. Let's get you some, Mr. Sly."

He chuckled as he walked past the hammock to join her. "Yes to the lemonade, but no to Sly. It isn't even my real last name. I'm actually Edward Sylvester. Eddie Sly was made up by an agent who thought it would sell more records. Who knew Sly and the Family Stone would make it so much bigger? Then along came that Stallone guy and he stole the brand."

"Oh, music industry folklore," she cooed. "I like that. But you registered at Coquina House under that name."

"I kept it for business," he said.

"Performing?" she asked as they started walking.

"Nope. Haven't been on a stage in more years than I care to admit. After my one hit—thank you very much, Lovely—I moved into production and started a label, Sly Records."

Not sure why he'd thank her, but the way he said her name gave her a little thrill. And so did the fascinating business of a recording label.

"I've always had such a passion for music," she told him. "Wait until you see my vinyl collection. My great-granddaughter says it's worth a fortune. A small one, but still."

As he followed her toward the stairs, he looked up at the cottage, slowing his step to take in the home she'd lived in for more decades than she really wanted to admit.

"Speaking of worth a fortune, this is a dream piece of property, Lovely."

She loved the reverence and respect in his voice, looking up to see the unassuming beach bungalow from his perspective.

"Well, it's aging, humble, and comfortable," she said, smiling up at him. "Much like her owner." She tapped her chest. "I've lived here so many years, the locals just call it Lovely's cottage."

He tore his gaze from the house to study her. "Humble

and comfortable, maybe," he said. "But clearly young at heart."

"Oh, good gracious, you *are* a poet." She beckoned him to the stairs. "Now you get all the lemonade you can drink."

Laughing together, they went inside, and she headed to the kitchen for glasses and ice while he took a look around the living area attached to the kitchen.

"It's small, but the view's nice," she said, angling her head toward the sliders and the water vista.

"It's beautiful," he said. "Decorated by the same designer that did the B&B?"

"Designer?" she scoffed. "The B&B is all my talented daughter, who has quite an eye for décor. So, yes, she's had some influence here. This place has been through a lot of iterations—everything from my seventies earth tones era to the Y2K glitter bombs. Now, apparently, I'm in my coastal chic phase, or at least that's what they say on HGTV. Like, if you haven't shiplapped, have you even decorated?"

Good gracious, she was rambling. She clenched her jaw and poured lemonade while he meandered through the room.

"Whoa!" He stopped in front of the bookshelf, which was really a floor-to-ceiling record collection, holding out his hands as if he might need to drop to his knees and worship.

She laughed at the reaction. "It's vinyl or nothing for me."

"Amen, sister!"

"Although I admit to getting a thrill from how easy it is with that Spotify stuff," she added, hoping she didn't sound too old school. Or just plain old.

"Easy if you hate your ears. Wow, this is impressive." He

reached for an album jacket and slid it out. "*Hotel California*. Of course, a fan favorite." He slid it back into place and skimmed the dust jackets. "Crosby, Stills & Nash. Carly Simon. Buffalo Springfield." He nodded with approval. "Oh, Poco. So glad to see they made someone's collection. And Carole King's *Tapestry*. A classic of a bygone era."

"My bygone era," she said. "I'm a seventies folk-rock junkie."

"I see that. And here's Queen Joni. Lovely woman but, whoa, she can have a withering stare when she's not happy."

She gasped. "You've *met* Joni Mitchell? Now I am officially impressed. Possibly faint." She rounded the kitchen counter, holding his tall glass. "I'm sorry you won't find Electric Breeze. I don't know why I don't have a copy of...whatever album your song was on."

"Because there never was one," he said. "They only produced a single, and by the time we were able to get to a studio and record an album..." He shrugged and accepted the lemonade with a nod of thanks. "Label politics and band drama killed that career."

"I'm so sorry," she said, picking up her own lemonade from the counter.

"Don't be. It opened my eyes to where the real power and money is in pop music. The fall of Electric Breeze led me to a far steadier and more lucrative life on the production end."

Reaching toward the middle shelf, he pulled out a well-loved copy of *The Sounds of Echo Canyon*, her favorite album from Rust & Harmony. Turning it over, he pointed to a small logo and the words Sly Records underneath. "I actually produced this one."

"Really?" She glanced at the album cover with an image of a dreamy red-dirt canyon road that she'd studied for countless hours, memorizing every song—every note—on the vinyl disc inside. "*Wildflower Dreams*? *Lullaby for the Lost*?" She closed her eyes and nearly swooned. "And please —*When Embers Fade*? I cry at the first three notes."

Pressing the album cover to his chest, he smiled. "I wrote that song."

She nearly dropped her glass. "No!"

"I did. It's about Lani, my first wife."

"But it's so sad!"

He chuckled. "We broke up once and I wrote that song while lost in a Hawaiian cornfield under the moon. We got back together a week later because we were fated mates—"

"Another one of my favorite songs from that album."

He angled his head, silent, but he didn't have to say anything.

"You wrote that one, too?"

"Those songs all came out the year we decided to get married, so it's close to my heart, too. John Rust had a haunting voice, rest his soul, and he nailed my lyrics."

She stared at him, knowing she must be slack-jawed and starstruck, but she really didn't care. "I can't tell you how many, many hours of pleasure that album gave me. Solace and joy and inspiration to paint."

"You're a painter?" Both brows rose with interest.

She shook her head. "A dabbler who never sold much. Nothing like you." She raised her glass to him, a huge smile pulling. "I absolutely don't know how to thank you for writing songs that moved my heart so frequently—still, to this day. Thank you, Eddie. I am in the company of greatness."

He toasted with his glass, giving her a smile that was humble and wistful and...wary, though she couldn't imagine why.

"My glory days are long gone, Lovely, so it's really nice to meet...a fan."

She took a sip, then put her glass down and stepped toward the records, more comfortable with each passing minute. And far less lonely.

"Would you like to hear anything special?"

"I'd like to hear a yes."

"Yes? The band?" She crinkled her nose. "I'm not sure I have any of theirs. It's a little hard rock for me, but I..." At his amused expression, she let her voice trail off.

"I meant an actual yes," he explained. "To the question I'm about to ask. Forward and bold, but they say you never hit a homerun if you don't take a swing."

"*Oookay.* Ask away."

"I was talking to Beck before she left this morning," he said, shifting from one foot to the other. "I understand there's a table on the beach and a caterer that can't be canceled and fireworks for New Year's Eve and..." He bit his lip in a sweet expression that reminded her of someone. Beck, maybe. "Would you like to have dinner with me tonight, Lovely?"

She blinked at him, knowing a feather could have knocked her over.

"With your daughters?" she asked, because...well, was this a *date*?

"Those two are just young enough to want to hit the Key

West scene for New Year's Eve. Personally, I'd rather have my eyeballs plucked out with sharp scissors. But dinner on the beach with a beautiful woman who loves the same music I do? Now that's my idea of a good time."

She drew back, a tiny bit breathless.

"I'd love to," she said, softly and without hesitation. "What a wonderful way to end the year."

"And..." He lifted his glass again. "Start a friendship."

Instantly, her mood lifted. Goodness, how fast a day could shift from sad to sunshine and...Eddie Sly.

A TINY PART of Lovely was disappointed that Beck wasn't here to help her pick a dress and dish about her dinner date. Her daughter could fortify her with verbal encouragement and maybe one tiny sip of a "momosa," as Savannah called Beck's favorite drink.

Probably better this way, Lovely decided as she flipped through her array of maxi dresses, looking for something simple and understated. This wasn't a serious *date*—it was two people who'd been ditched by their daughters and wanted company for New Year's Eve.

That didn't mean it wasn't fun or special. That didn't mean it wasn't her first date in...this century.

Drawn to a pink and purple V-neck maxi with bits of gold threads in the fabric, she pulled out the dress and pressed it to the front of her bathrobe, looking in the mirror.

"Too...try hard-y, as Ava would say?" she asked the most faithful of her companions.

Sugar shuddered out a sigh and flopped her tail.

"I agree! You only live once, baby girl. Let's wear it!"

She slipped on the dress then added a bit of makeup, covering the mostly-faded scars that reminded her that, actually, she *had* lived twice. And that was all the more reason to go on a dinner date with the man who'd written some of her favorite songs.

Next, she fluttered the long silvery hair she'd washed and dried earlier, separating sections for her standard braid. Then her fingers stilled. She inched back and looked at herself in the mirror, and, on a whim, abandoned the braid.

Nope. She'd wear it loose tonight. At the end of December, even Coconut Key wasn't crazy humid, and she wanted to be a little free tonight. This long-haired songwriter brought that out in her, she admitted to herself. He made her feel...something.

She just couldn't figure out what it was.

Slipping on a pair of gold sandals, she grabbed a bag, gave the dogs some treats, and headed out to the Beach Table, where they'd planned to meet.

The caterer had called and said they'd completed the set-up for the dinner that had been booked for Beck and Oliver. So Lovely wasn't surprised to see the table arranged for two and covered in a soft linen cloth. There were warming dishes, an ice bucket, and lanterns flickering along the boardwalk that led to the intimate spot on the beach.

A few feet away, Eddie stood with his hands locked behind him, staring out at the water, seemingly unaware she'd arrived. He wore a white linen shirt with the long sleeves rolled up his forearms and khaki pants, the look perfectly casual but not sloppy. She appreciated that.

Lovely slowed her step and studied him, struck one more

time by that indefinable feeling she got when she looked at him. And, oh, how she wanted to define it.

Was this a spirit-to-spirit pull that some called chemistry and others called attraction? Yes...but it was different, too. It was a tap on her heart when she noticed a gesture or expression, a sensation when she looked into his eyes.

He seemed...familiar.

And that begged a whole host of questions. Of course, she'd never met him before and she didn't believe in past lives, but...she believed in the one that came after this one. After all, she'd been there.

Could she have met this man in that two-minute brush with the afterlife? In that time, she remembered seeing faces. Some she recognized, some strangers, and some were people she knew to be alive, which she didn't understand. She'd only talked to her sister, Olivia, in her brief brush with the Great Beyond, but she had seen...others.

That otherworldly experience had convinced her that she simply wasn't done here on Earth. As her life changed and her relationship with Beck blossomed, she'd always assumed she'd been sent back for that reason. But...what if there was more?

Maybe Eddie was here to teach her a lesson. Or perhaps he was the "soulmate" she'd long ago given up hoping to find. Maybe...maybe...he was *her person*! Her own fated mate.

She nearly whimpered at the idea.

Lovely Ames had spent a lot of her life waiting, wondering, hoping, and aching for what she believed was her One True Love. He never showed. There'd been men in her life, a suitor now and again, even some who'd risen to the rank of... boyfriend.

Like she and Beck joked, the word seemed inappropriate now, especially for Lovely so deep in her very golden years.

She'd given up hope of ever finding him. Still, she listened to the music of her "younger girl" era—some of which this man actually penned—and longed for something that never—

He turned and sucked in a soft breath, ending her thoughts. "Wow. You look beautiful."

A shiver whispered over her skin, despite the warm evening air.

"Thank you," she said, angling her head and fluttering the skirt with one hand. "I hope I didn't overdress."

"For New Year's Eve? There is no such thing." He came around the table and held out his hand. "You're perfect."

She smiled at the compliment. "I'm going to have to remember you are a wordsmith and not take anything you say tonight too seriously."

He'd started to pull out a chair for her, but froze at her statement. "Please don't do that, Lovely. I want you to believe everything I say tonight. I want to—I *have* to—be honest."

She hesitated for a second, looking into his crystal blue eyes. She wanted to ask what he meant by that, but she was suddenly transported...somewhere. Those eyes, that expression, it was...yes, familiar.

"What is it?" he asked, sounding concerned by whatever expression she wore—probably confusion.

"Oh, it's nothing. I just..." She studied his features, certain she'd never seen him before yesterday, not in person, at least. But those eyes reminded her of... *Dang*, she couldn't think of who it was.

"Thank you," she finished, slipping into the chair and looking over the table while he took the seat across from her, taking in the cloche covers, the crystal and china, and two tall green bottles perched in ice.

"Goodness. Two bottles of champagne?" She laughed. "You *do* intend for honesty."

"That's sparkling cider for me," he said, sliding his chair closer. "And you, if you prefer. I actually don't drink."

"Ah, okay." She eyed him as he lifted the bottle, nodding. "I'll try that cider, then, yes, thank you."

He popped the top and poured two flutes with hands that...why, goodness, he was trembling ever so slightly. Age or anxicty?

He looked over the bottle and followed her gaze. "Guess I'm more nervous than I realized."

Leaning back against the chair, she gave him a warm and genuine smile. "I promise you, if anyone is intimidated by this, it's me. I'm terrified I'll go all fan-girl, as the kids say, and start reciting your lyrics."

He poured a glass, let it fizz, then topped it, repeating the move on the other one without saying a word.

On a sigh, he handed her one glass and took the other, still silent as he looked at her with an expression she simply couldn't read. All she could see was...fear.

Why?

"Eddie," she said, suddenly longing to rid him of that. "There's no need to be tense. There are no expectations." She lifted her glass. "What should we drink to?"

He looked across the table, his eyes glistening with... tears? What the heck?

"I'm...sorry, Lovely."

She lowered her glass, her heart crawling into her throat. Something was very, very wrong with this moment and this man. Chills exploded on her arms and the hairs at the nape of her neck rose. A deep, dark foreboding pressed on her chest.

"I wanted to have dinner first," he said in a gruff, thick voice, which only made her more concerned. "I wanted to have a light conversation and get to know each other and laugh some more. I love your laugh," he said. "It's musical. It hits a minor note that appeals to me."

She took a steadying breath, barely hearing anything after his first sentence. "Dinner...first... Before what?"

He visibly swallowed, his eyes cast down again. "Before I tell you...but I can't just *chat* over dinner until I do."

"Tell me what?"

He finally looked up, his gaze so direct and powerful it felt physical. Like he could touch her and affect her and... What was this all about?

Silent, a tear rolled from his eye down his cheek, shocking her, stealing her next breath, and making everything in her feel all those same feelings of attraction and familiarity and...and... Oh, heavens, *no*!

That's who he was!

"I'm sorry," he whispered, already pushing back his chair. "Lovely, I'm so, so sorry for what happened that night. It was wrong and unplanned and wild and...and I don't know how to ever make it up to you."

With a soft cry, she pressed both hands to her lips, her

whole being transported and lost and vibrating with disbelief. "You are..."

"Ned." He breathed the short, distasteful three-letter name that was always synonymous with shame and regret and fate and...and...

How was this *possible*?

He was up and around the table before she could comprehend what was going on. He dropped to his knees next to her, reaching for her, his tears real.

"Please forgive me. Please don't be angry. Please, Lovely. I came to find Beck and I had no idea...I thought you were...it said her mother was...gone."

She shuddered a sob of shock and disbelief, fighting the urge to...run. Everything in her wanting to throw her body out of this moment and tear down the beach, away from her mistakes, back to the safety of solitude and the life she'd built.

She didn't want to face this! She didn't want to face *him*.

But he held her in place with strong, steady hands that didn't tremble now. He looked at her with blue eyes that had once seduced a young girl and never really left her memory. He wouldn't let her run away, so she did the only thing she possibly could...

She grabbed his shoulders with two hands, squeezed with all her might, and cried.

CHAPTER NINE
EDDIE

*E*ddie had no idea how long they stayed in what might have been the most uncomfortable position a seventy-six-year-old man ever held, but it was just the right amount of time.

Long enough for them to both let the emotion out, long enough for the cider to go flat, and long enough for Lovely to let go of the urge to cut out and end a moment she clearly hadn't been expecting.

And, thank God, long enough for them to decide they could take the next step and talk this out.

That, Eddie decided, was a big fat win.

"I'll take the real bubbly stuff now," she said on a wry laugh as he got up on stiff legs and returned to his seat, satisfied that she wouldn't bolt.

"I'll get it for you." He sat down and pulled out the champagne, tearing the foil as he met her gaze. "Are you okay?"

She sighed. "You're a kind and tender man," she said softly. "Thank you for—oh, my goodness!" She put her hand to her lips. "The song! It was...about me!"

He popped the cork, the celebratory sound somehow the perfect punctuation to her realization.

"It certainly was," he said. "After you left my tent, the sun hadn't even come up, and I tried to find you."

"I had to get back to Coquina House, climb the old trellis, and get back into my room before my mother woke up. She had refused to let me go to an outdoor concert but I couldn't bear to miss it."

"While you were sneaking back in?" He emptied one of the cider glasses onto the sand, then refilled it with champagne. "I was marching around Mallory Square, climbing over sleeping bodies, asking everyone if they'd seen a girl with golden hair and bangs, and big green eyes. 'Her name was Lovely,' I kept telling them. 'Her name was Lovely,' I said over and over. And then I went back to my tent, defeated, and wrote the lyrics to *Her Name Was Lovely*, a song that didn't get recorded for years."

Her jaw loosened and she rubbed her arms as if the story had given her chills. "I...I don't know what to say. I was shocked by my own behavior, terrified I would get caught, and deeply ashamed of my complete lack of control. I still am, if I'm being honest."

"Don't be," he said. "We were kids, smoked a joint, had an incredible connection, and...acted human. Really, really human. Don't be ashamed, Lovely. Don't punish yourself for a mistake you made."

He saw her shoulders sink and hoped that was because they were letting go of a weight she'd carried far too long.

He handed her the glass with a wistful smile. "You gave me a number one song."

"And you..." She took the glass, but this time it was her hand that seemed a little unsteady. "Gave me Beck."

"Then you won," he said, picking up the flat cider for a silent toast, the connection as they gazed over the table as strong as anything he could remember.

She took a sip, set the glass down, and studied him. "Why don't you drink?"

The question surprised him—so far removed from the real topic on the table—but he respected it.

"You want the truth?"

"Tonight, that's all I want."

He tipped his head in concession. "Of course. For the three years after our, uh, first meeting, I tried to be a recording star. I hitchhiked—wish I was kidding—from Tampa, where I'd grown up, to Los Angeles, and gave it everything I had. I hit every brick wall imaginable and...I used alcohol and weed to dull the pain of my failure."

"You're clearly not a failure."

"And I have you to thank," he said, getting a surprised look.

"It was spring of 1968, and I had about fourteen bucks to my name. I'd formed Electric Breeze with some buddies, but we were all lost, miserable, broke, angry, frustrated, jealous, and mostly drunk or high. We played some gigs in bars with six people ignoring us. I wrote a few decent songs, but the other guys didn't share my love of pop music. The drummer wanted to sound like Pink Floyd, and I wanted to sound like The Mamas and The Papas."

"What happened?"

"We got a shot to make an audition tape and somehow I convinced the band to record *Lovely*. A producer heard that tape and offered to release *Lovely* as a single, with another one of our songs on the flip side."

"*Voices in the Void*," she said without a second's hesitation and the perfect eye-roll. "Very Pink Floyd. Of course, I had the forty-five, but I lost it along the way."

He chuckled at that. "Well, my side won because a couple of radio jocks loved the song, and we got our big break when it got played on *American Bandstand*."

She clapped once, letting out a squeal. "I saw that episode! I was so excited to have my name in a song!"

Laughing, they toasted again, the tension of his confession fading like the evening light and a connection sparking with the first few stars in the sky.

"That song hit number one on August sixth and that was the last time I took a sip of alcohol—I decided that reality was too good to alter in any way, shape, or form. And we stayed at the top of the list for a few weeks." He grinned. "Until those hacks from Liverpool put out *Hey, Jude* at the end of August."

She laughed. "How dare they?"

"Right? Nice to know we were knocked off our pedestal by one of the most popular songs of all time." He finally took a drink of the cider. "With my act clean, I could see where the real money could be made in music. Not pennies on plays, and I knew I didn't have the charisma or, frankly, the voice, to go solo. I loved the production side and found I was quite good at spotting talent and trends." He shrugged. "But I would never have survived—literally and financially—if you hadn't inspired that song."

"Oh." She breathed out the word. "That's good. I'm glad."

"And, as you said, not the only thing to come from our, uh, ill-advised liaison. There is Beck, your—*our*—beautiful daughter. I still can't wrap my head around that."

"Beck is...everything," she said on a sigh. "Even though I

didn't raise her, she hit the world and never stopped making it a better place from the day she was born until today."

"That was clear from the moment I met her," he said, then leaned in, dreading this last bit of news, too, but it had to be said. "She knows."

"What?" She sputtered the question and the champagne she'd just sipped.

"She figured it out—"

"*What*?" she repeated, incredulous.

"Actually, I think you have a granddaughter named Savannah? She was the one who figured—"

"They *all* know? How?"

"I think my daughters asked one too many probing questions when we checked in and alerted Beck that something was up," he told her. "Beck and I talked last night, and it came out fairly quickly. That's when she told me her daughter had guessed it."

"Why wouldn't she tell me?"

"Because I asked if I could have this time with you privately," he said. "I felt strongly that I owed you an apology for my bad, bad behavior, and to be the one who told you who I am."

"Ned." She looked toward the sky again, letting out a long sigh. "I never liked that name."

"You and me both," he said on a dry laugh. "I left that name in Florida and have been Eddie ever since."

He watched the wheels turn in her head as she processed all this information. "Now I understand why Beck was scarce all day," she said. "Wait. Did you send Beck to Miami? I'm confused and don't know what to believe anymore."

"No, she really had to go there, and it all fell into place."

Gesturing to the covered dishes, he asked, "Do you still want dinner, Lovely?"

"I do," she said. "And I would like you to tell me just how you figured this out and found me."

"Happily."

Over slow bites of tender salmon and sips of their drinks, he told her the whole story, from the moment his granddaughter had discovered the genetic connection to Rebecca Foster right up to last night, when he and Beck opened the floodgates.

When he was done, and their plates were nearly empty, she dropped back on a long exhale, seemingly satisfied with dinner and his explanation.

"I suppose it was inevitable," she finally said. "With all the DNA business these days, a secret like this is impossible to keep."

"I'm glad we didn't keep it," he said simply. "I'm so happy to know you, and Beck. I should warn you that Beck invited us—all three of us—to your family gathering tomorrow. Are you okay with that? Does everyone know the truth about Beck?"

"Oh, everyone knows she's the result of a younger, wilder Lovely. Not exactly the details…" She flushed and gave an embarrassed smile. "Or that I didn't really know your name."

"Well, you know it now." He reached over the table and took her hand, glancing at the sparkles in the sky behind her. "And it looks like some fireworks are starting."

"They'll go all night up and down the beaches," she told him.

"Then why don't we continue this date with a walk in

the moonlight? Or would you like to call it and go home and...process?"

"A walk in the moonlight," she said with a smile, giving his hand a squeeze. "It sounds like a song you might write."

He tipped his head. "That's two great song titles since I got here," he said. "A first."

"Will you write them?"

"I wish I could," he said. "But I don't write much music anymore."

"Why not?"

He shrugged. "Writer's block, I guess. Old age. Lack of inspiration. And, of course, I'm retired." He drew her a little closer. "But if I spend more time in Coconut Key, who knows? I may be inspired and unblocked."

She laughed, but he wasn't kidding.

"Okay, I think I've got all of Beck's kids and their kids worked out," Eddie said as they strolled the cool sand, pausing when a particularly nice firework lit up the sky. "Kenny is the oldest—was adopted but now is part of this family—and he has a daughter, Ava. Kenny is marrying..." He dug for the name. "Hailey?"

"Heather," she corrected. "At the end of the month. I hope."

He shot her a look. "Kind of getting late to be hoping."

"Long story and I've told you so many of those."

"I love them all," he assured her. "But let me finish the daughters before I forget. Callie is the youngest, in law school in New York. A go-getter."

"Of the highest order, if you know the type."

"Oh, I know the type," he said. "Peyton is early thirties, an aspiring chef, married to Val Sanchez, living here in Coconut Key and expecting a baby girl, right?"

"Any day now."

"I hope I'm still here for the birth of a great-grandchild, because that is so cool."

"Well, she's not due for about three weeks, but I suppose she could be early."

Smiling, he draped a casual arm around her shoulders, determined to learn all about the family he'd meet tomorrow. "And Savannah, Beck's middle daughter, is really married to that heartthrob Nick Frye? That's wild. I heard he fell off the face of the earth."

"Just off the face of Hollywood. He was happy to leave the life," Lovely told him. "He was disillusioned with that world and very satisfied living here, and madly in love with Savannah. And they're having their second child in late April. Little Dylan is their son, who's a year and a half."

"Ah, yes, the one you call French Frye."

She trilled that melodic laugh. "You are a great listener," she observed.

"Still have my hearing." He tugged on an earlobe. "My knees feel like they belong to Methuselah, but the hearing's good."

"Aging isn't for the faint of heart," she agreed. "Everyone who says it's just a mindset hasn't crossed sixty-five."

"The kids keep you young," he said. "Lark and Kai do that for me."

"Melody's children, right? Now tell me about them, please."

He beamed with pride. "Don't get me started, 'cause I'll never stop. Lark is twenty-six going on forty, another high achiever who never met a deadline she couldn't crush or a task she couldn't dominate."

"She and Callie could rule the world," Lovely said.

"And probably will someday. Now, Kai? He can barely rule his life. He's a twenty-three-year-old surfer who is supposed to be working at the label, but doesn't always show up if the waves are good at Half Moon Bay. But in some ways, he's a carbon copy of his grandmother, my late, great first wife, Kailani Kahue."

"She was Hawaiian, I take it?"

"Born and raised. I met her when one of my recording artists was doing a live album in Honolulu and she was hired as the photographer for the cover art. She wanted to take the photos from the top of a volcano, and dragged me up there." He chuckled at the memory. "It was, if you will allow me a cliché—and you should, because there's nothing a songwriter loves more—love at first sight."

"Ahh. That's sweet." She leaned into him ever so slightly, smiling up. "She was your fated mate."

Oh, was she ever, he thought. "Fated, all right." He sighed, knowing he was smiling, as always when he talked about Lani. "Gone far too young."

"I'm so sorry," she said, her voice soft and reverent. "Was she sick?"

"Lani was a thrill-seeker who never met a risk she wouldn't take." He felt a familiar and sad weight in his chest, as he did anytime he told the story. "She died in an accident, hang-gliding to get the perfect shot over in Ka'ena Point in Oahu. The place is known for its unpredictable wind gusts and wretched terrain. She was hired to get a photo of someone else gliding with her, and they were, sadly, both killed."

Lovely let out a soft groan. "You must have been devastated."

"Beyond. Also furious. I hated her obsession with living life on the very hairy edge. Her fearlessness and incredible eye made her a sought after 'extreme adventure' photographer." He added air quotes for the job that hadn't existed back then, but there was no other way to describe what Lani did. "In the end, she took one risk too many. Mel was only three, which was the real travesty."

"Oh, so sad."

He gave her shoulder a squeeze, hating the subject and not wanting to bring down their magical reunion. "Enough about me."

"But you remarried," she said, clearly not having heard enough about him. "Jazz's mother?"

"Victoria," he said. "She's still a close friend and business partner. She was an early investor in Sly Records, and a genius chemist, and we were always friends. After Lani died, she was the one who picked up my shattered pieces and helped me with Mel." He shrugged. "I thought I was in love again, but I was just in need. Victoria was part therapist, part friend, part nanny. A great friend and vintner—we own a small winery together in Napa—but not a life partner. We divorced on amicable terms and are still quite close."

"That's the way to do it."

He looked down at her, studying her face in the moonlight, curious about the nearly invisible scars he saw but, again, wanting to keep the conversation a little lighter. He suspected they were related to the accident Beck had told him about, so he took a different direction.

"What about you? Love? Marriage?" He already knew Beck was her only child, but hadn't she had a partner in her life?

She shook her head and, for some reason, his heart dropped.

"Never married," she said.

"I'm sorry," he said softly. "You're such an amazing woman, I can't help but think someone made a big mistake along the way not snatching you up."

"I'm the one who made a mistake," she said, turning toward the water so he couldn't see her face.

He didn't respond, waiting for more, wondering if she'd let one get away or...or...*Oh*.

He was her mistake. "Lovely. I feel like I...like that might be my fault."

"Any decisions I made in my life were fully my own," she told him turning back, but he could see the shadow of pain in her eyes. "But it was a dark secret to carry, and I always believed if I found my...my *fated mate*, if you will, then..." She shrugged. "It couldn't be very *fated* if I wasn't completely honest. And with Beck not knowing for all those years, and my promise to Olivia that I wouldn't tell her? I just couldn't. And I didn't want to lie to someone, so it was easier not to fall in love."

He let out a soft grunt and shook his head at the weight of what she'd carried all by herself for so many years.

"I'm so sorry. You deserved to be loved, Lovely. You deserved more children and a husband and that forever love." He sighed and squeezed his eyes shut. "Wow. It's just not fair that one night in Key West—one stupid, crazy, immature decision—would change your life that way."

"I told you, Eddie, my decision, not yours."

He pulled her in closer to him, knowing that to any of the people along the beach, they probably looked like an old married couple slipping out for a New Year's Eve date.

And that couldn't be further from the truth.

"I'm in awe of you, Lovely," he said, leaning his head on hers. "You know, I'm here for two weeks and all I want to do is somehow make it up to you. I want to spend time with you, take walks with you, listen to music, dance, laugh, share stories, and...and...and somehow make up for what I took from you."

She smiled up at him. "You didn't take anything. But I'll accept that offer and spend the next two weeks doing all that with you."

Stopping in the sand, he turned her to face him, both of them holding each other in the most natural way.

Under any other circumstances, he might kiss this woman, but these were not normal circumstances. Instead, he looked into her eyes and made a silent vow to somehow repair the damage done by the sins of their past.

A loud, bright blue firework filled the sky, and they both looked up and laughed, filling his heart with hope that he could do just that.

CHAPTER TEN
HEATHER

"Happy New Year, Mommy!"

Heather looked up from her pen and paper at the kitchen table, drawing in a breath at the sight of her teenage daughter.

"Maddie! Happy New Year, angel. You're up early."

"New Year's resolution," she said, her long blond hair swinging as she grabbed a glass from the cabinet and headed to the fridge to fill it. "Along with water before coffee, homework before social media, no more cookies after dinner—"

"Cookies? Now you've gone too far," Heather cracked.

She turned to look over her shoulder, the angle accentuating her high cheekbones and true beauty. "I mean it. And you'll love my last resolution. I'm going to church with you and Kenny and Ava every Sunday."

"Church?" Heather blinked at her, quietly spreading her hand over the page of the Bible in front of her. "That's awesome, honey."

Water in hand, she sauntered to the table, looking like a supermodel despite her PJs of choice—a faded SpongeBob SquarePants T-shirt and Santa Claus sleep pants.

"Credit—or blame, if I hate it—goes to Ava. She convinced me it's a great church and she likes youth group a lot. So I said I'd go."

Heather smiled at her, a warmth filling her as she fought the urge to fist-pump the air and praise the God of surprises.

Her children had not been raised with any faith, since Drew had been an ardent non-believer. Almost immediately after he'd died, Heather had given in to a tug on her heart, starting to read everything she could about Christianity, then finally cracked a Bible.

She'd met Kenny in those early days of finding her faith —a man who'd been raised with plenty of it, but had drifted far away, and for good reason. The loss of his wife and son had left him disillusioned with God.

Together, they'd found their way to a beautiful place, joining Our Redeemer, a church where they were both happy and active. She invited her kids all the time, but understood that teenagers raised with an atheist father had to make the decision to go—or believe—on their own.

She never hid her faith from them, but she didn't force it, either.

"God bless Ava," she said, containing her joy.

"Speaking of the Big Guy..." Maddie tapped the open Bible, then glanced at the notebook page covered from top to bottom in writing. "Taking some serious notes, Mom."

"Not notes," she said, slowly turning the notebook. "I'm writing the Bible."

"You're...what?" She choked softly. "Handwriting it? The whole thing?"

"Yep. I started about four months ago and I'm a third of the way through Exodus, which is the second of sixty-six books."

Maddie's soft blue eyes popped. "Dude. You got a long way to go."

"I'm giving myself ten years."

She propped her elbows on the table and stared at

Heather's writing, which wasn't that bad, but was no work of art. "Why would you do this?" she asked.

"Because it's a way of imprinting the words on my heart," Heather said. "I heard about people who do it because they learn by writing and remember things better. I read fast and I miss a lot, and this slows me down and forces me to focus. Plus, I feel like it's a way to honor God."

While Maddie read, Heather scooted closer, imagining this moment might be a gift from the Holy Spirit to help her open her daughter's heart. The rest was up to Jesus, Heather knew, but if she could just help her see—

"The parting of the Red Sea?" Maddie scrolled her finger over the page. "I'd imagine that was a high point so far."

"One of them," Heather said. "And I hadn't expected it to hit me so hard, but right in the middle of all the action—Egyptians chasing Israelites and such—God hit me with a verse that just, wham. Gobsmacked me. I look for those when I'm writing it out."

"Which one?" Maddie asked, genuinely interested.

"Right there in Chapter Fourteen. Verses Thirteen and Fourteen." Heather turned the Bible toward her daughter so she could read the words that had just squeezed her own heart. Would they have the same impact?

Maddie's long lashes brushed her cheeks as she looked down at the page and read. "'Moses answered the people: Do not be afraid. Stand firm and you will see the deliverance the Lord will bring you today. The Egyptians you see today you will never see again. The Lord will fight for you; you need only to be still.'" She waited a beat, then looked up. "Okay. That's...Bible-y. Moses and everything. Not quite getting more than that."

Heather nodded. "God is saying that He will handle my troubles, all I have to do is stand firm and be still."

"Do you have troubles, Mom?" Her brows knit in concern. "Is everything okay?"

She let out a sigh. "Everything's fine, honey. I just..." She swallowed, hating that her throat got thick, but not surprised. Ten minutes ago she'd been crying.

"You got Egyptians on your tail?" Maddie joked, not realizing how close to the truth it was.

And, goodness, she needed to share her burden with Maddie, of all people. This affected her as much as Heather.

"Aunt Blanche," she said softly.

"She's Egyptian?"

Heather laughed softly, but her smile faded. "She's determined to get us back to South Carolina where, in some ways, I was as much a prisoner as the Israelites were. And I guess Coconut Key is my Promised Land."

"Wait, wait. What?" Maddie waved her hand, not following. "Why the heck would we go back to South Carolina?"

"Why wouldn't we?"

They both spun around at the completely unexpected sound of Marc's voice—always a shock that it was so low now that, at fifteen, it had truly changed. But the real shocker was seeing him awake, since he normally used any non-school day to sleep in as late as humanly possible.

He did look like he just woke up, with his wavy brown hair tousled, some pillow lines on his cheek, and his glasses a little crooked since he, of course, hadn't put his contacts in yet.

"Why *would* we?" Maddie demanded, rising from her

chair as if everything else in her world was forgotten. "Life is perfect here."

"Perfect for you," he countered.

"Marc, aren't you happy in Coconut Key?" Maddie asked. "You're going to play varsity ball this year, as a sophomore."

"Life is not just baseball, Maddie." He pulled open the fridge and reached for the milk that only he drank—but keeping it in stock was a challenge.

"What's wrong, honey?" Heather asked softly, knowing her boy wasn't the open book that Maddie was, and this could take a little digging.

"I don't know," he grumbled. "I walk down here and you two are talking about Moses and moving? What the hell?"

"Hey." She narrowed her eyes, not caring that he didn't think "hell" was that bad a word; it wasn't. But she wouldn't tolerate anything worse.

He gave the fridge door a hard push, then spun around to them. "Why couldn't we go back to Charleston? Kenny would go. He told me he would. And Maddie's going to—"

Heather gasped softly. "He *what*? You talked to Kenny about it?"

"Yeah, after we got back. I did." He sloshed some milk into a glass and gave her a defiant look. "I talk to him, you know. And I talked to Grandpa Andy. We talked last night, as a matter of fact."

She spoke "teenager" well enough to know that they "talked" meant they texted, but she longed to know what was said. And suspected they were getting to the heart of Marc's bad mood.

"Is he okay?" she asked, always concerned about Andy's welfare.

"Yeah, I guess."

"What does that mean, Marc?"

"It means...he's fine. He's sad. He's lonely. He's fishing all by himself and Aunt Blanche says that's not safe. Caught some redfish, though, so that's cool."

Blanche says it's not safe? Why doesn't she go with him? Heather tamped down the unkindness. The bottom line was a seventy-year-old man probably shouldn't go fishing alone in the Lowcountry marshes and creeks.

"We're not moving back there," Maddie proclaimed, not interested in fishing. "That's insane. It's my senior year and I'm in the play and I'm going to college in Florida and this has to stop."

"You're right, you're going to college," Marc fired back. "So will Ava. You two cozy new stepsisters won't even be here. And if Kenny thinks it's a good idea, why shouldn't we?"

Cozy stepsisters? Was he jealous? And Kenny thought it was a good idea? Heather practically reeled at the thought. And why would he talk to Marc about it and not her? She had barely shared what Blanche had said, playing it down, but apparently...he was willing to move?

Was that God opening a door?

"Grandpa Andy should move here," Maddie said, dropping back and folding her arms. "Ava and I think he and Lovely would make a great couple."

"Oh, my God!" Marc smacked his hand on the countertop.

"Marc, don't take His name in vain," Heather said.

"Come on, Mom! What's wrong with you two? That's all you talk about—people falling in love, and Mom getting married, and now you're going to church?" He pointed at his sister, making Heather wonder just how long he'd been eavesdropping on their conversation.

"If either of you cared about God or what was right," he continued, "you'd make Grandpa Andy more important. You'd care about what was happening to him. He's still our grandpa, even though Dad's dead. But all you two care about is weddings and church and dumb stuff. I care about *him*!"

He thunked his empty glass in the sink, making Heather flinch. It didn't break, but her heart did when he marched out and called, "I'm going back to bed and not going to that stupid party. I told Grandpa we could talk later."

The next sound was his door banging closed, making Heather flinch when it echoed like a gunshot.

"Nice way to start the new year," Maddie muttered.

Heather let out a groan. "I was worried about this. But I honestly didn't expect Kenny to agree, especially without talking to me first."

"Those two are thick," she said. "Which is cool, but..."

"I don't want to leave," Heather admitted on a whisper, dropping her head in her hands. "I do not want to move back there."

"We need to get Grandpa Andy here." Maddie stood up. "I'm telling you—he and Lovely? Match made in heaven. How cute would they be? Old people love! Ava and I have been plotting the whole thing. Will he be here for your wedding?"

She looked up. "I don't know. I think coming to my wedding is a lot to ask of a man who lost his son less than two years ago. It's hard for him. You can't imagine what it's like for a parent to lose a child."

And no one knew that like Kenny, she thought, forgiving him for having the conversation with Marc. Her son filled a hole in Kenny's heart and, normally, she counted that as a blessing.

"Well, you know what to do, Mom," Maddie said as she pushed in her chair.

"I do?"

She leaned over and pressed her fingertip to the Bible page. "Stand firm. Don't let them Egyptians get ya."

With that, she left and, despite all odds, Heather felt a smile pull. Sometimes God sent his message through the most unlikely sources.

THROUGH THE DISCUSSION of typical travel logistics for the party—Maddie wanted to drive over with Ava, who would bring Kenny's truck, so Mom could pick up Kenny in the van—Marc was the one who stood firm.

He wasn't going to Savannah's house for a party. The discussion—and door—was closed.

So Heather drove alone to get Kenny, fighting a battle with the devil, who loved nothing more than for her to feel uneasy and uncertain.

"Get out of my van," she muttered as she parked in Kenny's driveway, leaving the door open to symbolically boot the enemy from her heart and head.

Replacing all thoughts with a prayer, she walked up to

the house and tapped on the door, barely waiting a moment for him to open it.

And as soon as he did, she felt better. The tall, strong, faithful, handsome, wonderful man who'd changed her life always looked at her with just enough adoration that she felt whole and beautiful.

Today was no different.

"Morning, gorgeous," he said, reaching for her with a smile that sparked his dark eyes, the same one that had been there last night when he'd stayed until midnight so they could have their first kiss in the year they were getting married.

For reasons she'd never understand, her heart dropped as he pulled her in for a hug and another light kiss. Then he looked over her shoulder, drawing back with a frown.

"Where's Marc?"

"He's not coming."

"Whoa." He studied her face, always able to read her emotions. Without another word, he brought her into his small house, a rental he and Ava would be leaving in February when they moved into Heather's house. "Come on, we're early. Talk to me, babe."

Following him to the leather sofa in the living room, she sat down and told him everything, from Blanche's diatribe to Marc's temper-tantrum.

"Oh, and your wonderful daughter has convinced mine to start going to church," she finished.

His jaw dropped. "Well, that's the real news, Heather. That's awesome. Way to go, Ava."

"I know, you're right," she agreed. "Maddie knowing

Christ is a way bigger deal than us moving. Did you really tell Marc you would?"

He let out a sigh and leaned back. "I told Marc the truth —that I would do anything to keep this little family we're creating together and happy. Why didn't you tell me about Blanche? You've been back for a few days."

"I don't know. Because, deep inside, I knew you'd probably say if I wanted to move, you'd move. Especially with Maddie and Ava going to college."

"Maddie going," he said. "Ava? We'll see when the acceptances come in."

"What do you mean? They both applied to the same schools."

"And Maddie will get in anywhere, even UF, which is like Ivy League these days. But Ava doesn't have her grades or test scores or the extracurricular stuff Maddie has. She might not get into the same level school."

"Then Maddie won't go to that school," Heather said. "She wants to be roommates."

He choked softly. "Maddie is not going to pick a junior college just because Ava didn't get into a four-year university," he said. "That's crazy."

She held up a hand, waving off the discussion for when it became a reality. Now, she had to think about the problem at hand.

"What's crazy is moving to South Carolina," she said. "You've built a thriving construction business, I love my job at the café, my house is perfect for all of us, the kids are happy at this school, and we have an extended family here that— Well, trust me. It beats the one I have there. Why would we go?"

But even as she said it, she knew. Grandpa Andy.

Kenny rubbed his clefted chin, freshly shaved for the day. As always, he took a moment to consider his response, no doubt mentally skimming scripture for guidance. It was something she loved dearly about him, but right now, she wanted a simple, "We're not going."

"You know I have a weak spot for Marc," he said instead.

"It's one of the many reasons I love you. He's lost a dad and—"

"And I lost a son," he interjected. "We both fill a need for each other. And that kid loves his grandpa so much. I respect that."

"He can love him from afar."

He nodded. "I know, but I can't help spoiling him a little, you know. When I think about Adam..." He worked to swallow. "He'd be a sophomore, too, now, and..." Turning to her, she could see his brown eyes fill with tears. "I want to give him everything he wants."

"And me?"

"You?" he scoffed. "I want to give you the sun, moon, stars, and...and...anything. Anything in the world. I love you so much I can't even breathe when I think about it."

She laughed at that, both of them hugging in a move that had become as natural as breathing. "I don't know why I ever doubted this marriage."

He whipped back. "Excuse me?"

"You know doubt is my worst trait."

"Not about me you don't doubt!"

She smiled, always touched at the fervor he put into this relationship. She hated to let herself think how much she'd longed for that from Drew, but never got it. And he'd been a passionate man about a lot of things—just not Heather.

But Kenny was more than making up for what that marriage had lacked.

"I don't doubt you, but..."

"But what?" he asked, stroking her hair back with his large but oh so tender hand.

"It's fast. Getting married, I mean. It feels very fast."

He nodded, no stranger to this concern. "It also feels very right, blessed, and certain."

"But to my in-laws in Charleston? Drew hasn't been gone that long."

"He hasn't," Kenny agreed. "And you know I've given my word that he won't be forgotten by your kids, just like Ava and I talk about Adam and Elise all the time."

"You don't talk about them all the time," she said gently. "And there are full days in our house when Drew's name is never even mentioned."

"We'll change that," he promised. "And I'll talk to Marc. I'll tell him that moving is not a reasonable request and, hey, maybe over spring break the four of us can drive up to Charleston and take ol' Grandpa Andy fishing."

Her heart eased at the offer. "You, Kenneth Gallagher, are the greatest man to ever live."

"Not even close, but I love that you think that." He leaned in for a kiss, then held her close. "Let's swing back to your house and see if I can talk Marc into changing his mind and joining us today."

She sank deeper into his arms. "I love you."

"Darn right you do," he teased, kissing her head. "You're

marrying me this month, Heather Monroe, and nothing is going to stop that."

She kissed him again, and felt the doubts lift and float away.

CHAPTER ELEVEN
BECK

*B*eck arrived at The Haven, her daughter's breathtaking waterfront property, itching to share the news. She wanted to get her daughters alone first so she could confirm their suspicions, which turned out to be rather easy.

When Nick went upstairs to get Dylan from his late-morning nap, and Peyton's husband, Val, headed to the beach to set up the volleyball net and fishing rods for the kids, she had the perfect opportunity.

But before she could gather the girls, Savannah swooped into the kitchen and grabbed her arm. "To the deck," she said, where Callie and Peyton were setting a long table. "I have news."

"So do I," Beck said, earning a look.

Outside, when they spotted Savannah and Beck, Callie rushed over and Peyton—well, Peyton didn't rush anywhere, but she moved as quickly as a woman could in her ninth month.

"Get this, you guys," Savannah said, bringing Beck closer and lowering her voice. "Lovely texted and asked if she could bring the three B&B guests today. What do you think that means?"

All three of them looked at Beck, who angled her head and smiled, waiting a beat to enjoy the moment of anticipation and the warmth of the sun on her skin.

"It means that those guests are your biological grandfather and aunts."

They squealed, gasped, and generally reacted exactly as Beck expected they would.

"How do you know?" Callie asked.

"He told me outright when I came home that first night they checked in. And then Mel and Jazz came back, and we talked for hours! I had to take Oliver to Miami, as you know, so Eddie and Lovely had dinner last night at the Beach Table and he told her, too."

Another noisy gasp came out in sisterly unison.

"And what did she say?" Callie demanded.

"To him? I don't know," Beck told them. "I told him about the party today and obviously, Lovely wanted them to be here. I talked to her this morning, and she just seemed a little...giddy. Happy, I think. Pleasantly surprised."

"That's so amazing," Peyton said on a sigh. "I've been worried about her."

"No need. Honestly, I think he's a really a nice man and he handled the whole thing with grace and tenderness and a remarkable amount of humor."

"He must be great," Savannah said, "or she wouldn't have invited them here."

"And she's being the class act we know and love," Beck added. "She told me to come alone and that she'd drive over with them so she could make them all comfortable walking into this family party. She also said she'd come a little late, so we have a chance to break the news to everyone else and save her the awkward explanations and raised eyebrows."

"Who's going to raise a brow?" Peyton said. "It's not like we don't know the history."

"She's just being careful and kind," Beck replied, turning when she heard Maddie and Ava's laughter floating up from the beach. "She'll want us to gently explain it to the kids. Oh, and Kenny doesn't know he has a grandfather, and I think he and Heather should get here any minute. He texted me about going back to her house for Marc, who probably wanted to sleep in late."

"Jessie, Chuck, and the hooligan will be here, too." Savannah said, shrugging at their looks. "Sorry, Beau's a handful."

"I can't wait until you have a kid who misbehaves," Peyton said. "Then we'll see who's a hooligan."

"What about Josh and Julie?" Beck asked, trying to figure out just how many people would be finding out this earthshattering news today.

"He said they are going to a party at her family's house," Savannah said. "So that's the guest list."

At the loud cry of a child's voice, Savannah slid them a side-eye. "I hear the call of the wild, er, Beau."

Beck walked to the railing to look down at the beach just as Heather, Kenny, and Marc walked up to the group down there.

"Once Nick comes down, we'll have a quorum," she said.

"I'll go get him," Savannah said. "He's dressing Dylan. Callie, can you get that crew up from the beach so we can try to explain the latest shockeroo in Coconut Key?"

"Of course." Callie rose on a happy sigh. "I can't get over the fact that we have another grandfather. I think that's so cool."

"It is cool," Savannah agreed. "But wait until our kids have to make a family tree for a school project. 'Oh, honey, that's your grandfather who knocked up Grandma Lovely... Why, yes, just like me and Dad. And Grandpa Oliver and Grandma Beck? Well, one is my mother, and one is Daddy's father, so...'" She groaned. "I think I'll homeschool just to avoid the gnarled branches."

"Or you tell the kids the truth," Peyton said, rubbing her belly with one hand. "We do have a lot of branches, some broken, but Val's big Cuban clan is just as—well, maybe not *just* as complicated—but that's what families are—messy and wonderful."

Savannah patted her sister's belly as she passed. "You'll love her, McFatFace, but she's a little naïve. Come to Auntie Savannah for reality checks."

Peyton flicked her away, laughing, while Callie took off for the beach.

"So, Mom," Peyton said to Beck, "you have two sisters. Can I say from experience, that's a gift? Usually. Unless one's Savannah."

"I heard that!" Savannah called as she stepped inside.

"I wanted you to!" Peyton shot back.

Beck laughed at them, sliding her arm around Peyton to guide her to a comfy rattan sofa. "I'm overjoyed, a little shocked, and excited. I can't wait to get to know them even more."

"What should we expect?" Peyton asked. "I mean, what are they really like?"

"Awesome, all of them," Beck said without hesitation, sitting next to her. "Mel is just a ball of fire and hilarious. She's half-Hawaiian, gorgeous, and very protective of her father. And Jazz is like a long, cool icicle who I think could easily thaw. Also beautiful, in that highcheekboned blond way. And Eddie? Oh, I really like him."

"Apparently, Lovely did, too, which surprises me," Peyton mused. "I don't know why, but she's so squirrelly on the subject of your less-than-noble conception, so I imagine she's a little embarrassed to come face-to-face with him."

"She'd tell me if she didn't like him, trust me," Beck said. "And she wouldn't have agreed to ride over here with them."

"Well, that's good," Peyton said. "They'll have to be Coconut Key regulars."

"I don't know." Beck shrugged, thinking about all she knew about the successful sisters and Eddie's two homes out West. "They've got full and busy lives in California. I doubt they'll be spending a lot of time here, but I do really want to get to know them before they leave."

"Oh, she's moving." Peyton grabbed Beck's hand. "Feel this little girl kick."

Instantly, Beck put her hand on the rise of Peyton's belly, a big smile pulling when a tiny foot jabbed her palm. "Oh, there she is! Hello, sweet..." She made a pretend frown. "Name My Daughter Won't Tell Me." She leaned in close to whisper, "I know you have a name picked."

Peyton just smiled, then looked past Beck. "Oh, look. Here come the troops. Get ready to tell the tale, Momma."

Little Beau came tearing onto the deck with a running lead, then Jessie and Chuck came up the stairs, followed by Val, then Maddie and Ava, and Heather and Kenny.

Marc stayed way in the back, looking at his phone, a little disconnected from the group, although the rest of them seemed intrigued, peppering Beck with questions about Callie's announcement of "big family news."

Before he could run off, Callie snagged Beau's hand. "I'll get Dylan, too," she said. "We can hang in the playroom while you talk, Mom." She winked at Beck, who beamed in gratitude at her youngest daughter's considerate thinking.

A minute later, she looked from one to the other as they gathered in a semi-circle around her, making Beck suddenly feel like the matriarch of this clan.

"Where's Lovely?" Jessie asked.

"Well, that's what I want to tell you—"

"Is she okay?" Val asked, concern in his dark eyes as he put an arm around Peyton.

"Yes," Beck assured them. "She is fine. But she's bringing some people today who...who might surprise you. They're guests at Coquina House, but they're also..." She fought a smile, surprised at how happy this news made her and hoping for the same reaction from them. "They're also my biological father and two half-sisters who arrived in Coconut Key two days ago."

At first, there was silence, then a lot of questions. Marc just shook his head and walked away, looking disinterested. Kenny bolted right after him, and said something no one heard.

Beck answered the questions as best she could, sensing that Val and Nick had already been clued in by their wives, but soon everyone was chatting with theories and opinions. Before long, they reached the obvious consensus that more family could only be a good thing.

"I knew I could count on all of you," Beck said, overwhelmed by how much she loved this group.

"Of course," Nick said, her son-in-law coming closer with a supportive arm. "We love you and Lovely and this whole family. I've done my share of upsetting the apple cart, what with my long-lost father discovering me the weekend of my wedding. How is Olipop, anyway?" he asked with a smile.

She smiled at the "grandfather" name that Savannah had hung on Oliver that, like most of her nicknames, stuck like glue.

"On his way..." She made a face. "I almost said 'home.' But that's here, I hope."

"Well, he's selling the manse in Sydney," Nick said. "So that's a step out of Australia and closer to us."

"But he's keeping the beach house," Beck reminded him.

"Which is smart," he said. "You can go hang there all summer long, which is winter here, so..."

"Which would mean leaving my business in the middle of the high season," she said, the argument she'd given Oliver a dozen times when he suggested they split their time between two continents.

"Don't you want to retire, Beck?" He leaned closer to add, "I have to tell you, it's a good life."

But she'd just started working after a lifetime of being a wife and mother, and kind of hated the idea of giving it up. "I love every minute of running Coquina House," she said. "Why would I quit now?"

"To spend more time with Olipop," he replied. "The guy loves you, you know."

She nodded slowly. "And I see him a lot."

"He wants you to go to Australia. To spend time there and soak up his homeland."

How much time, she wondered. "And I will, I promise," she said. "But I—"

"They're here." Savannah whizzed by, passing Dylan off

to Nick. "Watch him. I went to get him in the playroom and Beau the Barbarian was teaching him the fine art of nose-picking."

"Eww." Nick took his toddler and made a gross face. "Dis*gusto*!"

Dylan giggled and snuggled into his father's neck.

"Anyway, Beck, one life change at a time," he said. "Incoming new family in five, four, three..."

Beck turned to the stairs that led up from the driveway, getting a flash of déjà vu from the day Oliver had appeared at the top of the steps—a sixty-one-year-old version of his great-looking son. From the moment they met, he'd made Beck a little weak in the knees.

She'd certainly felt weak yesterday, kissing him goodbye at the airport. When he'd pressed his lips to her ear and whispered that if she had her passport, he could whisk her away... she darn near buckled.

If Peyton wasn't literally days from giving birth, she might have—

"Happy New Year, everyone!" Lovely's sweet voice easily reached the whole group on the deck, since they'd grown quiet in anticipation. "I'm thrilled to introduce you all to Eddie Sylvester and his daughters, Melody and Jazz."

As the greetings rose and people slowly closed in for introductions, Beck held back, caught by something in her mother's voice. And her expression—a look of wonder and exhilaration that Beck was certain she hadn't seen before.

Goodness, Lovely was happy about this reunion.

She watched her mother put a light hand on Eddie's shoulder, gesturing as she introduced him to Savannah and

Peyton and Callie. Instead of looking at her granddaughters, though, Lovely's gaze was on Eddie.

A look of...

Oh, dear. Oh, my. Oh...*wow*.

They both laughed at a joke Savannah made, and Eddie turned to Lovely, leaning close to her ear to say something private to her, and getting a look of...well, Beck couldn't follow the exchange. She had no idea what they'd said.

But she was quite fluent in the concept of infatuation. And, whoa. Lovely Ames, her seventy-five-year-old mother who'd been single for a lifetime, was...one smitten kitten.

THE FIRST TIME Beck got Lovely alone—passing each other in the hall on the way to and from the bathroom—she grabbed her mother's arm and stated the obvious.

"You like him."

Lovely flushed like Ava did when Maddie teased her about that Levi boy in their calculus class. "I do, yes. Don't you?"

"Very much." Beck leaned in and whispered, "Maybe not as much as you do."

"Oh, dear." She put her hand to her lips. "Am I making a fool of myself?"

"Not even in the least. No one in the world knows you like I do, Lovely." Beck took her hand. "I just think it's sweet and fun and wonderful that you two have talked and connected."

With a sigh, she tugged Beck closer. "He's very attractive, isn't he?"

"Oh, yes. I mean, considering he's my biological father." And seventy-six, Beck added mentally, not wanting to say anything to take the smile off her mother's face.

"Well, yes, that's weird, but..." Lovely giggled a little. "I mean, those eyes! And he's so poetic and...just dear. At least it explains how he, um, *wooed* me in the first place. The chemistry is like nothing I've ever experienced before."

This whole thing was like nothing she'd ever experienced before, at least as far as Beck knew.

"I'm glad you're having fun," Beck said, wanting to add a warning but, again, the spark in her mother's eyes was too delicious.

"And we're going to continue having fun," Lovely said. "It's just not going to end."

Beck blinked at her, not sure how to take that.

"I mean for two weeks," Lovely added quickly. "He said he wants to spend the time he's here with me. We're going to go up to Grassy Key to swim with the dolphins and he wants to go out on Chuck's charter boat. Oh! And he wants to go kayaking to see manatees, all the things that tourists do."

"Kayaking and swim with the dolphins?"

"Well, not on the same day—we're too old for that." Lovely laughed, then her expression grew serious. "I know that means I won't be around much to work at Coquina House, but this feels like something that happens once in a lifetime."

"Don't even think about it," Beck assured her. "With Oliver gone, I've got nothing but time, and I want you to have fun. I really do, Lovely."

She squeezed Beck's hand again. "I don't want to give up this opportunity."

"And I don't want you to," Beck whispered, gripping her hand right back. "I can totally handle everything while he's here with ease. You just...be careful."

"Me? Of course. I can kayak and I'm not afraid of swimming with the dolphins."

She meant be careful with *him*. Beck had never seen Lovely give her heart to a man, but she assumed it would be like everything else her mother did—with full commitment, passion, and trust.

And what would happen when it was over? Would Lovely be shattered by that goodbye?

"Just so you know what you're doing," Beck said vaguely.

But not so vague that Lovely didn't get the message. "Pffft." She flipped her wrist. "I'm not going to fall in love and get my heart broken, Beckie. I'm not a teenager, as if that isn't obvious to everyone."

"I know," Beck said, pulling her mother in for a hug. "I'm so, so happy for you. I want you to sink into the whole thing and enjoy every minute."

"I will! I am! I..." She felt Lovely straighten a little in her arms, sucking in a soft and silent breath at whatever—or whoever—she saw over Beck's shoulder.

As if Beck didn't know.

"There you are." Eddie's voice was low and warm and had the same note of pure joy that Beck heard in her mother's.

And, she noticed when she turned, the same light in his eyes. Well, at least the feelings were mutual. Shocking as all get out, but...why not?

"Eddie, have you had a chance to talk to everyone?" Beck asked.

"I have and will continue, but..." He tipped his head and smiled at Lovely, not saying what his expression clearly communicated—he'd missed her.

"I was just on my way back," Lovely said, taking a step toward him. "But Beck and I had to whisper in the hall."

He lifted a brow. "Have we passed the family test?" he asked, as if there was no question what they'd been discussing.

"With flying colors," Beck assured him. "And have we?"

"Are you kidding? Your daughters—my *granddaughters*," he corrected, lowering his voice and fighting a smile, "are spectacular. Savannah is a hoot with a heart of gold and Mel is already in love with her. Callie is clearly a genius who has bonded with my go-getter, Jazz. And Peyton is going to slay motherhood, which, if you ask me, could be any day now. Oh, and Kenny. Such a fine man, and so is his growing family."

Beck smiled at him, almost unable to process his dead-on assessment of her kids, and Lovely looked delighted by it—and him.

"He does have a way with words, doesn't he?" she asked.

"He does," Beck said on a laugh. "And I can't disagree with any of it. I'm so proud of all of them."

"As you should be." He put a light hand on Lovely's shoulder. "Did you negotiate for the time off, or should I plead your case to Beck? We have to do the dolphins if nothing else."

"No negotiating necessary," Beck told him. "Lovely is my partner, not employee, and she can—and should—take as much time off as possible. Everything she mentioned sounds tourist-y and divine. We encourage everyone visiting to swim with the dolphins."

"Yes!" He fist-pumped. "Definite bucket list item and the number one reason to come to the Keys. Well..." He smiled at Lovely. "Number two."

Beck looked from one to the other, aware that she might just as well not even be standing in this hall with them. The chemistry and connection was off the charts.

Good heavens, she never saw *this* coming.

In her back pocket, she felt her phone vibrate and pulled it out. "I bet that's Oliver, who should've made it to L.A. by..." She frowned at the screen. "No, it's Serena McFadden."

"The real estate agent?" Lovely asked. "Funny day to call."

"Probably wants to wish me Happy New Year," Beck said, holding the phone and stepping back, feeling like she needed to leave these two alone anyway. "'Scuze me. I'll just be a second."

Turning, she slipped into the dining room and tapped the screen. "Hello, Serena. Happy—"

"Oh, it will be happy when you hear what someone wants to pay you for Coquina House."

Beck choked a laugh. "It's New Year's, not April Fools'. You know the B&B is not for sale."

"Everyone has a number, Beck, and I think someone might have yours."

For a moment, she was tempted, just to hear it. "No, thank you. Coquina House is not, and never will be, for sale, my friend. Thank you so much for letting me know. And Happy New Year."

"I'll call you next week."

Serena was nothing if not relentless. Beck chuckled. "I'll be very busy taking care of happy guests, but thanks."

With that, she tapped the phone and stepped back into the hall—just in time to see two not-so-young "lovers" silhouetted in the door frame, conveniently under a mistletoe that still hung for the holidays.

Lovely and Eddie stood face to face, with her looking up at him and him gazing down. They weren't touching, but even from ten feet away, Beck could feel the electricity arcing between them.

This was, she had to admit, a spectacular diversion for Lovely, who deserved all the love in the world. She'd never had her one true love, or fated mate, as she'd heard her mother refer to the concept of a soul mate.

But this also was...two weeks. Then what? Would Lovely be able to let go once she'd found him or—

In her hand, the phone buzzed again, and Beck glanced down to see a text.

Serena McFadden: *7 figures. First is not a 1.*

She stuffed the phone in her pocket. "Please," she muttered to herself. "You can't put a price on Coquina House."

Just then, Lovely tipped her head back and let out a laugh that sounded like wind chimes in the ocean breeze.

She couldn't put a price on that, either.

CHAPTER TWELVE
LOVELY

*L*ovely couldn't remember the last time she'd walked through a tourist attraction holding a man's hand, giddy with their banter and bathed in sunshine and good feelings. Maybe she'd never had the experience, other than in books and her imagination.

Which was all the more reason to cling tight to that hand and this memory-in-the-making. After a beautiful, laughter- and music-filled drive up to Grassy Key, they'd spent the morning meandering the Dolphin Research Center. They'd listened to a presentation, learned a bit about the protection and care of the special residents, and now wandered a warren of weathered docks that surrounded large salt-water lagoons.

As much as she wanted to give Eddie her full attention, it had to be divided between him and the remarkable gunmetal-gray creatures. A dozen or so dolphins zipped through the pools or bounded in the air, side by side, squawking at tourists in what they now knew was a language that no human had ever been able to decipher.

"Look, he's waving!" Eddie exclaimed, nudging her closer to the water where a dolphin spun for them and flapped a fin, delighting a small crowd. The kids squealed in response, getting the dolphin to blow some bubbles, then offer his snout for a pet.

All of it was orchestrated by one of the many trainers

both in and out of the water, blowing whistles, calling instructions, and supervising the dolphins.

Lovely adored every magical minute.

She and Eddie never ran out of things to talk about, with no awkward silences or even a moment of discomfort. This day felt so natural, like they'd done things like this all their lives, which made everything all the more wondrous.

And his stories were fascinating. He'd met so many famous people, been to exotic places, and lived a life chock full of more experiences than Lovely could even imagine.

Although, right now, stepping into the shade of a long thatched-roof overhang to watch some of the dolphins perform a duet dance, hers felt pretty darn fascinating—at least right now.

This experience might not last that long, but she honestly didn't care. It was exquisite.

Laughing and clapping as Wendy and Muffin arced in synchronized perfection into the air, Lovely dropped her head back and sighed noisily.

"Ah, this is heavenly, isn't it?"

"I don't know," Eddie said, giving her hand a squeeze. "You're the one who's been there."

She peered at him from under her lashes. "Been..."

"To heaven."

Oh, *that*. She managed a smile, not sure how to tell him she kind of hated the topic. Once she'd learned that Beck had told him of her near-death experience, she'd purposely avoided it—no small feat, considering this was the third day they'd spent in each other's company, and he'd mentioned it more than once.

"I don't want to prod," he said quietly, his tone gentle, as if he understood her reluctance. She didn't know how, but so far, he'd shown a tremendous ability to guess what she was thinking or feeling. "But it sounds quite remarkable."

"It's not that remarkable," she said, even though having experienced something few humans do was that and much, much more.

The whole thing was so deeply and shockingly personal, Lovely was reluctant to drop her protective barrier and talk about what was probably the most pivotal event in her life—even with him. And that was ironic, because he was at the center of the other most pivotal event in her life—having Beck.

"But will you tell me about it?" he asked.

"Over lunch," she said, not willing to change the lovely vibe of this day. Not yet, anyway. "It's no big deal, really."

"No big deal?" he scoffed. "You died and went to heaven, came back and have a new life. That's a huge deal. I could write a song about that—heck, I could write a whole album about it." He froze for a second, and then leaned in to whisper, "Can I?"

She regarded him for a moment, taking in the light on his skin, which had the same laugh lines and crow's feet as hers had, but no scars from an unexpected run-in with a truck.

"Are you embarrassed?" he asked when the silence lasted a beat too long, his eyes as penetrating as his question, and just as dizzying. And again, she marveled at his ability to read her emotions, even when she didn't quite know what they were.

"Yes," she admitted. "But I will tell you everything...if you tell me about meeting Joni Mitchell."

He laughed. "Deal. But she's not as interesting as—"

"Are you the Sylvester party?"

Relieved for the interruption, Lovely turned to a perky young woman wearing a navy-blue one-piece suit, a bright white visor, and a whistle hanging around her neck.

"We are," Eddie confirmed.

"Awesome! It's time for your Dolphin Encounter. I'm Gabrielle, your friendly dolphin trainer and your escort into a magical world. You ready to romp?"

They shared a look and laughed, the conversation about Lovely's experience instantly forgotten. Those were dark days, facing her mortality and her sister, and she was always happy to leave that memory behind.

Especially to make one as perfect as this.

"Water's chilly," Gabrielle told them. "So I'm going to recommend you change into wetsuits over your bathing suits, which you can do right by that dock. My assistant, Billy, will size you up, lock your stuff, and bring you to me in Lagoon Number Four. The water is fifteen to twenty feet deep, so you better not have lied about being able to swim when you signed the waiver."

"We can swim," they both assured her, sharing a look when they answered in unison.

"Good. So meet me there to romp with three of our most playful dolphins, Nyx, Vesper, and Gilligan. See you in a bit!"

She bounced off with a wave, leaving them to find Billy and... Oh, dear. Lovely would have to take off her coverup right in front of Eddie. She slowed her step and let him lead the way to the hut where they would don wetsuits.

"Mr. and Mrs. Sylvester?" Billy said from behind the desk.

They both froze at that, shared a look, and Eddie shrugged. "It's just easier," he murmured, then turned to the man. "That's right," he said. "Suit us up, Billy."

He gauged their sizes with a quick once-over, digging out two wetsuits and pointing to the corner of the structure. There was a bench, a railing, and nothing that looked like a ladies' room.

"Suit up over there and bring me your stuff and I'll get you a locker key." He turned, leaving them facing each other with armfuls of rubber and mirth in their eyes.

"You just pull it on over your swimsuit, Lovely," he told her. "And it's not like I haven't seen...some of you before."

She felt a flush on her cheeks. "I was...barely eighteen then." Truth was, she'd been seventeen, but he didn't need to know that little detail.

"And now I'm barely eighty." He leaned so close she thought he was going to kiss her for the first time. "This is fun!"

Yes, it was, so she laughed her way through the awkward process of pulling on a wetsuit, then they got their key, and made their way across the long decks to find Gabrielle.

She was tooting her whistle at one of the smallest of the dolphins and seemed to be talking to another one.

"Come, come," she said as she waved them over. "Nyx is our baby girl and she's in rare form today! Blow some bubbles, Nyxie!"

Without a second's hesitation, the baby dolphin stuck her snout in the water and made a loud, hilarious noise.

"Sit here." Gabrielle patted the floating deck, inviting them to sit down on the edge. "Nyx is a calf still, just two years old. And Vesper is her mother. And you are..."

"I'm Lovely and this is Eddie."

"All right, Lovely and Eddie. Brace for a good time!" With a quick whistle, the other dolphin rushed over, leaping and then shoving her long bottlenose right into Lovely's lap, gazing up with the deepest navy-blue eyes she'd ever seen.

"Do you know that dolphins never sleep?" Gabrielle asked. "They just rest one side of their brain. Oh, look, there's Gilligan. He's not Nyxie's father, but he'd like to be her stepfather. Vesper isn't so sure."

Lovely let out a soft laugh, leaning in to stroke her hand over Vesper's sleek skin. It was cool to her touch and slippery, like latex, and the dolphin responded with what had to be the biggest, brightest smile, showing all her teeth.

"Oh, she likes you!" Gabrielle said. "That means you're good to go in and swim with her baby, Nyx. She'll let you. And Eddie? You swim with Gilligan, but be warned—he's a goofball." She leaned in to whisper. "And a ladies' man, so expect him to try very hard to impress Vesper."

Slowly, they both slid into the water, laughing as their dolphin escorts sidled up next to them.

"This is unreal!" Eddie exclaimed, getting a happy wave from Gilligan's fin.

"He wants to take you for a ride," Gabrielle said. "Lock your arm around his dorsal fin on the top and off you go!"

He followed the instructions, and Gilligan took him zipping away, leaving Lovely right next to the little calf. In a moment, Vesper joined them, lifting her nose in the air and squawking more like a duck than a dolphin.

"She wants to play tag," Gabrielle said. "Just swim and she'll chase you. You're it, then tag Nyx!"

Lovely took a few strokes away and, sure enough, Vesper

shot over and poked her snout into Lovely's arm, adding a squeal.

"You're it," Gabrielle called. "Tag Nyx!"

She did and pretty soon the three of them were playing a game of tag as real and competitive as if she were running on the beach with her great-grandchildren. Every time her legs got tired, one of the dolphins offered to hold her up, which was simply the most magnificent feeling.

Gilligan and Eddie came back and joined in, leaving them breathless with laughter and disbelief.

Every time Vesper was alone, Gilligan swam to her. After a few tries, he brought Eddie with him.

"I'm his wingman," he joked. "Come on, Vesper. Give the guy a chance. He's a goner for you."

Vesper swam in a circle, then came back to Lovely, looking right in her eyes. Holding Nyx for support, Lovely stared right back at the mother dolphin. Under the wetsuit, chills rose as she realized they were communicating, loud and clear.

"This is amazing," she called to Eddie, glancing over to see he was looking at her with the same expression Gilligan used on Vesper.

She turned back to Vesper, feeling so connected to the animal that she had to reach out and put both hands on the side of the dolphin's head.

"You're beautiful," she whispered.

Vesper replied by making a clicking sound, then dove into the water, disappeared, and suddenly popped up twenty feet away, cutting a perfect semicircle in the air.

The move got a noisy response from the crowd, but Lovely just stared at her, marveling at what just happened.

A second later, Gilligan came flying over with Eddie, both man and beast wearing insane smiles.

"All right, buddy," Eddie said to the dolphin. "You know what to do!"

Lovely grinned at him, delighted by his playfulness, enchanted by his personality, and swamped by what Ava would call "the feels"—a jumble of euphoric emotions that could be the dolphins, the sunshine, the experience, or... the man.

Just as she was about to respond, Gilligan dove forward, straight into Lovely's side, gently nudging her...right into Eddie's arms.

"Oh!" She wrapped her arms around his neck to keep from going under, face to face with the most attractive man.

"Maybe he's *my* wingman," Eddie joked, tightening his grip as they both kicked their legs to stay afloat.

"I'm sinking," she said.

"Same. Falling so hard, so fast, I'm sure to drown."

Just as they dipped under the surface, his lips brushed hers and Vesper came whipping back to offer her whole body to lift them back up for air.

Not that Lovely could breathe. Or think. Or do anything...but fall a little more in love with each passing minute.

THE DAY SLIPPED into evening and time passed in a blur for what had to be the best "date" of Lovely's life.

As they drove back to Coconut Key, holding hands over the console and listening to Van Morrison croon *Tupelo*

Honey, Lovely let her eyes shutter so she could, once again, cling to the moment and the memory.

"Can you tell me now?" Eddie asked, letting go of her hand to tap the volume on his phone and lower the music. "I politely didn't ask again, even over lunch, but I'm dying to know. No pun intended."

She shifted in her seat, seeing the sign announcing the entrance to Coconut Key. They'd be home in a few minutes, which might not be quite enough time to tell her story.

"Come in for some lemonade and we can walk the dogs and talk," she said.

He nodded and shot her a smile. "Great day, huh?"

"Amazing," she agreed without a moment's hesitation. "Are you really going to go back to swim with Gilligan again with Melody and Jazz?"

"If they want to," he said. "They're both more about lounging on the beach than doing the touristy things. I'm shocked to see Jazz so...mellow. She never takes vacations."

"It's the magic of Coconut Key," Lovely said. "And you don't have to come over if you want to spend time with them. I'd understand if you'd prefer to go straight to Coquina House."

"And miss a chance to walk three dogs with the most beautiful woman on this island? No way."

She smiled, still enjoying the glow of his company but wondering, not for the first time, if all this attention was... genuine.

"Are you always so flirtatious?" she asked.

"Yeah, but I don't always mean it." He shot her a grin. "I'm kidding. No, I'm not generally flirtatious and I'm not flirting with you. Not in the cheap and meaningless sense of the word, anyway. I just...like you." He lifted their joined hands to his lips and kissed her knuckles. "I'm probably not supposed to admit that so easily and openly, but, hey, I'm seventy-six. I don't beat around bushes, dance around the truth, or pretend I have all the time in the world. We're long past being coy, don't you think?"

She couldn't disagree with that. "Does age make you want to...rush a relationship?"

"There's a difference between rushing things and not wasting time," he said. "I have two weeks here, and I want to make them count."

A few minutes later, they were barefoot on the beach, wearing sweatshirts because some chilly air had moved in during the day. Night had fallen but an almost full moon lit their way as they walked with the three dogs unleashed and trotting ahead of them.

Sugar stayed close. And Eddie stayed closer, putting his arm around Lovely as they strolled.

"Okay, don't make me ask again. It's starting to get weird."

"I won't," she said. "I'm just gathering my thoughts."

"And, full disclosure, I might hear something that makes it into a song."

She slowed her step and blinked in surprise, looking up at him. "A song?"

"Too bad *Stairway to Heaven* is taken."

"There were no stairs," she said on a sigh. "Just wheels and metal and a terrible, terrible sound that I never want to relive."

Instantly, he pulled her even closer. "I'm sorry for

making light of it," he said, the apology touching something deep inside her.

"It's fine. I probably should be more 'light' about it."

"The outcome was happy, after all."

"Oh, so very happy," she assured him. "But sometimes, it's shocking to realize how close I came to...not coming back. It was hard in the ensuing days to face the fact that I am not, after all, immortal. And last year, I had a slight—turned out to be nothing but still terrifying—cancer scare."

He groaned. "I hate not being immortal," he said. "At least, I hate facing it."

"Well, I did. Lying on the side of the road, on Christmas Eve, making a left turn on US 1, because of an impulsive decision to stop into Joshua Cross's furniture store on the way home from one last shopping errand. For the record, I have not driven a car since that day."

"Oh, Lovely." He added some gentle pressure on her shoulders.

She took a long, slow breath, wondering which of the many details of the event she wanted to emphasize in this retelling.

Sometimes, she remembered that horrible split-second realization that the truck going at least fifty-five was coming directly at her. Sometimes, she got stuck on the moment she hovered over her own bloody, battered body, utterly without pain. Sometimes, she focused on the trip through the light—the yellow and lavender flowers, the familiar faces, the fact that she remembered her sister was wearing a blue dress that once belonged to Lovely.

"A truck hit my little Nissan so hard I was thrown...far,"

she finally said. "I kind of remember the sound and the impact, but not really. Then I was dead."

He slowed his step. "What did that feel like?"

"Really nice," she said on a laugh. "Much better than I would have felt being alive, based on the way I looked."

"You could see yourself?"

She nodded. "Classic out-of-body experience, looking down, floating off to..."

"The good place?" he guessed.

"Very good, if that's measured in light and beauty. Lots of flowers in my heaven, and my sister. My parents, too, and many other people, but I just remember my sister." She smiled. "Wearing one of my dresses, which is a weird detail, but it stuck with me."

He resumed the walk. "Were you there long?"

"The emergency room report said I was dead for three and a half minutes, but it felt like scant seconds. Just as I hugged Olivia, I could feel myself being pulled back. It was like a physical yanking and as it happened..." She frowned, deep into the memory now. "I started to feel pain. I didn't want to feel that pain. I...I would have been perfectly happy staying right there in the afterlife."

He nodded. "Before that, what exactly did Olivia say?"

"She gave me permission to break the promise I made when I gave her Beck to raise. She said I could tell Beck the truth. Getting that permission was...well, it was like a key unlocking my soul. Honestly, there's not that much more to tell about the heaven part. It was beautiful, and quite real. I have no real fear of dying now. But it wasn't my time. I still had more to do here, even with pain and scars and paralysis."

"You were paralyzed?"

"In so many ways," she said, longing to bring some levity to the moment. "I knew I had a purpose, and I knew that purpose was to tell Beck the truth. But I couldn't walk, and I couldn't bring myself to pick up the phone and wreck her life. Of course, I had no idea her ex-husband was already doing that."

Eddie nodded. "She told me he took up with his partner at his law firm."

"The timing was right," Lovely said. "I invited her here, and she came, with Peyton."

"She told me a little bit about that," he said.

"I didn't tell her at first. I was so scared she'd be furious, but..." She shook her head, the long story not feeling like what she wanted to share this time. "It came out, eventually. She found the written contract I'd signed for my sister swearing to never tell a soul that Beck was my daughter. Yes, she probably told you she was upset that I'd kept the secret, but..." She smiled, remembering how Beck had come around after Lovely had taken a tumble.

"Beckie and I are destined for each other," she said. "It might have taken fifty-some years to become mother and daughter, but we are connected at the soul and heart and spirit. She's the greatest thing that ever happened to me. Have I thanked you enough for her?"

He chuckled. "I need to make time for her during these two weeks," he said. "I got so wrapped up in you, I have put her on the back burner. Let's plan to spend more time with her."

"I think she'd like that, Eddie. And so would you. She's

such an extraordinary woman. Strong, loving, kind, smart, and her heart is just good."

"Obviously, she takes after her mother."

"And there he goes flirting again," she teased.

He stopped and turned to her, putting tender hands on her shoulders to get her to face him.

"I'm not flirting," he said simply. "I'm not rushing, either. I'm...taken with you. Completely and utterly besotted."

"Oh." She looked up at him. "Now, those are words I never dreamed I'd hear in my lifetime."

"Why not?" he asked. "You're amazing. You're delightful. You're—"

She put her finger on his lips. "I get the point. But I'm also an old woman who never met...my one true love."

"Yet." He whispered the word so softly, she wasn't sure she'd heard it. And he punctuated it with the sweetest, lightest, most caring kiss.

"Eddie..."

It was his turn to put his finger on her lips. "Shh. I'm writing lyrics in my head."

She smiled at that, studying his serious expression as he looked right at her. She could practically see the wheels turning, rhyming words, spinning phrases, creating poetry.

After a moment, he stepped back. "I think I'll call that song...*Yet*.'"

"I can't wait to hear it," she whispered.

"Then I better get writing," he said. "We have, what? Ten days left?"

Ten days?

And right at that moment, she knew the truth. The awful, gut-wrenching, shocking truth. This wasn't enough time with him. She wanted more. She wanted it all.

She wanted…forever.

CHAPTER THIRTEEN
EDDIE

There really wasn't a feeling like this in the world, Eddie thought as he looked up from the page of lyrics he'd madly scribbled since sunrise. Nothing like hitting the hooks, capturing the emotion, and making the whole thing rhyme.

But for the past hour—maybe more, judging from the height of the sun glinting on the water—all that had happened and more.

He'd opened his eyes this morning with a chorus fully formed...

I found her by the sea,
Where waves meet destiny,
A heart I thought had drowned in time,
Now dances with the ocean's rhyme.
It's late, so late, but no regret,
Haven't met my one true love...haven't met her yet.

And from there, nothing could stop him. Beck had already brewed coffee when he'd gone downstairs and was off to pick up breakfast at the local café. He'd grabbed a cup, come out to the deck with the mostly empty notebook he carried so optimistically...and the magic happened.

Yet could be a beautiful love song, and he hadn't written one of those in what felt like forever.

Sipping the now-cool coffee, he scanned the words again, certain phrases jumping out because they delighted him.

She watched the tides rise and fall
But never heard her heart's call.

Wait, did tides rise and fall or go...in and out? But what rhymed with *out* besides...*doubt*? No, too sad. This song was the opposite of doubt. It was the embodiment of hope. Something with no doubt?

He scratched out tides and scribbled "ocean" in its place. Sea? Gulf?

"Don't let the technicalities block you, Eddie," he muttered, refusing to hit the wall he'd been banging against for too many years.

"Talking to yourself is a very good sign."

He turned at the sound of Mel's voice, smiling at his daughter as she stepped through the sliding glass doors with a cup of coffee in hand.

"Good morning, my beautiful girl," he said, waving his pen in greeting.

"Oh, that is my dad's happy voice. Are you writing?"

"Yes. Join me."

Beaming at him, she crossed the deck and slipped into one of the other chairs, her brows flicking with surprise at the words in front of him.

"Goodness. Haven't seen *that* for a while."

Sighing, he nodded. "I haven't written for so long, Mel. It feels great."

"Ready to share? Or are you still deep in draft mode?"

He cocked his head, considering the question. "This one didn't really need a draft." He turned the notebook and inched it closer to her. "Needs some tweaks, of course. And I'm aching for a melody, so I don't suppose you saw an acoustic hanging around here?"

"No, but let me read." She looked down at the page and he turned to study the horizon, surprisingly tense for a man who'd written a hundred or more songs. A thousand rough drafts that would go to the circular file. And Mel, his sweet angel of a daughter, had probably read, critiqued, then helped him with every one of those songs.

He glanced at her, unable to look away while she read, his heart wrenched with love for his girl. Yes, she was a fifty-year-old woman with silver streaks and a few lines on her face. But Mel would always be that little three- or four-year-old who didn't have a mother and attached herself to him. His little buddy. How did time pass—

She looked up, her dark eyes as mesmerizing now as when she'd been as a toddler.

"'Secrets she had kept alone'?" she recited. "Dad. This is about Lovely."

It wasn't a question, and he didn't bother to deny it. Instead, he shrugged. "I'm inspired."

"You're...more than that."

He chuckled and leaned back. "She's awesome, Mel. I forgot what true chemistry felt like." At her arched brow, he flicked a hand. "Oh, I know, it's been a while. Haven't kissed a woman since that sweet Irish lass who recorded her fiddle album in our studio."

"Nora? She was in her sixties, so not a lass."

"Also age appropriate and I liked her, but..." They'd fizzled fast. "This is different."

She eyed him. "You do seem...sparky."

He chuckled. "I feel sparky. Like..."

When he didn't finish, she tapped the page. "Like 'maybe love is waiting...yet'?"

"Dumb line?" he asked. "I really want to end on 'yet' for the final punch."

"I like it. These lyrics are buoyant and upbeat."

"Exactly what I wanted."

"And so are you," she added, reaching across the table. "I'm happy you're in love."

"What? Love?" he snorted. "Slow down, missy. We just met."

She lifted a shoulder. "Who cares, if it's destiny?"

"And we're in our mid-seventies," he added with a wry smile.

"Exactly." She pointed at him. "Time holds no sway over the love of people who are in their golden years."

"You've always been such a diehard romantic, Mel," he said. "Also, write down 'time holds no sway'—I like that and will find a home for it."

"I come by my diehard romantic nature from my father," she teased, taking his pen and jotting the words dutifully. "You are the king of diehard romantics."

"Maybe once," he agreed. "Now, I'm a diehard realist."

"And what does the realist say about this new romance?" she asked.

"It says...while this is a wonderful woman who touches something very tender in me, we live three thousand miles apart."

"She can move," Mel said, sounding cavalier.

"Lovely's roots may be in the sand, but they are deep," he replied. "I'm not going to pull her away from her home and family."

She angled her head. "For love?"

"It's merely *like* at this point, and I plan to make the most of what time we have left. After that?" He shrugged.

She leaned in. "You're not moving," she said with all humor gone from her expression. "Lark and Kai would never forgive me for bringing you here to meet your long-lost daughter only to lose you in the process."

"Nobody's moving anywhere—"

"Greetings! I come bearing breakfast!" Beck's voice floated from the kitchen, then she came out with a covered tray. "Would you like it out here in the morning sun or inside?"

Eddie rose instantly to take the tray. "Out here, and I hope you'll join us."

"I'll have coffee. And refills for you? Is Jazz coming down?"

"She's doing something workaholics never do," Mel said. "Sleeping in. But she'll smell the coffee and show up soon enough."

They chatted and set up the breakfast, all laughing and fussing over what a beautiful spread they'd made at the Coquina Café.

"Jessie is a genius and so is Heather, my future daughter-in-law and gifted pastry chef," Beck told them as they all settled at the outside table. "You met her at Savannah's party, remember?"

"Absolutely," Eddie said, sliding his notebook to the side. "Jessie is your childhood best friend."

"You have a wonderful memory," Beck said, but her gaze was on his writing. "Are you journaling?"

"In a sense," he said, sharing a quick look with Mel. "I was working on a song."

"He's *inspired*." Mel dragged out the word and leaned into Beck for emphasis. "It's a, uh, *lovely* song."

Eddie rolled his eyes. "Sometimes you are fifty going on fifteen."

"Hey, she's my sister. We have no secrets, as the song says." She grinned at Beck. "Cool, huh?"

Beck lowered her coffee cup and gazed at Mel. "Beyond cool," she agreed. "I still can't believe I have two sisters. And a father." She smiled from one to the other. "Thinking about it makes me downright dizzy."

"Same!" Mel exclaimed.

"But can we go back to the song?" Beck raised a brow.

"Speaking of dizzy," Mel cracked.

Beck looked interested. "Does it have a title, or do you do that after it's finished?"

"It does," he said. "For me, I can't write a song without a title. That comes first, then usually the chorus, and I work from there. This one's called *Yet*."

"Fascinating," Beck said, inching in. "It looks like you wrote a lot."

"The whole thing. But it's just poetry without a melody." He narrowed his eyes. "If you have a guitar handy, I can do something rudimentary."

"And then he can go down the beach and serenade the woman who inspired *another* song," Mel added with a wink.

"I don't have a guitar," Beck said, glancing at the notebook again. "But...I'm dying. Can you share or not?"

"Let me work on it some more," he said. "Mel's read it, though, as my beta listener. She always sees my work first."

"How frequently do you write songs?" Beck asked.

"It's been a while, so I'm really happy for the breakthrough," he said, considering how to share the trouble he'd had writing.

It was hard for people to understand how capricious the creative brain could be. But then, this was his daughter, and he didn't keep anything from the other two. Why would Beck be different?

"I actually have had quite a dry spell," he added, plucking the crust from the croissant on his plate. "But that seems to have changed."

"A good woman always has that impact on Eddie Sly," Mel said, making Eddie wince.

Beck laughed softly. "Coconut Key is known to inspire," she said, too classy to pursue Mel's comment.

"The song is obviously about Lovely," he said, not wanting to keep that from her. "And if it's as big a hit as the first one she inspired, we will all be celebrating."

Beck frowned, looking confused. "You said you've had one hit, but you've written a lot."

"Oh, I've had many songs top the charts for other artists," he explained. "But only one that I sang."

"Then maybe you should sing this one, too," Beck said.

He cleared his throat. "I don't think I have the pipes anymore, if I ever did. This one..." He angled his head toward the notebook. "Is purely as a gift to Lovely."

The high-pitched sound of barks broke through the quiet morning.

"And she's here," Beck said. "She'll be coming up those stairs right behind the pooches."

The news gave Eddie a jolt of pleasure as he rose to meet her. Sure enough, Pepper and Basil came romping up the stairs just before he heard Lovely's voice and footsteps.

"Holding Sugar, no doubt," he joked as he walked to the top of the landing.

"Of course," she replied, smiling up at him.

She looked beautiful and happy, with a gleam in her eyes, her long braid hanging over one shoulder. Having just looked at Beck, who shared so many facial characteristics, he could suddenly see the very young woman he'd met all those years ago.

The memory of her had faded over the years, but now, seeing her again, the girl he'd been with that night was, after all, burned in his memory. Same eyes, same smile, same delicate cheekbones. Time told its story on her face, but the woman inside never changed.

She never changed…

New lyric?

"You look happy," she said as she reached the top step, a long pink skirt swirling around her ankles.

"I am," he said, reaching out his hand to take hers. Her fingers were narrow and cool, clasping his instantly. "Good morning, Lovely."

"Hello." She smiled up at him, then lifted Sugar so he could give her a little love, too. "Did you sleep well?"

"Next level," he said, drawing her an inch closer but not wanting to hug her in front of Mel and Beck. Their relationship, if it could be called that, was too new and he didn't want to make her uncomfortable. "Coffee or tea? A scone?"

"Yes, please." She lowered the small dog to the wooden deck and blinked in surprise at the women seated around the table. "Oh, I'm missing a sunrise party. Hello, ladies."

They greeted her with hugs while Eddie stepped into the

kitchen to get Lovely some coffee and a fresh cup for himself. There, he found Jazz inside pouring some of her own.

"Well, the gang's all here," he said, putting an arm around his younger—well, young*est*—daughter. "Morning, Jazzy."

"Hey, Pops." She turned and smiled. "I slept in. It was... out of this world. I still haven't turned my phone on. I feel... untethered."

He chuckled at that. "Welcome to life, my friend. And the foreign concept of a vacation."

"I really thought I'd hate it. In fact, I really thought I'd hate this place and this whole state." She lifted her coffee, inhaled but didn't drink, looking out the window at the water. "I just love Coconut Key." She took that sip, thinking some more, no doubt her logical mind clicking through why she'd feel that way without considering the powerful tug of emotions. "I'm in love."

Well, that made two of them.

"It's a very special place," he said. "Very special people, too. Something has me writing songs today."

"You are?" She drew back, smiling. "You must *really* like this woman."

He laughed, shaking his head as he poured Lovely's coffee and jutted his chin toward the deck. "Come join the party, Jazz."

Outside, they all talked for a while, getting into the topic of running a B&B. Mel was fascinated by the constant flow of new people actually living in one's home, while Jazz seemed more interested in the business end of things.

As for Eddie, he mostly sipped hot coffee and enjoyed the

pure pleasure of being surrounded by strong women, including one who made his heart stop every time she glanced at him.

Where warm breezes blow...something... something where hearts go.

Lovely turned to him, a question in her gaze. She knew he wasn't thinking about a reservation system or how frequently guests returned.

Why keep it from her?

He put his hand on Lovely's shoulder and moved in closer.

"I wrote a song," he said, reaching down with his other hand to retrieve his notebook leaning against the chair leg. "I wrote...*Yet*."

With a soft inhale, she put her fingers to her lips, the gesture bringing the other conversation to a halt as they turned and looked at them.

There was an awkward beat of silence, then Lovely smiled. "We're going to Key West," she announced, getting questioning looks from everyone, including Eddie.

"We are?" he asked.

"There's a music store you'll love, and we can buy an acoustic guitar. Didn't you say you needed one to really write a song?"

He had, in passing, and he was touched that she'd listened so intently. "Yes, I actually do need one."

"Perfect. The place is called Island Guitar, and you'll love it. More importantly, they'll love you. A record producer!" She pushed up, that unstoppable spirit he liked on full display. "They'll have something used, so you won't have to spend a fortune." She smiled at the others. "Who wants to come with us?"

"I'd love to, but I have a long-awaited video call with Oliver and errands to run," Beck told her.

"Errands, schmerands," Mel said. "Talk to Aussie man, then you're going to show us around Coconut Key and take us to the most fun waterfront joint there is for some day-drinking and sister-bonding. You in, Jazz?"

"So in."

Beck laughed, hooking her arm around both of their necks for an awkward but precious group hug. "I love that idea."

"Hold that pose!" Lovely scrambled for her phone and took a picture of the three of them, getting a few with silly faces, making them all laugh.

As they stood to end the impromptu gathering, Eddie turned to Lovely, about to ask her to text the pictures. For a beat or two, neither of them could do anything but look into each other's eyes. The pull was purely magnetic and the sensation was the best high he'd ever felt.

"You..." He inched closer, at a loss for words. "Are perfect."

She gave her melodic laugh. "Far from it." But she didn't look away, holding his gaze. "Did you know that your eyes are the exact color of the sky right now?"

He just smiled, his fingers itching to pick up that notebook as a line of lyrics danced around in his head.

In my eyes
she sees the shore
and a life she's longed for.

Oh, boy. He was in trouble. The good kind. The creative kind. The kind that ended with terrific music.

And a broken heart.

He just hoped that, this time, it was his and not Lovely's.

CHAPTER FOURTEEN
BECK

*B*eck pressed her chin to her knuckles and leaned toward the laptop screen as if one inch could get her closer to the man on the other side of the world.

True to the time difference, Oliver sipped a beer, and she finished the last drops of her coffee while they talked about the massive job ahead of him.

"Trust me, I'd like to chuck the whole thing, hit the Grand Pacific and head up to the Gong," Oliver said, his Australian accent sounding a tad more pronounced the common nickname for the beach town he loved. "The drive alone is a game-changer. And a *mood* changer."

He'd told her about the scenic route between Sydney and his beach house many times, with enough longing in his voice that she knew he missed the gorgeous part of the world where he'd spent most of his life.

Wait a second—did he say...

"Chuck the whole thing?" she asked, incredulous. "Do you mean selling the house? And...does your mood need to change?"

He gave a wistful smile. "It would be whole lot better if you were here."

"I'm sorry," she said, and meant it.

"No, no, Beck. I'm just being whiny. I'm not chucking anything, but the whole process of moving out of this place is daunting and it's late here. I'm wiped out."

"Oh, honey." This time, they both moved closer to the screen. "It's a big job and I so wish I could be there to help you. I do have a bit of Coconut Key gossip that might cheer you up."

"Yes, please," he said on a soft laugh. "Something about the new family, I hope."

"Something, indeed. Lovely is..." She shook her head, not sure how to describe it. "Whoa. Gone. And so is Eddie."

"Pardon? Gone? You mean, like..."

"Crushed," she finished for him. "Both of them are like infatuated teenagers, unable to stop staring at each other, holding hands, whispering. It's so adorable. Terrifying, but adorable."

He looked shocked, then pointed at her. "Didn't I call that one?"

"You kind of did," she said on a laugh. "There's whirlwind romance happening right under our noses and the parties in question are both in their mid-seventies."

"I guess the Beach Table worked its magic," he said, then made a face. "It could have been us."

"We're already in love," she said. "But this—"

"Ah, say it again, Rebecca. I love to hear that we're in love."

Laughing, she blew him a kiss. "You know we are."

"Do you think she's in love?" He locked his elbows on the desk, riveted. The move made her smile, reminding her that he was as much a friend as a boyfriend, even though she hated that term at their ages.

"I think she's got a massive crush," Beck said. "And he seems to be just as enchanted. He wrote a song about her this morning."

"Really? Another 'Lovely' ballad?"

"I don't know how it sounds, but Melody implied that a woman can inspire him. A good woman, I believe she said. And he said the song was a gift to Lovely."

"That's so precious."

"And now they're off to Key West to buy a used acoustic guitar," she told him. "He's on a songwriting roll and she's his muse."

Oliver considered that, studying the label on his beer for a moment. "What if it isn't a crush, Beck?" he asked. "What if this is the real deal and she's ready to run off with this mate?"

She stared at him, hating that he put into words her deepest, darkest fear. "Run *off*?" she scoffed. "Lovely? She's barely left this island her entire life."

"Maybe it's time," he said. "She's only seventy-five and healthy. She's got a good twenty years left."

She sure did, and Beck wanted to spend every one of them with her mother at her side. But...what if Lovely fell in love and wanted to...

Sighing, she stifled a grunt, definitely not ready to go there.

"Now you're upset," he said, searching her face even though a world and a screen separated them. "Of course she's not going anywhere. Maybe he'll move to Coconut Key."

She rolled her eyes. "He's got a ranch outside of San Francisco, a winery in Napa, and a business, not to mention kids, grandkids, and a life. He's not picking up and moving here."

But what if Lovely got serious about him? Again, she tamped down the thought.

"I'm sorry I mentioned it, Beck," he said softly. "I'd like to wipe that worried look off your face with a kiss."

She smiled, trying to erase any grimace that came with the idea of losing Lovely. "It's fine. It's just...no, it's fine. And I just wish you were here to see the whole thing unfold."

"I'll be back soon, I promise."

"Unless you realize you're so happy to be Down Under that you don't come back," she said, giving in to a new punch of self-pity, made worse by the conversation.

"I'll come back," he said without a nanosecond of hesitation. "But it isn't a bad time to be here. It's the heart of summer and the weather's quite nice. Sydney is bustling with life, and just an hour north is my own personal oasis on the water."

His deep love for Australia wasn't exactly helping her mood, but she smiled brightly. "Are you going to get up to the beach this trip? Or is this just an emptying out this house and closing the property deal?"

"Oh, I have to visit my place in Wollongong. My soul wouldn't survive if I didn't spend a few days there." He glanced around what looked like a mostly empty office in his home. "I love Sydney, but this is just another big house. However, that place? Oh, you'd love it so much, Beck. Mountains and water and miles of sky. It's like nothing you've ever seen and all I want to do is take you there."

"I promise I'll go. Between babies, maybe?" But even as she said it, she knew she'd be hard pressed to leave after Peyton's baby was born this month. Yes, Savannah had four more months, but last time she was pregnant, she ended up on bed rest. What if that happened again? Savannah had Nick, but nothing—not even the world's greatest husband—could replace a mother.

"You're already second-guessing that suggestion," he said, a knowing glint in his dark eyes.

"Just the timing," she assured him. "I will go. I want to go, but I just don't know when."

"I get that, Beck. And I won't pester you. Hopefully, this property closing will go smoothly, and I'll be back in a few weeks. Think you can hold off Peyton?"

"Who knows?" She laughed. "I think she's got at least two more weeks. Oh, and speaking of property deals, guess who called me? Serena McFadden."

"The woman who found my rental? What did she want?"

Beck took a deep breath, almost afraid to say the words, and she wasn't sure why. They were so...monumental. To own something worth so much was daunting and, well, tempting.

Not that she'd ever sell, but still.

"She has a client who wants to buy Coquina House."

"I'm sure she has ten of them," he replied on a laugh. "That's some prime property you're on."

"Well, this one made an actual offer. Seven figures, and, as she said, the first isn't a one."

He let out a whistle. "Well, they're not making any more beach, and that sliver of Coconut Key is beyond unique. And your house is gorgeous." He leaned back and crossed his arms. "Would you consider it?"

"Oliver! How could I even think about selling this house?"

He lifted a brow, silent, but she knew him so well. She knew what he was thinking.

If Lovely wanted to leave and Beck were willing to live half the year in Australia like he wanted...

She literally felt a little sick at the thought.

"I've upended my life once already," she said softly. "Divorced my cheating husband, discovered my biological mother, reinvented myself in the Keys, and started a new business."

"And you've fallen in love with an Aussie."

"That, too," she agreed. "Enough change for one middle-aged woman."

He smiled. "No one would ever expect you to sell, move, or change a thing. Except..." He leaned in to whisper, "Six months in Wollongong, and six in Coconut Key. Doesn't it sound perfect?"

"It sounds..."

Her cell phone flashed and vibrated on the desk in front of her.

"It sounds like Serena McFadden is texting me again."

She picked up the phone and read the text, an invitation to have coffee later this week "and just chat."

Chat about *changing her life*.

She took a breath and stared at the screen, then something caught her eye outside the window overlooking the wraparound porch. There, she saw Lovely and Eddie, their heads close in conversation, then both leaning apart with hearty laughs over some shared joke.

She moved her gaze back to the computer screen, to Oliver's handsome and hopeful expression.

Everything could change. *Everything*.

"Beck?" Melody called from the living room. "Where are you?"

"I better go, Oliver," she said, pushing back. "And you need to rest up for all that packing tomorrow."

"Amen to that. Good night, beautiful Beck." He blew her a kiss. "Trust the process, love, and don't worry."

She just smiled, holding onto his two-dimensional gaze until the screen went blank, unsettled by the whole conversation.

"Beck?" Melody tapped on her door. "Your sisters are out here looking for fun."

Her *sisters*. Talk about life changes. "Come on in," she called.

The door opened and Melody and Jazz stood side by side in sunhats and shades. "We're ready!" Jazz said.

"For anything," Melody added.

Laughing, she tucked her phone in her pocket without answering the text.

THEY EXHAUSTED the sights of tiny Coconut Key fairly quickly and made a few stops for B&B supplies, and by one o'clock, Beck, Mel, and Jazz needed food and a break.

Beck texted Peyton and got a recommendation for the perfect outdoor waterfront restaurant on Summerland Key, the next island over. Before long, the three women were happily ensconced at a four-top on the deck of the Blue Heron, gazing at the shallows of a channel that separated this island from Ramrod and the Torch Keys.

"Margaritas for everyone," Jazz announced as the server approached. "Because isn't this, like, *actual* Margaritaville?"

"Wait a second." Mel leaned in and narrowed her eyes at Jazz. "Who kidnapped my workaholic sister and where is her phone?"

Jazz snorted. "Deep in my bag and call it the Jimmy Buffett Effect. Didn't Dad meet him a few times?"

"Yes, but seriously, Jasmine Sylvester. I've never seen you like this."

Jazz gave an easy smile that softened her features. "Because I don't think I've ever been on vacation. I finally get it."

"Then you need to come back again and again," Beck said. "You will always have a place to stay at Coquina House."

The other woman leaned over and put her hand on Beck's. "Be careful what you wish for, sister of mine."

Beck laughed, loving the term of endearment and the fact that she had sisters. While they chatted, the waiter came back with three massive margs, salt glistening on the rims.

They toasted their sisterhood, and Beck took what would probably be her one and only sip, because she was driving, but relished the tangy taste of the drink.

"So," Mel said, leaning in with a conspiratorial glint in her dark eyes. "What do we think about Dad and Lovely?"

"Ooh." Jazz's brows shot up. "I guess Beck has to tell us what she thinks. After all, they are her biological parents—both of them—and only one is ours."

Beck exhaled and looked from one to the other, trusting them but also knowing their respective loyalties ran deep.

They would love and defend their father, and she would basically die for Lovely.

"Is he a ladies' man?" she asked, not surprised it was the first question to pop out. She couldn't stand it if Lovely got hurt.

The other two women shared a look and didn't answer with a resounding, "No!" like Beck hoped they would, but she could tell that was because they wanted to be fully honest.

"He's not a *player*," Mel finally said. "Not in the love 'em and leave 'em sense of the word."

"He is, however," Jazz added, holding her drink umbrella to make her point, "a man who falls in love easily. He's basically in love with the idea of being in love."

"But that's not a fault," Mel insisted quickly. "It makes him passionate and enthusiastic and probably the best boyfriend ever, but, yeah, falling for a woman is his happiest place. Not that it happens frequently, but when it does..."

"He's all in," Jazz finished.

"Hence, the songwriting," Mel added.

Listening to it all, Beck considered a second sip. She really didn't want Lovely to get hurt.

"So...he writes music when he's with someone," she said, choosing her words carefully. "So a woman is like...a muse?"

"Not exactly," Mel said. "He can only write when he's happy, probably because his songs are mostly happy love songs, very upbeat and optimistic. When he's in love, the dopamine flows, then...he writes."

"In love?" Beck scoffed. "They literally met a few days ago."

"They met fifty-seven years ago," Jazz corrected.

"But they didn't know each other's last names," she countered. "I think this is more of a crush than love, don't you?"

They stared back at her, neither one agreeing. Melody had a bit of amusement in her eyes and Jazz looked quite serious.

"They can't be in love," Beck said. "That's not...possible. Or sustainable. Or realistic."

"Anything's possible," Mel retorted.

"And sustainable, if they want it badly enough," Jazz said.

"But not realistic," Beck insisted. "They live three thousand miles apart with completely separate lives and families."

"You're family to both of them," Mel reminded her.

"And I'm here," she said. Unless she spent half the year in Australia like Oliver wanted her to do. Maybe Lovely would want to spend half of her year in California.

Her heart twisted and she gave in and took that second sip.

"They could do long-distance," Mel said.

"Or someone could move," Jazz suggested.

Beck felt her eyes widen. "Would he?"

"No," Mel replied.

"Yes," Jazz said right over her in the same tone, then they laughed. "Obviously, we don't know," Jazz assured her. "Mel would flip out, though."

"And so would Lark and Kai," Mel said. "My kids are so attached to him, it would kill them if he left. They both live at his ranch most of the time, which is twenty-five acres, just a few miles from Half Moon Bay. No one *leaves* that."

"Well, my kids are attached to Lovely," Beck said,

suddenly feeling like she was drowning. "As am I. And no one leaves Coconut Key. Not willingly, any—"

"Beck? I found you, Rebecca Foster!"

Yanked from the conversation, she turned, not knowing who to expect here, a good half-hour from home.

"Serena?" What was she doing here?

The Realtor breezed over, her cream-colored silk dress that hugged her curves and sky-high heels looking out of place for the Blue Heron but perfect for the hard-working agent.

"You don't return my texts and now I know why! You're socializing!" She flattened them with a blinding smile. "Girl! It's like you don't want money."

Laughing, Beck stood to greet the other woman with a warm hug. "Is this a coincidence?"

"I could lie and say yes, but I'm not capable of it. I tracked you down by way of Peyton, who told me you were coming here. I had to see a house on Summerland Key anyway, so I thought I'd force myself on you." She turned to the other women, extending her hand to Jazz first. "Serena McFadden, licensed Realtor and maker of dreams."

"Jazz Sylvester...in awe of your beauty."

Serena gave a hearty laugh. "Back atcha, Blondie." Then she turned to Mel, who shook her hand.

"I'm Melody Davidson. Jazz and I are Beck's sisters. Well, half, if we're getting into specifics."

"Sisters? Who knew?" Serena dropped right into the only empty chair as if the invitation had been extended. At least it ended the uncomfortable conversation they'd been having, Beck thought, even if it opened up another one that wasn't exactly welcome.

"None of us knew," Melody said. "You're looking at a twenty-first century family—found on Ancestry.com."

Serena's jaw dropped. "Get out of town!"

"We were just talking about that," Jazz joked. "I take it you two are friends?"

"Beck is my friend and client," Serena explained. "I found Oliver's rental and her daughter's home. No baby yet, I heard."

Beck shook her head, still processing everything. "But then you've talked to her more recently than I have," she added with a teasing voice. "We're literally looking at days now."

"She certainly didn't sound like she was in labor," Serena said, flipping open her bag without taking her eyes off Beck. "But, girl, you'll be in pain if you don't at least consider this offer on Coquina House."

"An offer?" Jazz and Melody practically sang the words in unison.

"A waste of everyone's time," Beck corrected. "I'm not selling Coquina House, not now, not ever. It was built by my grandparents and will be going to my daughters."

Serena wasn't listening, or at least not responding. Instead, she grabbed an unused paper napkin and wrote on it with a ballpoint pen. Then she folded it into a much smaller square and slid it across the table with the flair of a poker player.

"Just look at the number and know that this man will negotiate."

Beck didn't touch the napkin. "I don't care what the number is. You can't put a price on Coquina House."

"Everyone has a price," Jazz said with the air of a woman

who'd been in many such negotiations as a venture capitalist. In fact, whatever that number was, add a zero or two for the kind of deals Jazz did.

"Not me." Beck slid the napkin back, tucking it under the edge of a plate. "But thank you, Serena. Your determination is a thing of beauty."

Far too classy to overstay her welcome, Serena stood, pointing a bright pink nail in Beck's direction. "You haven't heard the last from me."

"I hope I never do," Beck said. "You're a treasure. But I can't make anyone's dreams come true because mine are all wrapped up in that house."

Serena smiled and tilted her head with a sweet, pouty lip. "You're the cutest, Beck. And you two? When you want to move here, call me." She flipped open her bag and produced business cards, handing them out like candy on Halloween. "Bye-bye, long-lost sisters!"

She blew out with the same spirited breeze that brought her in. When she was gone, Beck just swept her hand to stop that conversation and, hopefully, the previous one.

"Now, I want to hear about Kai and Lark," she said to Melody, who visibly brightened at the idea of talking about her kids.

Without much encouragement, Mel shared stories that painted a picture of two very different, but very lovable, offspring. She didn't talk much about Gideon, her husband, but couldn't stop gushing about her kids.

When it was time to leave, Beck snagged the check and slipped her credit card in the folder as the conversation easily moved to the fascinating business of running a record label and life in Northern California.

A long hour or so had passed when they finally stood and gathered their bags for the drive home. As they were walking back into the dining area to get to the parking lot on the other side, Beck remembered the napkin.

Should she leave it there? Should she see that number after all? Surely Lovely would want to know what the offer was, and she owed it to her partner to tell her.

"Hang on a sec," she said, holding up a finger. "I forgot something."

"Oh, good. I have to hit the ladies' room," Mel said, spotting the sign near the hostess stand.

"Same." Jazz followed her.

Beck darted back through the restaurant to the outdoor deck, happy to see the table hadn't been bused yet. She reached under the plate where she'd stuffed the napkin, but it was gone.

Frowning, she scanned the whole table, the only napkins used, crumpled, and on their small appetizer plates.

Maybe it had been bused. Maybe it had been scooped up by the server when they brought the check. Maybe it had blown into the water.

Maybe...she wasn't supposed to know that number.

Satisfied with that, she joined her sisters and headed back home.

CHAPTER FIFTEEN
HEATHER

"God, give me wisdom. Give me answers."

But as her wedding date grew closer, all Heather heard from her beloved Father was... silence. She'd prayed, she'd listened, she read the Word of God, she dug through old sermon notes. Nothing gave her the guidance she needed.

She had no idea how to handle the family that used to be her in-laws, how to show them the grace of Jesus, honor their status in her life, and include them in what should be a happy day...but might not feel like that to them.

Was the reason she didn't know how or even if she should invite them to her wedding the obvious one? Because it was too soon for her to remarry.

That was at the very core of her discomfort, and it was that doubt and disturbance that woke her up at night and made her wonder if the Holy Spirit was trying to tell her something.

Should she invite them to the wedding? What was protocol? What was the best thing for this family? If they came, would it be awful? If they didn't, would she and the kids lose them forever?

The fact was, she didn't particularly want Drew's sister there, but Blanche deserved an invitation, even though she'd likely not come. And Grandpa Andy? He could fly alone, easily. But would he want to? Drew had an aunt and uncle and a few distant cousins on his mother's side, but she wouldn't bother to invite them.

She stared at the phone and the short guest list in front of her, then checked her watch, knowing Blanche would likely be finishing up her non-stop meetings right about now.

Marc had baseball practice for at least another hour, and Kenny, the team's assistant coach, was dropping him off and staying for dinner. Maddie and Ava were racking up their service hours volunteering at the local library, so this really was her opportunity to make the dreaded phone call.

Leaning back from the small kitchen desk that she used to run her household business, she closed her eyes and pinched the bridge of her nose.

Was this the right thing, the right time?

With a slow, deep breath, she hit her phone contacts, found Blanche, and tapped the speaker button so she could move around the kitchen and burn off nervous energy as they talked.

"Hello, Heather." Blanche answered on the first ring, erasing Heather's high hopes that God—and Blanche—might give her voicemail.

"Hey, Blanche." She infused warmth into her voice. "How are you?"

"Fine."

She waited a beat for the normal response—"How are you, Heather?"—but Blanche was dead silent.

"Good, good," Heather said as if she had asked. "Um, are you busy?"

Blanche snorted. "Am I awake? I live busy, Heather."

Of course she did. "And Andy? How's he?"

"Don't get me started."

"Oh, is everything okay?" Heather asked, rising to get cold water for her parched throat. "Is he sick?"

"He's not well, that's for sure."

He wasn't? "What's wrong?"

"Hold on, I'm leaving a meeting. Let me find a place to sit down."

Heather could hear the click of high heels and pictured Blanche Henderson in a sharp business suit, her dark bobbed-cut hair swinging as she walked with the confidence of someone who knew she was important and respected.

Had Heather ever walked through a room with that much swagger? Blanche didn't know the meaning of humility, and Heather pretty much wore it as her only outfit.

Drew's older sister by less than two years was the quintessential driven and successful career woman. She'd been married briefly, though Heather had never met her husband. It hadn't lasted because he'd wanted children, and she adamantly did not.

Now, Blanche curled her lip at the very idea of a man in her life. Fiercely independent and downright disdainful of stay-at-home moms, Blanche was driven by her ambition and success. Heather respected that, but it sure seemed like an empty life to her.

Still, she reminded herself as she waited, it wasn't her place to judge the woman, only to love her and show her the love of the Lord—no matter how challenging that was.

"All right, I have about two minutes before my next appointment," Blanche said, slightly breathless. "Crazy day, honestly. Just wall to wall sales calls and problems to solve. What did you need?"

Heather came back to the desk with a bottle of water, feeling very much like Blanche's next problem to solve. "You were going to tell me about Andy. He's not well?"

"He's a mess and his doctor, who's a genius, by the way, thinks Dad needs a sleep study, ASAP."

"Oh?" Heather frowned, parsing the words, as she balanced the phone on her desk and listened through the speaker. "A mess? What are his symptoms?"

"The man doesn't sleep, Heather. He's got so many aches and pains and bags that could carry groceries under his eyes. I know sleep apnea when I see it—or hear it, as I did when he stayed in my guest suite—and I finally got him in to see the best sleep expert in Charleston. There are ways to fix this."

Heather winced, knowing Blanche's go-to for every possible situation was to address the problem with pharmaceuticals. They had their place in the world, no question, but Heather always hoped for a natural solution first.

"He needs a CPAP machine," Blanche finished.

At least it wasn't a drug. "I think I know what that is. Very uncomfortable, isn't it?"

"There you go, always with the negative," Blanche shot back. "He'll deal with it and live longer because he sleeps better. But in the meantime, I have to drive him to the sleep study and pick him up at an ungodly hour and—"

"He can't drive himself?" Heather asked.

"And risk a seizure at the wheel?"

"A seizure? Has he had one?"

"No, but sleep apnea can bring them on. It's a very common side-effect. Never mind, you don't have the healthcare background I do. Why did you call?"

Healthcare background? The woman was a pharma rep, not a physician's assistant. Heather pushed the unkind thought away and cleared her throat.

"Well, I'm calling because we've set the date and we're having a small wedding in a few—"

"No, thank you. Next question?"

Did she have to be that horrible? Heather swallowed the lump in her throat and took a sip, gathering her thoughts.

"If you don't want to come, I understand," she said. "But I didn't want to be rude and not invite you or Andy, so maybe I'll just call him."

Blanche waited a beat, then replied with a noisy sigh. "Heather, listen to me and listen good, okay? You *are* rude—getting married less than two years after my dear brother died is beyond rude. It's actually offensive and nothing short of reprehensible, if you ask me."

Well, she hadn't asked her. Heather just closed her eyes and took the tongue-lashing, since it wasn't nearly over. She didn't want to offend anyone or act *reprehensibly*, but—

"I'm not going to your so-called wedding, and neither is my father."

Her so-called—

"If you wanted to make our lives better, Heather Monroe, you would come back and help with the burden of caring for my aging father."

"Blanche, Andy is only seventy. He's not aging."

"You don't know how sick he is!" she practically shrieked. "And I don't want to have this conversation. Goodbye and good luck. I guess I'm supposed to say 'best wishes' for a wedding. Well, my wish is that my brother was still alive, but we can't all get what we want, can we?"

With that, the phone went dead, like a punch in the gut.

"No, Mom, we can't."

She whirled around at the sound of Marc's voice, gasping at the sight of him in his practice uniform, standing in the door from the garage. Was he constantly eavesdropping these days? She bit back the question and settled on something that wouldn't cause a fight.

"You're home early."

"Coach cancelled practice because there's a storm coming. Kenny stayed in his truck to take a call. What is sleep...*what*nea? Just how sick is Grandpa?"

She closed her eyes on a grunt. "He's not sick, honey, he's—"

"You heard her, Mom! He has to go to specialists and can't drive."

"He can—"

"I don't get why you don't care about him!"

She shot up. "I do care about him, Marc! That's why I called. I want him at the wedding so very much, but I thought I should talk to her first since she's like a gatekeeper. I'll call him myself—"

"Just leave him alone," he fired back.

"Do *not* talk to me that way."

"Sorry, Mom, but hearing your voice upsets him."

"Grandpa? What? Why? How do you know that?"

"He told me," he said, toeing off his cleats to kick them into the mudroom behind him.

"He told you my voice upsets him?"

"It reminds him of Dad," he said, heading to the refrigerator. "I think I do, too, but in a good way."

"And I remind him...in a bad way?"

"It just makes him sad, I guess."

And the hits just kept on coming. She crossed her arms and swallowed, uncertain how to handle this while Marc stared into the fridge, silent for a long while.

"I don't know, Mom," he finally said, pulling out the ubiquitous container of milk and heading toward the cabinet to get a glass. "He just said it once."

"Said what?" she pressed.

"That it was hard to hear you laugh because...honestly, I don't want to talk about it. I'm going to call him."

"Can I talk to him?"

He spun around, his eyes full of hurt. "Kenny said we can't consider moving back."

She didn't quite get the change of subject, but she knew her fiancé had made a promise to have that conversation with Marc, and she knew he'd keep that promise.

"He said it doesn't feel like a good time to consider something like that." He shrugged then turned back to pour his milk. After filling the glass, he walked to the pantry, opened the door and did the staring thing again.

"You understand that, don't you, honey?" she asked.

Huffing out a breath, he closed the door without getting anything, or answering the question.

"I brought brownies from the café," she said, stepping to the table to pick up the overflowing Tupperware she'd snagged from work.

"I'm fine. I have to do homework." He took the glass, left the milk on the counter, and walked out.

She stood stone still for a long time, then put the milk away and went out to the garage.

Clouds had moved in, darkening the sky, but she could

see Kenny in his truck in the driveway, talking on his cell. As he caught sight of her, he gestured emphatically for her to join him.

She walked out, feeling the first drops of rain, then pulled the passenger door open.

"She's right here, Pastor."

Was he talking to Pastor Allen? Frowning, she climbed into the truck. "Can you hold for one second, Pastor? Thanks." He tapped the phone, presumably muting the call. "Practice was cancelled. There was some lightning like twenty miles away, but the good news is that Pastor Allen can squeeze us in now for the premarital meeting we have to have for him to marry us. Can you..." He inched back. "Hey. Are you okay?"

Someday, she'd learn to keep her emotions off her face. Not today, apparently. "I'm...yeah. I'm fine. A meeting right now?" She glanced down at her jeans and sneakers. "I guess."

"He doesn't care what you're wearing, Heather. He had a cancellation, and we should take it. An hour or so, at the most, since he knows us so well. Marc's okay alone." He squinted at the sky. "This'll blow over fast."

"Oh, I know, I know." She exhaled, not certain she wanted to quietly sit and be counseled on marriage right now, but then...God always opened the doors He wanted you to walk through. "Of course. We can go now."

"Perfect." He started to tap the phone, but he moved his hand toward her and lightly touched her chin, lifting it. "It's going to be okay, Heather. Trust the process."

She smiled. "I'll get my bag and tell Marc we're leaving."

As she walked inside, she sighed and thought about the hour ahead—a long hour about the holiness of marriage.

Maybe she'd get her answer there. After all, it was church.

Pastor Allen Armstrong was one of the most calming and kind men that Heather had ever met. Nothing riled him—except salvation, of course—or made him lose a gentle, honest sense of humor.

Well into his sixties and the pastor of Our Redeemer for nearly half of those years, Heather would have expected him to be a little bored during the process of preparing a couple to join in a holy, Christ-based marriage. On the contrary, Pastor Allen practically vibrated with the joy of his mission.

Or maybe that was the window in his office, shaking as a noisy thunderstorm rolled over the Lower Keys.

"Ephesians!" he announced, the fifth of such direction through the Bible.

His counseling was simple—taking the Word of God, identifying the scriptures that addressed the very foundation of a Christian marriage, and directing Kenny and Heather to read and pray together during the time leading up to their wedding.

That was it—no ministerial advice, no structural guidelines, no dos and don'ts. Just chapters and verses to read and consider.

"Ephesians Chapter Five holds the key to a lasting and loving marriage," he said.

"'Wives, submit to your husbands,'" Kenny said, shifting in his seat without even tapping the Bible app on his phone.

Heather slid him a slightly surprised look as she turned a

page of her much more traditional version of the Good Book. "Look at you, memorizing," she teased.

"It was one of, uh, Elise's favorites," he explained with the wistful smile he always used when speaking of his late wife. "When we disagreed on something or even had differing opinions, she'd say, 'Wives, submit to your husband,' and give in. Then I'd probably back off because, well, the next verse is, 'Husbands, love your wives.'"

"See the difference?" Pastor Allen asked. "God asks men to love and women to submit, but not in the way we think of 'submission.' He's saying that in a Christian home, the man does lead, but he leads with love. And you're called to respect him. Are you good with that, Heather?"

She thought about that, turning to stare at the downpour that obliterated the view of a cloud-darkened parking lot. For a moment, she drifted back to her own marriage, her own late spouse, and what shaky ground that marriage had been on.

Drew had not led with love. He'd led with bullheaded certainty that he was right about everything. Sometimes that was fun—he had an adventurous spirit and demanded they "seize the day" so often, both kids could yell, "Carpe diem!" by the time they were four. No, he didn't quote scripture, but he knew every line from *Star Wars* and *Dodgeball*.

Had she respected him? Mostly, she'd stewed with resentment because she felt that, deep down, he didn't love her the way she wanted to be loved.

The way Kenny loved her.

"It's complicated," she finally said. "I'm not sure I completely understand the concept of submission in the Biblical sense, but will compromise do?"

Pastor Allen smiled. "It's close. The real meaning of the word is to, well, be a team player because you are now on a team together."

She nodded and looked down, but the words on her Bible blurred as unexpected tears welled. She'd blamed Drew for so many things, from his short temper to his ardent atheism to the way he brought out the worst in her.

But she hadn't fought to bring God into that marriage, not even in the end when she'd become "Christian curious." She certainly hadn't been a team player many times. Yes, when he was sick, she'd cared for him, but maybe she hadn't been a good wife. Maybe getting married eighteen months after he died was another example of that.

Maybe she was rushing into this marriage only because it was so, so different from the last one.

"And the final place I want you to go in this book is First Thessalonians," the pastor said, pulling her from her deep, dark thoughts. "Chapter Five, Verse Seventeen."

She forced herself to concentrate and find the chapter, but then she realized what he'd said and smiled as she flipped the tissue-like pages.

"I actually know that one," she said. "It was the first verse I memorized because it's only three words long—'pray without ceasing.'"

The pastor beamed. "Absolutely. And as God is my witness—and He always is—if you start and end every day in prayer, make every decision after praying, and cover each other with prayers of protection and peace, you cannot fail. And I'm not saying that because it sounds nice—having a prayer life will improve all of your life."

Without speaking, she and Kenny joined hands again,

and she felt his strong fingers thread with hers and tighten the grip.

"You have my word, Heather. That's how I want to live with you."

Swallowing hard, she looked into his eyes and saw the tears that she felt in her own. How could she *not* marry this man?

"I feel like this union is blessed," the pastor said, softly breaking into the moment. "And it will be my honor to marry you in, what? Just a few weeks, right?"

"Three weeks tomorrow," she said.

"Not a moment too soon," Kenny said sweetly.

But was it? Was it too soon?

The pastor stood and reached out a hand to both of them, offering to close the session in prayer.

As he spoke, though, Heather didn't hear all of the words. She tried. She squeezed her eyes closed, listened to the calming voice, and tried to lift her heart to join in Pastor Allen's heartfelt request for a blessed marriage that honored God and each other.

But what if it wasn't blessed? What if—

A bolt of lightning and simultaneous cannon shot of thunder felt like it shook the whole church, shaking the window glass and frame.

"Whoa." Pastor Allen laughed softly. "He has spoken."

Had He? And what was He saying? Was that...a *warning*?

She knew better than to even think that. God speaking through lightning bolts and thunder was far more clichéd and really Old Testament, but she'd spent most of this day looking for a word from above. Maybe that was it.

"Would you like to wait for this storm to pass before leaving?" Pastor Allen said as they walked toward his door.

They glanced at each other and Kenny shook his head.

"Let's get you home to Marc," he said, misreading her look of worry. "No one wants to be home alone in a storm like this. I'll go pull the truck under the overhang and pick you up."

He shook the pastor's hand and walked out, giving Heather the perfect opportunity to ask what she simply couldn't bear to bring up while Kenny was here. But here was her chance, so...

"Pastor, I do have one more question for you, if you don't mind."

"Anything," he said.

She took a deep breath and looked up at him. "You know my husband passed away eighteen months ago, from brain cancer."

He nodded, quiet.

"Do you...well, please be candid. Do you think we're rushing this or getting married too soon? Is a year and a half enough time to properly mourn him? Would...Jesus approve?"

He considered the question for a few seconds before answering. "I can't speak for Jesus. Do *you* think it's too soon, Heather?"

"I don't, no. I love Kenny, and I know we're going to be together forever. My kids love him, and they're already like a family with his daughter. I just...want to do the right thing in God's eyes."

"He doesn't have a timeline," he replied. "He gives you the Holy Spirit for guidance and discernment, so I would urge you to listen. And our Lord shows you the path he wants you to take, but you have to decide whether or not to take it. To do that, you have to trust Him completely and pay attention to all the words and directions He gives you."

She nodded, knowing all of that already. "How will I know which path, which door is closed, and what is His will? How do I know what's my voice and what's His?"

"I promise you, Heather, if your marriage isn't part of God's plan, He'll make that perfectly clear."

She sighed and gave him an impulsive hug. "Thank you."

"Just listen and trust Him."

Holding that thought, she left and followed the hallway toward the side portico where she could see Kenny already parked and waiting for her, rain sluicing over his truck. Without so much as a drop getting on her, she climbed in, noticing that the walk through the parking lot had left him soaked.

But he was smiling from ear to ear.

"Why are you so happy after a run in the rain?"

"Because..." He huffed out a breath. "It hit me like that bolt of lightning that if it hadn't been for you, I would still be so angry at God. I would still blame Him for my pain and my loss. Without you, I would never have set foot in a church, lifted that book, or said another prayer."

"Oh, Kenny. You might have, eventually."

"No," he said. "It was you. You walked me right back to Him and I'm so grateful. And I'm smiling because I'm marrying you, Heather Monroe. You! Perfect, beautiful, precious you. I probably won't remember what I'm saying when we exchange vows, but I know what I'm saying right now. I am going to do everything in my power to protect and love you, but first and foremost? This marriage is built on our faith and that will never waver. I promise. I see your doubts. I know your fears."

"You do?"

"Babe, you're an open book." He kissed her lightly. "This marriage is blessed and lasting. Amen?"

Her eyes filled and she leaned over the console to give him a kiss, tunneling her fingers into his hair and pulling him even closer to add pressure.

As they kissed, another bolt of lightning flashed, followed a few seconds later by thunder, a long rumble that shuddered the truck.

Kenny pulled back and gave in to another smile. "See? He agrees."

"Amen," she whispered, her prayers finally answered.

CHAPTER SIXTEEN
LOVELY

The entire dynamic of Lovely's home and life had shifted over the past few days, taking on a new rhythm that seemed to cover the cottage in a shiny haze of happiness. The days slipped by, each one a little sweeter than the one before.

After a long morning walk, they squeezed in something active and fun, like an hour of kayaking in the canals or a short charter on Chuck's boat, which they'd both loved.

Back at her cottage, they'd share lemonade and a delicious mid-afternoon meal, happily agreeing that they preferred that to a large dinner, laughing about how age changed everything.

Then they settled in for the best part of their time together, always shared with three very content dogs. They took their respective seats on the screened patio—he on the rattan sofa with the coffee table covered in notes, a guitar in hand, and her facing the water with a paintbrush and her canvas—and got creative.

He worked on a few different songs—*Yet* and *Whisper of Truth* were her favorites—and she slowly painted a "beachscape," capturing all the colors, the sweet hammock hanging between palm trees, and the comfort of the sun on the waves. Eddie promised the painting would hang in the den at his ranch.

During these hours, as the sky shifted from bright blue to soft lavender, they basked in each other's company. He jotted notes, made up lyrics, strummed the worn walnut Gibson he'd found in Key West, and sang to her with a deep but raspy voice that she swore she would hear later in her dreams.

It's the whisper of truth that sets us free,
The gentle breeze that lets love be.
No more pretending, no more shame,
Hear me calling out your name.

All the while, she stroked her brush over the canvas, capturing the colors of Coconut Key. Each shade somehow reflected the beautiful, warm, tender emotions that were taking up residence in her heart.

Lovely, though she'd probably never admit it out loud, was falling in love, and it was the most exhilarating and soul-lifting sensation she'd ever known.

"Whatever happened to your bangs?"

She turned from the easel at the question, frowning as she tried to figure out what he meant. "My...bangs?" She tapped her forehead with the back of her hand. "These bangs?"

"You had bangs...back then," he said, squinting at her like he was seeing eighteen-year-old Lovely in his mind's eye.

"I also had light brown hair with blond streaks, courtesy of lemon juice I squeezed on it every day."

"I liked the bangs. And your hair was just to your shoulders, and I remember when I saw you walking, it swung all in one smooth move, like a shampoo commercial."

She laughed at the image. "Well, your hair was dark and barely touched your shoulders. When did you grow it?"

"When I retired from the label," he said. "I stopped getting haircuts and finally looked like the rock star I never got to be. When did you grow yours?"

"I stopped cutting my hair the day my sister drove off with Beckie in her car."

He blinked at the answer. "Why? Protest?"

She lifted a shoulder. "Sadness, I suppose. A sense of... giving up? I knew that no one, including Beck, would ever know she was my daughter, but by then I was almost twenty-nine and kind of figured I'd never have another child. I was so broken that year."

"I can't imagine," he said softly.

She let her eyes close. She'd forgotten that was when she'd grown out her bangs, well over forty years ago.

"When Olivia took her away," she said, "she told me in no uncertain terms to stay away from her so Beck couldn't see the remarkable resemblance between us. And I just..." She tried to swallow, but tears threatened at the memory of those dark days. "It was a sad time."

"Oh, Lovely." He made a move to put the guitar down, but hesitated, looking uncertain. "I don't know if I want to write a song about that or come over there and hug you."

"Hug," she whispered without a moment's hesitation.

He stood immediately, placing the Gibson on the sofa and rounding the coffee table, arms extended as he walked to where she was perched on a stool.

"I'm sorry you were sad."

"It wasn't your fault," she said, taking the embrace.

"But it was." He inched back and looked at her. "How unfair that your whole life bore the brunt of that night, and I didn't even know it."

She sighed, acknowledging that, then shrugging. "It's over and it's fine. All's well, as they say. And, you know, now that Beckie's back in my life, I suppose I should get a decent haircut. I got into the habit of just trimming and braiding."

He lifted the long braid that was so frequently hanging over her shoulder, taking it to her forehead. "And bangs," he said. "I thought they were the cutest thing I'd ever seen."

She laughed, weirdly unselfconscious by his close attention. "I liked them, too."

"I'll cut it," he said. "Let's do it now."

Gasping, she shook her head. "You will not cut my hair. No, siree, not for love or money, as Beck and I like to say."

"I'll do it with love and charge you no money," he promised. "I know how to cut hair. I have two daughters. I cut Melody's bangs her whole childhood."

"I don't know..." She stroked the braid. "It's tempting, but I'll make an appointment. And what about yours? Will you ever cut it?"

"Do you want me to?" he asked, turning to show her his ponytail.

"I do," she said, getting a surprised look over his shoulder. "I like a nice, short-haired look on a man, to be honest."

"Then cut it. You have scissors?"

"Now? You want me to cut your hair right now?"

His whole face lit up. "Let's cut each other's hair."

She felt her jaw loosen. "That's so..."

"Intimate?" He smiled.

"I was going to say risky. And..."

"And fun," he finished for her.

"Fun if we don't mind wearing hats for the next few months."

Still smiling, he cupped his hand on her cheek, rubbing his thumb under her lip. "You are so pretty, Lovely."

She almost made a joke about her age, wrinkles, or the slightly soft jowl he held, but something stopped her. The look in his eyes, maybe, or the way her heart felt like it was simply melting in her chest.

"Thank you," she whispered. "You make me feel..."

He lifted his brows, interested and waiting.

"I don't know how to describe it," she said.

"Try."

Laughing, she shook her head. "I'm not you. I don't know how to put feelings into words like you do. You take feelings and make them words and music, and I can barely form a sentence."

He tipped his head toward the canvas. "You paint them."

She didn't look at the art, gazing up at him, lost. Completely and irrevocably lost.

"What are you thinking?" he asked softly. "Describe it. That should help with the words."

"I'm thinking that..." She swallowed. "Honestly?"

"Nothing but, Lovely."

"I'm thinking things that will just make you say you're sorry."

He drew back, confusion clouding his blue, blue eyes. "What do you mean?"

"I don't want you to take responsibility for things that happened nearly six decades ago."

Nodding, he slid his hand from her face and held her shoulders. "I promise I won't. But tell me what you're thinking."

Searching his face, she gathered her words, so very much

wanting to tell him that she'd never been in love, never even close.

She'd never felt so tender toward a man, even protective, and fascinated and enthralled and close but every minute she simply wanted more. She walked around with him in her head and on her heart and she'd never known that this kind of connection was possible for her.

How could she tell him that?

She exhaled. "I'm thinking I do want bangs. And I have good scissors. Yes?"

A slow smile pulled. "That's not what you're thinking at all, but yes. Let's cut our hair and recapture our youth."

That made her laugh. That and all the dizzy, wild, unexpected and wonderful things she was thinking but couldn't say.

Dusk was falling by the time he finished his work.

"If you try to look in that mirror one more time," Eddie said, "I'm gonna screw up and you won't be happy."

Lovely bit her lip at the order and closed her eyes to resist the temptation to peek. She could certainly see plenty of silver strands on the ground where they sat, just under her upper deck. She'd let him take off about six inches at the bottom, but from this vantage point? It looked like six feet.

And the hair on her forehead tickled, and took her back to the past when she would let her mother cut her hair, always outside just like this.

He stepped back, snapping the shears with the flair of a professional, eyeing his work and nodding.

"Is it straight?" she asked.

"Sort of."

"*What?*"

He laughed and leaned over, giving her nose a kiss the way Nick frequently pecked Savannah. The very idea of that made her heart twist.

"Yes, my lovely Lovely. It's straight and adorable and I think you're going to love it. Hang on, one little…" He lifted his scissors, peered closely, snipped, and backed up. "All right. You may look."

"Really?" Now she was scared. What if it was awful? She could be dead by the time her bangs grew back.

He handed her the mirror. "Trust me."

She inhaled, took the handheld and turned it. "Oh!" she exclaimed, blinking her eyes wide at the unexpected sight. "Oh, look at that."

"I am," he said, smiling as he stared at her. "Now you look like…her. That girl I remember. The one that got away."

She glanced up at him, then back in the mirror, beyond pleasantly surprised. She fluffed the bangs, and they fell right into place, then shook her head so her hair—which looked thick and soft—brushed over her shoulders. Her shoulders! It was short, but…

"I love it," she said, lowering the mirror to look at him. "I really love it, Eddie. Thank you."

"Good. My turn." He flicked his hand to get her off the stool he'd carried down for the project.

"I don't know if I can do this as well as you. Where did you learn to cut hair?"

"I told you, the girls. Especially Mel, who was always attached to me." He lifted the towel from her shoulders and shook off some hair, then draped it around his own. "Just cut the ponytail. One snip. Then we'll clean it up a bit and get back to business. I think my next song will be called...*A Cut Above*?"

"No, that's a terrible title," she said on a laugh, standing up and giving him the seat. "How about...*Cut Loose*?"

"Oh, getting better. We could go with *Snip Out the Past*."

She smiled and got behind him, easing the elastic from his hair. "*Clean Cut, Messy Past*."

"I like it! Emotional and clever. Or...*Fresh Cut, Fresh Start*."

"Optimistic," she said. "Cheesy as all get out, but hopeful. Just...straight across?"

"Yeah. It's no biggie, Lovely. Just hair. Oh! I know. *The Cutting Edge*."

"*The Final Cut*," she offered, picking up the comb they'd brought to slide it through his hair, which was surprisingly silky and so perfectly silver. The very act was, yes, intimate, but she nearly purred with how good it felt.

"I like that, but it's sad. How about *Shear Decisions*?" he countered, making her snort.

"Don't make me laugh or it'll be...*A Bad Cut*."

The puns flew as she trimmed, very slowly at first, then with more and more confidence. Silver locks fluttered to the wood deck while he sat perfectly still, not the least bit afraid she'd mess up his beautiful hair.

"How short?" she asked as her scissors approached the very top of his shoulders.

"Whatever you like," he said. "This is for you."

"For me?" She froze mid-snip. "Why?"

He tipped his head and looked up at her. "I want to look good for you."

"You already do."

"But you don't like long hair." He flipped his fingers over what was left of his. "I like this. Keep going. Just clean it up."

"Okay." Narrowing her gaze, she approached the hair like art, looking for ways to shape it and make it look fuller and thicker—which it was, surprisingly for his age.

After about ten or fifteen more minutes, she ran a comb through it again, positively delighted with her work. But would he be?

"All right. Big change," she said. "Are you ready?"

She handed him the mirror and held her breath. He lifted it and looked at himself for a long time, silent and staring.

"Oh, Lovely."

Her heart plummeted. "You hate it."

"It's too short. It's way, way too short." He lowered the mirror and stood as she took a step back, putting her hand over her lips.

"Eddie, I'm sorry. I just wanted to—"

"Not my hair. It's great. It's hair. It's actually quite comfortable."

"Then...what do you mean?"

"I mean...this. Us. This time we have together. It's just not enough," he said, reaching for her. "It's too short. A few weeks in the scheme of the ten or twenty years we hopefully have left? It's just too short."

She gave a sad smile, relieved that he didn't hate the haircut, but feeling the punch of pain for how right he was.

"I guess that's your song title. *Too Short*."

His eyes shuttered. "What are we going to do?" he asked on a gruff whisper.

She took his hand and drew him closer. "Enjoy every moment we have together," she said. "That's what I'm going to do."

He closed the space left between them, pulling her into his chest, planting a soft kiss on top of her newly-cropped bangs. "It's just not enough time when you find something like this. Unless..."

Holding her breath, she waited for what he'd say next. Dreaded it and longed for it and didn't know how she could possibly respond.

"Unless?" she asked when he was quiet too long.

He looked down at her. "You come to California."

"Of course I'd love to visit and—"

"For good," he said before she could finish her thought.

The rest of her sentence stayed trapped in her throat as she stared at him.

"Why not, Lovely? I have the most beautiful place. Half Moon Bay is one of God's most beautiful works of art. And the winery is spectacular. The whole state, really. We could go up to Mendocino or into the mountains and have so many adventures. We could—"

"Stop." She put her fingers on his lips. "I live here."

"I know you do," he said, undaunted. "Now. But I'm seventy-six and you're seventy-five."

"Too old to move," she countered.

"Too old *not* to," he fired back.

"And too soon to have this conversation," she added.

He shook his head, which looked so different and, yes,

younger. She loved the short hair. Oh, God. She loved *him*. Now what? Now what was she supposed to do? A low-grade panic crawled up her chest as she stared at him, unable to talk.

"Nothing's too soon at our age, Lovely. Everything's too late if we wait. Why would we find this amazing thing and then just let it go? Why would we do that? This gift? This surprise? This unexpected late-in-life joy? I'm not willing to just give it up because of...of geography. Are you?"

She took a step back, unable to answer and suddenly needing to breathe or run or hide.

"Are you okay?" he asked, genuine concern in his voice, which touched her.

"I'm...yes. I'm fine. But I think...the sun's going down. And I need to just be...alone."

His shoulders sank with a sigh as he nodded. "I understand. And I haven't seen much of Mel and Jazz, so I should go sneak in a bite of dinner with them. Join us?"

She shook her head. "I'd like to stay here and..."

"Think," he finished for her, leaning in for the lightest kiss. "About the future."

The future? She didn't answer, so he started to pick up the towel and brush the fallen hair through the deck cracks.

"Let me get it, Eddie. You get back to Jazz and Mel. Please."

As if he heard the soft note of determination in her voice, he stopped and set the towel on top of the stool, then gave her another light kiss.

"I'll leave the guitar here. I can't write without you anyway."

She smiled at that, hugging her arms against the lightest

winter breeze off the water, watching him take off down the beach for Coquina House.

Standing stone still for the longest time, she felt that gentle wind flutter her new bangs and shorter hair, blowing change all over her. Finally, she swept away their hair, picked up the towel, scissors, and mirror, and walked up the stairs to the screened-in porch where the dogs were sleeping.

She put the items on the table, stopped to pet Sugar, and looked at a few golden clouds hovering over the horizon.

California? She could never leave Coconut Key.

But...she was in love. For the first time in seventy-five years on this Earth, she was deliriously and genuinely and completely in love.

And didn't she deserve that as much as anyone?

She turned and looked at his guitar, his open notes, and the remnants of him. On a sigh, she went to the rattan sofa and inched the guitar over and sat, glancing down at what he'd written last.

The years go by, they slip away.
Next thing you know, it's your dying day.
Chorus:
Love happens fast or happens late.
You might regret it if you wait.
A second chance, a second time.
If only

He'd crossed out the next few words and she couldn't read them.

If only...what? If only she'd turn her life upside down, leave her family, her home, her newfound life...for love?

Dropping her head back, she gave in to a sob. She'd

waited her whole entire life to find this kind of love…and now she couldn't have it. How was that fair?

It wasn't. If she was being honest, life hadn't been terribly fair to her. A teenage pregnancy, an overbearing sister, a life apart from her daughter, and now…this.

No. It wasn't fair at all.

CHAPTER SEVENTEEN
EDDIE

His head felt weird on the walk back to Coquina House. Well, he'd just lost about seven inches of hair and there was no ponytail pulling at his scalp. But that didn't really explain how light and free Eddie felt just then.

He shook his head and ran his hand through the short hair as he walked along the shore, the sand between his toes, the fading light guiding him along a route he already knew by heart. Yeah, weird, but not because of his hair.

On a groan that came from his chest, he paused and looked out at the horizon, struck as always by how different the Atlantic Ocean was from his beloved Pacific. The West Coast wasn't "pacific" at all—this was. The waves didn't crash here, they rolled in like slow, steady breaths. The Atlantic—at least down here in the Keys—was as sweet and tender and calming as the woman he'd just left.

The woman he was absolutely and undeniably falling in love with.

How was that for life's big, fat irony? A woman he could have easily been with for fifty-seven years and—

"Hey, Pops."

He turned at the sound of Jazz's voice, not expecting to see her at the Beach Table where it all began. She lifted a glass of champagne and beckoned him closer.

And not have had her or Mel. So whoever ran this crazy

planet probably knew what they were doing after all. Still, the what-ifs of life really made him nuts sometimes.

"Hey, Jazz. You look comfy."

"Mel just ran up to get some appetizers that Beck— Whoa! Where is your hair?" She practically shot out of her chair.

"On the cutting room floor or, beach. You like?" He ruffled what was left of it.

"I love! Hang on." She picked up her phone. "I'll text Mel to bring you lemonade. Please, please, please join us."

"No need to 'please' me three times," he said, walking toward the boardwalk. "I'd love to share your cocktail hour. How was your day?"

She lifted a brow while she thumbed a text with the same lightning speed as Lark or Kai. "Not as good as yours."

"What makes you say that?"

She just laughed and pointed to his hair. "Sea change."

"Oh!" He threw his hands in the air. "Beautiful. Perfect title. Just perfect."

Still smiling, she looked at her phone. "She's on her way. She has ordered that you give no deets until she arrives." Putting down the phone, she propped her elbows on the table and gazed at him. "Wow. A whole new you."

"You should see Lovely." He pulled out one of four chairs and sat down, giving his head one more shake. "Yeah, I like it."

"You like *her*," she said.

He just smiled.

"Sorry, no deets, per Mel's request," Jazz said.

"All right, I'll hold on," he agreed, but he really did want to talk about his feelings. "How was your day?"

"Much, much too good," she said, her features set in a soft expression he couldn't remember seeing since...grade school.

"What does that mean?" he asked.

She let out a noisy sigh and threw open her arms.

"I love this place!" she exclaimed, making him laugh. "I love vacation. I love relaxing. I love doing nothing. I don't even know how this happened to me, but I am not waiting another ten or twenty years to take time off."

"That's great, Jazz." He beamed at her, always loving when either of his daughters grew and matured. It was a comfort he couldn't explain. "Why don't you back off at the firm and find more time for yourself?"

"I might," she said. "I very well might do that and—"

"Hey, who are you?" From behind him, he heard Mel's voice, making him turn. "Who stole my dad and replaced him with a short-haired Boomer?"

"Another long-haired Boomer." He stood to help her with the tray, laden with cheese, crackers, a large goblet of white wine, and an equally sizeable glass of Lovely's lemonade. Just looking at it made him miss her and he almost suggested he go get her so she could enjoy this impromptu party with them.

But he'd essentially ignored his girls on this trip, and he did want some time alone with them. They always helped him work things out.

"What did I miss, other than your new look?" Mel asked, ruffling his hair before taking a seat. "This was so long overdue."

"What? You didn't like my long hair?"

Mel and Jazz shared a look that spoke volumes that could be summed up in one word: *No.*

"Why didn't you tell me?" he asked.

"Because you liked it," Mel said. "You needed to recapture your rock 'n' roll youth. And now, you've done that with Lovely, so you can let go of never having been on the cover of *Tiger Beat*."

"*Tiger Beat*? Who said anything about that rag?"

Jazz pointed a finger. "You, frequently. Do you know how often you remind us that you weren't on the cover of that teen magazine all those years ago?"

He snorted and shook his head before taking a deep drink. "Man, the slings and arrows are flying down here. Maybe I should go talk to Beck. You know, my other daughter? The one who likes and respects me?"

"We *love* and respect you," Mel assured him. "Otherwise, we wouldn't tease you. Anyway, Beck went to see Peyton."

"Everything okay?"

"Mini contractions," Jazz said. "Probably false. Let's get back to Lovely. Before Mel came down, we were talking about how much you like her."

"No, we were talking about how much you like it here," he corrected. "I was told to wait for Mel before talking about my lady."

"Your *lady*..." Mel dragged out the word.

"Well, 'girlfriend' seems kind of ridiculous at our age."

"And after a week," Jazz added.

He didn't answer that, just smiled and took a sip. Then he exhaled, and looked from one to the other.

"Girls, when you know, you know. Time has no meaning." Although, to be fair, time had all the meaning right now. The only thing that mattered was the future, and how little there was left of it.

"When you know, huh?" Jazz tapped her fingers and looked expectantly at him. "What do you know?"

"I'm in love with her." It was so easy to admit, it had to be true.

"Does she know that?" Mel asked.

"Are you sure?" Jazz said right over her.

"No and yes," he replied. "I haven't told her, but I have asked her to consider moving to California." Now, they looked shocked, making him laugh. "You barely blink an eye when I say I'm in love, but I suggest she move, and you look like I suggested we all take off for the moon."

"Well, it would be easier," Mel replied. "Dad, she's not going to California." She waited a beat. "*Is* she?"

He leaned back and glanced at the water and sky, the sand and setting sun—the only home Lovely had ever known.

"She didn't seem too keen on the idea," he finally said. "She's lived here her whole life and has spent most of it pining for Beck. Now they're together, running Coquina House, and she has oodles of grandkids and extended family, so..."

With each word he said, he knew how absolutely ridiculous it was to expect her to leave.

"And you have a great life in California," Mel reminded him. "I mean, if you're thinking about living here, you have to remember *your* grandchildren, two incredible homes, extended family, and the business that you built from nothing and still control as chairman emeritus."

"I do remember all of that," he promised her. "So if she'd

move there..." But even as he said the words, they sounded like he was banking on winning the lottery. The odds were not in his favor.

Mel leaned in. "If she feels the same way about you, Dad, maybe she will."

"I just told you all the reasons she won't. Beck is here—"

"For now," Jazz said. At his surprised look, she shrugged. "We've talked a lot about her relationship with Oliver and you know what he wants? To split their time fifty-fifty between Coconut Key and Australia. Apparently, he has a beach house in some place I've never heard of and loves it there as much as she loves it here."

"And she'd do that?" For some reason, that really stunned Eddie. Everything he could see about Beck's life was rooted on this island. "What about Coquina House?"

"Someone could run the B&B for them," Mel said, flicking her hand.

"Or they could sell it," Jazz added.

Mel nodded. "True, they already have an offer on the table."

He looked from one to the other. "Does Lovely know that?"

"I don't think so," Mel said. "Beck refuses to even consider the offer. The house has been in her family forever and she and Lovely put their heart and soul—and Beck's whole divorce settlement—into remodeling it."

"You've gotten to know her more than I have," he said, hearing a note of sadness in his voice. "I came here to do just that, and I've been..."

"Distracted," Jazz supplied. "It's okay. You and Lovely had a lot of catching up to do. And we have spent quality time with Beck. As far as the offer? I'm with the real estate agent who said, 'Everyone has a number.'"

"Beck won't sell," Mel said. "She was absolutely clear about it."

"But, just for argument's sake," Jazz said. "If there was an offer that was, say, crazy high, then Beck would be free to live her fifty-fifty life with her Aussie. *And*...Lovely would be able to leave without the guilt of abandoning her business."

Eddie shook his head. "I think what keeps Lovely on this sand is far more than a business. Coconut Key is her heart, soul, life, and love."

"What if you were all those things to her?" Jazz asked.

"Well, if I were, I'd be the happiest man alive," he admitted. "But I'm not and I doubt I ever will be."

"Don't doubt, Pops," Jazz said, patting his hand.

He didn't doubt. He knew. Lovely wasn't leaving Coconut Key and he wasn't moving here, so their little romance, as perfect as it was, would come to an end eventually.

Unless one of them had a...*sea change.*

He reached up and touched his short hair. "Well, you know, anything can happen," he said.

"Or you can make it happen," Jazz murmured.

But she was just young enough to believe that was true. At seventy-six, he didn't know everything, but he knew that he couldn't make things happen just because he wanted them to.

If that were true, Lani would still be alive or he'd have made the cover of *Tiger Beat* or...Lovely would come running down that beach calling his name and saying, "Yes!"

He looked down the sand and squinted into the fading light, but no one was there.

WIDE AWAKE AT TWO A.M., Eddie finally threw off his covers and shook off the attempts at sleep. With his mind churning and uncertain, he sat on the edge of the bed and tunneled his fingers into his hair, not used to the feeling of it stopping so much sooner than he expected.

Not used to any of these feelings, to be honest.

He sat up straighter at a sound in the house, which was normally like a tomb. Water running? A dish on the counter? Way too early for someone to be preparing breakfast, but one of his three daughters—still getting used to that new number—must also have insomnia.

Whoever it was, Eddie wanted the company.

He opened the door slowly and glanced toward the stairs that led to the third floor where Mel and Jazz slept, seeing only darkness at the top. Padding downstairs, he noticed the owner's suite door was open, spilling enough light for him to easily find his way to the kitchen.

"Don't want to scare you," he called softly as he approached. "It's just me."

"Oh, Eddie, hello." Beck sat at the farmhouse table with a cup in front of her, the room lit only by a soft light over the stove and some moonbeams in the window. "Whoa!" She straightened and pointed to his hair. "You're a new man!"

"I kind of am," he said, giving the hair a quick finger comb. "You like?"

"I love!"

He rolled his eyes. "Don't tell me—you hate long hair and ponytails on men but would never tell me for fear of hurting my feelings?"

"Um...yeah?"

He snorted a laugh. "Why aren't the women in my life honest with me?"

"Because they care about you," she answered without hesitation, then lifted her brows to ask, "What are you doing up at this hour?"

"Couldn't sleep. You?"

"I just talked to Oliver. It's the middle of the day down there and he texted me a photo. I woke up and couldn't resist calling him." She pointed to her cup. "Can I get you a cup of decaffeinated green tea? It'll help you sleep."

"Sounds yummy," he said, only mildly skeptical. "I can make it, Beck."

She nodded, directed him to a drawer full of various flavored teas that all sounded like flowers and good health. He went with her recommendation, heating up the water in a comfortable silence that felt right for the middle of the night.

"Oh." He turned when he remembered why he hadn't seen her all evening. "No news with Peyton? I guess you'd have mentioned it."

She shook her head. "Braxton Hicks, which is baby language for false alarm. She didn't go to the hospital or anything, but it'll be soon, I think. Everything about her has changed. She's slow and settled, nesting like a mama bird, all ready."

"I like her husband," he said. "How did they meet?"

"Val used to bring the fish to Jessie's restaurant, back when it was Chuck's. It was Peyton's first cooking job."

He turned and leaned against the counter. "Ah, yes, the diner used to be called Chuck's, after Jessie's husband. Lovely told me that wild story."

"It was wild, all right. Chuck was believed dead at sea and Jessie was a deeply sad widow."

"And he was in St. Barts the whole time?" Eddie shook his head. "With amnesia? A gunshot victim?"

"Yep. It was quite the event around here when he showed up and then he helped the FBI bring in a money-launderer."

"That's pretty high drama for this place." He reached for the steaming teapot. "Oh, let me get this before the whistle wakes the girls upstairs."

"The girls." She laughed. "That's such a Dad thing to say."

"That's me. Dad to Mel. Pops to Jazz." He poured the water, bounced the bag, and carried the cup to the table, ecstatic at the quiet, private opportunity. "What would you like to call me, Beck?"

She screwed up her face, which looked young and sweet without any makeup. "Ever since Lovely told me the story, I've always thought of you as Ned."

He gave a quick laugh as he sat, then lifted his mug. "Then here's to Beck and Ned's very first father-daughter chat in the middle of the night. May it be fruitful, fun, and not the last."

"Aww." She tapped his cup with hers, a sparkle in her green eyes as she gazed at him. "You do have such a way with words. I understand why you're a songwriter."

"Didn't have enough of a way with words today," he admitted, blowing on the tea, which was far too hot to drink.

"How so?"

He shook his head, not quite ready to delve into that yet. "How's Oliver?" he asked instead.

"He's good, but..." She inhaled deeply and looked out toward the darkness, maybe not ready to delve into *her* insomnia cause, either. But his years of being a dad taught him that sometimes you had to press.

"He misses you?" he suggested gently. "And Coconut Key?"

"Yes, but he loves Wollongong."

"His pet kangaroo?" he joked, making her almost choke on a sip of tea. He'd also learned that humor went a long way with his daughters.

"Wollongong is where his beach house is. Have you been 'Down Under'?"

"I've been to Sydney and Melbourne," he said. "Honestly? Unless you're in the Outback, it feels pretty, well, American. At least it did to me. Where's Wollon...goner?"

"An hour or so from Sydney. It's a mountain and beach paradise that, yes, does look a lot like California, at least from the picture. Extremely picturesque and dramatic. His house isn't big, but the views are stunning and the surrounding area is just..." She let out a slow and wistful breath. "Anyway, he wants me to go there, and I'd love to, but not with Peyton days from delivery and Savannah hot on her heels."

"There'll be months between those babies," he said.

"Months when this B&B will be full and my oldest will have a new baby and my mother will need me and..." She flicked her hand. "It doesn't matter. What Oliver really wants is for me to live there half the year, and we'd live here the other half."

"What's wrong with that plan?" he asked, not wanting to reveal that his girls had already shared this with him.

"I don't want to live on the other side of the world for six months a year," she said simply. "My family and home and business and life are right here in Coconut Key. I only just got here two years ago, as you know. I don't want to leave, not even part-time. I'll visit, but..." She grimaced. "Nah. Not leaving."

He gave a dry laugh. "There's a lot of that going around."

"There is?"

He took a drink of the tea, now cool enough for him to —well, not exactly *enjoy* the taste. But appreciate the greenness of it. "Lovely won't leave, either."

"I should hope—" She caught herself, freezing mid-sentence. "Have you asked her to?"

"I did," he said, not surprised to see the flash of horror in her eyes. "But fear not. She turned me down."

"Well...*yeah*. She's lived here all her life and has known you for, what, ten days?" Her voice was tight enough that she could barely ask the question.

"The older you get, the faster time goes," he said.

She put her cup down and looked hard at him. "Talk to me in real words and not lyrics, Ned. Did you seriously ask my mother to leave with you?"

He studied her for a minute, liking that little bit of fire she kept back from the world. The mama bear in her—or, in this case, the daughter cub—was strong and admirable.

"Fair enough," he said, digging for clear and straightforward words that didn't sound like platitudes or poetry. "I'm falling in love with her. Might already be. I think it's mutual and what I'm saying about time is that it whizzes by a little faster every year. We're not young, Lovely and me. If we wait, or try to see each other long-distance, or just let these emotions die on the vine, I believe it will be one of the biggest regrets of both our lives."

"Are you *serious*?" she whispered, her face going bloodless.

"I am," he said.

"But...but...you fall in love easily," she said. "Mel told me that."

He laughed softly. "She's officially the bad daughter now. I am not one who, uh, runs from a relationship. I'm probably the opposite of a commitment-phobe, but that doesn't mean I don't really feel it. I have been alone for several years, and unmarried for many. I'd like to change that."

Her eyes nearly popped out of her head. "You want to *marry* Lovely?"

He hadn't put that into words—not yet. But wasn't that the very reason he was thrashing around upstairs, unable to sleep? "I want to...not live without her. Whatever that means."

"That means you move to Coconut Key, court her properly, and make sure she's one hundred percent on board."

He smiled. "Goodness, you love her."

"More than anything or anyone," she fired back. "Or certainly as much as my kids. She's *wonderful*."

"I know," he said. "And she's never been in love...yet."

"Stop it. This isn't a song. This isn't a game. This isn't... fair."

Suddenly, he felt his shoulders sink, punched by the panic in her voice. This was his daughter, despite being a stranger. And he had no right or desire to cause her any pain or discomfort.

"I'm sorry, Beck. I don't want to freak you out."

"Too late." She leaned across the table to make her point. "You cannot take my mother away from me."

He opened his mouth to reply, then shut it again, a lifetime of empathy making it entirely possible to see this from her point of view instead of his. And, once again, he reminded himself that this woman was *his daughter*.

He owed her the same level of sacrifice and selfless love he'd showered on Mel and Jazz.

"Then let's forget we ever had this conversation," he said gruffly.

"Not likely."

He closed his eyes and sighed. "I'm being selfish," he whispered. "I want my own happiness—and Lovely's—but I forgot about you in that equation. I'm very sorry. As your father, that's the wrong call on my part."

"Well, I mean...I get that you like her," she conceded, visibly touched by his words. "It's just awfully late in both your lives to make a change like that, isn't it?"

"I guess I was thinking it was awfully late in both our lives *not* to make a change like that. How can we ignore the unexpected and delightful possibility of meeting and loving and someday dying next to...'the one'?"

Her eyes filled as she stared at him. "Lovely has never..." She tried to swallow, but her voice cracked. "Lovely has never known that. Not ever, not once."

"I know."

"She's lived a solitary life and spent so, so many years apart from me, her only daughter. She kept her vow of silence, which is what stood in her way of falling in love."

"It is," he said. "She told me that keeping her secret meant she couldn't completely give her heart and soul to anyone. I feel awful she carried that burden alone."

"It wasn't your fault," she replied. "It was my moth—Olivia. She forced that promise in writing, and Lovely would have taken it to the grave, but...well, you know. She almost went to that grave, but God sent her back to this life so she could create this unbelievable bond with me."

He reached over the table, his heart breaking with every word. "Beck, I—"

"Or maybe..." She pulled her hand out from under his and pressed it to her lips. "Oh. Maybe he sent her back...for *you*." The words came out on a strangled sob.

"Oh, Beck!" He shot up and around the table, reaching for her. "Don't cry. I'm so sorry. I shouldn't have said anything. I shouldn't have imagined you'd—"

"But if you are her person, her one and only?" she managed to ask. "What if you're the reason she was sent back?"

He just looked at her, not wanting to hurt her any more than this conversation already had. "Beck, I—"

"Can't you come here?" she asked, easing him away to look into his eyes. "We would love that! You could be part of this family, and I'd have both my biological parents here!"

The magnitude and impossibility of what she was asking rocked him so hard, he almost lost his balance. Just thinking about the number of people he'd disappoint and miss—no, he couldn't.

"I would cause the same pain on the other coast," he said gruffly. "My grandchildren, my daughters... No, we haven't spent decades apart, as you and Lovely have, but we are a unit like you'd never believe. I don't... I can't..."

After a moment, he eased into the chair next to her, finally seeing the mess he'd gotten into and the fact that his needs were just making it worse.

"I should leave," he muttered.

"Leave...go back to bed or..."

"I should leave Coconut Key. Before things get...deeper. Before Lovely and I say the words we're both already feeling. Before you shed one more tear. I'll leave early and I'm sure—"

She grabbed his hand. "No, no. Not yet. You don't have that many days left. Please don't just disappear, it would break her heart. Give me a chance to talk to her, to think this through, to imagine...a different life."

"That's not what you want," he said.

"But I don't want..." She held up her hand, working to gather her composure. "I *really* don't want to stand in my mother's way of having something..." She moaned softly. "Something she's longed for her whole life. I've heard her say things here and there—about fated mates or one true loves. I've heard the melancholy regret in her voice, always comforted by the fact that she'd found me...if not...if not you. But now...there's you."

He took her hand and wrapped it between both of his, feeling an indescribable connection with this dear woman. She had inherited something of his, he decided. That soft spot. That need to please the ones she loved. A level of compassion that sometimes got him in trouble but mostly made him a better person.

"Then give me time, too," he said softly. "Let me talk to Mel and Jazz and do the same kind of reimagining, Beck. Maybe there's a solution we've both missed."

"Maybe my mother and I both have to live six months at a time in different places."

He shrugged, not a huge fan of that option, but not wanting to kick doors closed just yet.

"I am sorry that I missed witnessing you grow up, Beck," he admitted. "Lovely has told me what you were like as a little girl before Olivia took you away. I wish so much that I'd been there for you. For her, too."

She smiled. "I know. You're a good man, Ned."

"Not even close," he replied, feeling the sting of guilt he hadn't even known he should have felt these last fifty-seven years.

"You are," she said. "I can see you're genuine and you don't want to hurt anyone and you really, really care about Lovely."

"And you," he added. "You are my daughter, Rebecca. If I had been more responsible or Lovely hadn't left without giving me her number, you would have grown up Rebecca Sylvester and I would have been so incredibly proud to be your father."

She let out a choke, half laugh, half sob. "Really?"

"I'd have married Lovely if I'd known there was a child. At least I like to think I would have. But who knows? Lots of roads not taken."

She squeezed his hand. "We're standing at an intersection of a few right now," she said. "We have to decide which to take, and which to pass. I don't want to make a mistake, though. I want everyone to be happy."

"Sometimes that isn't possible," he said.

"Then I want Lovely to be happy," she replied, almost giving it no thought. "Of all of us, she's the one who deserves it the most."

"I agree," he said. "And she knows where I stand—sort of. You talk to her, Beck. You and Lovely decide what you want to do. I'll accept whatever that decision is and figure out a way to have both of you in my life."

"But not quite the way you want."

"At the risk of going too far too fast," he said, "I don't think I'll have what I want until she vows to love, honor, and cherish me until death do us part. I know it really is fast and I'm willing to do the work to get there, but honestly, Beck? I love that woman and want to spend the rest of my life showing her that love."

She closed her eyes as if he'd hit her. "Oh. She deserves that," she whispered. "No one deserves it more."

Yes, he thought, *she does*. But he didn't want to make things worse, so he just leaned in and gave Beck a kiss on the head.

"You're a good daughter. Good night. Thank you for the tea and company."

With that, he stood and left her, maybe in worse shape than when he'd found her. And, as her father, that broke his heart.

CHAPTER EIGHTEEN
BECK

"Knock, knock. Special delivery."

At the sound of Savannah's voice, Beck hustled to her bedroom door still fastening the last button on her blouse.

"What are you doing here?" she asked, reaching for her daughter, who looked awfully bright-eyed and bushy-tailed for the early hour.

"I woke up craving scones, so I left Dylan sleeping with Nick and slipped over to the café. Jessie had me bring your delivery, which I put in the kitch— What's wrong?"

"Nothing," Beck said quickly.

Savannah's look said she knew better. "Did the fake contractions stop or are they real? No, you'd be there if they were real."

"They stopped and I slept in." Beck slipped on her sandals and gestured Savannah toward the kitchen. "I was awake until three, so you're a godsend with the breakfast."

"Visions of a new granddaughter dancing in your head?"

She threw a look at her middle daughter, knowing she'd get humor and advice and plenty of support on the "Lovely Cannot Leave" train when—not if—she shared what Eddie had told her last night.

But shouldn't she talk to Lovely first?

"I had a long convo, as Ava would say, with my, uh, father. At two in the morning."

Savannah cocked a brow. "Do tell and don't dream of leaving out a detail, because something has trouble in your eyes." She glanced over her shoulder when they got to the kitchen. "I take it we're alone?"

"Yes. Jazz and Mel like to sleep late, and I suspect so will Eddie. Oh! Bless you, sweet child!" Beck exclaimed when she saw the boxes and bags from the Coquina Café. "One of these days I'll hire a cook and stop having Jessie handle the breakfast part of my bed-and-breakfast." She lifted a box lid and inhaled the buttery smell of fresh pastries. "Or not."

"Because who can bake like that?"

"Because..." She closed her eyes and battled the temptation to tell.

"Mom."

"It's nothing."

"Mom."

"Really, it's—"

"*Mom.*"

Beck groaned. "It's the third 'Mom' that always gets me."

"Gimme a scone and tell me what's going on." Savannah breezed around the island to get her tea.

Beck took a deep breath and then spilled the awful truth as fast as she could. "They're in love and he wants her to move to California."

"What?" Savannah whipped around so hard, her long hair swung over her shoulders. "What did you say?"

"My reaction exactly."

She gave a soft hoot. "Can you spell 'preposterous'? Because I can. It's N-O, two capitals, one giant exclamation point. Next problem?"

"Savannah, you have to understand something."

She dipped her chin and gave a dubious look. "Please don't tell me you agree with this insanity."

"I love Lovely."

"Who doesn't? Everyone, it would seem. Mom, she can't leave this place and go to California! For a man? What kind of nonsense is that? I won't hear of it, end of story."

Beck pulled a platter from the cabinet for the pastries. "It might not be the end of the story," she said. "It might be... the beginning." And that's what kept her thrashing around in bed for the few hours she slept last night.

"*I can't hear you...*" Savannah sang, covering her ears, only half joking.

But she had to hear her. Beck needed Savannah and everyone else to understand what was at stake here.

"Just imagine, Sav," she started. "You never met Nick. No, no. Scratch that. Imagine you met him exactly as you had and never saw him again after your...your..."

"Hookup," she supplied. "It's fine to say it out loud, we know what happened."

"After that," Beck continued. "But you had Dylan."

"Different life, but—"

"And you gave Dylan to Peyton to raise and agreed—no, you *swore* on your family name and the Bible *in writing*—to never tell Dylan or anyone else that you are his mother."

Cup in hand, Savannah came a step closer, quiet for once in her life.

"And then, during the next fifty-five years, you never fell in love with anyone," Beck said. "Not ever. No strong man at your side. No deep affection in your heart. No one to love and cherish or worry about or wake up with. Ever. But you wanted to. You longed for it."

She swallowed. "Did she ever really try? I mean, Lovely's beautiful and sweet. Surely there were men lined up to fall in love."

"Lovely made a promise to her sister not to tell *anyone* the truth," Beck said. "And if she did find that man, she knew she'd have to keep the truth from him. She'd never be able to be truly honest. So, no, she didn't try."

"Oh, Grandie. A control freak to the end, wasn't she?"

Beck nodded, having nothing good to say about the woman who'd raised her, especially now that she knew what Olivia had put Lovely through.

"All her life," Beck continued, "Lovely had a hole in her heart and a longing for something she knew she'd never, ever have. But now…the truth is out and…Eddie is here. And they are, whether we want to like it or believe it, falling hard for each other."

"So, Lovely has a shot at finding The One," Savannah said.

"Yes, she does."

"I see where you're going with this. Which is, sadly, to California." She frowned and shook her head. "Which is untenable. Impossible. Unthinkable. No."

"I agree with all that," Beck said. "But I, for one, will not stand in the way of Lovely Ames finding her one true love and enjoying her last ten, fifteen, or twenty years on this Earth next to him. I won't."

Savannah turned when the kettle whistled, lifting it and bringing the room to a heavy silence.

"Permission to state the obvious?" she asked.

"Why doesn't he come here?" Beck replied.

"Exactly."

"Because his family ties and property connections and lifestyle are all just as strong."

"What about this B&B?" She gestured around the sun-washed kitchen. "It's not only the Ames family home, it's a thriving business now, and Lovely is half-owner."

"Well, maybe it's time to...change the management structure."

"What does that mean?" Savannah asked.

Beck felt the blood drain from her face, terrified to put into words the thoughts that had plagued her long after Eddie went to bed. "I could hire someone full-time or sell it—"

"Mom!"

"And spend half the year in Australia the way Oliver wants me to."

Savannah stared at her, blinked, and stared some more and, once again, the room was filled with a rare silence.

"I'm just considering all the possibilities," Beck added. "Trying to make the people I love happy."

"Oh, okay. Am I on that list? Is Peyton and Val and...and Baby McFatFace? Is Nick and Dylan and this fetus currently the size of that scone?"

"Savannah." Her voice cracked and as it did, her daughter's whole face collapsed.

"Oh, Momma! I'm so sorry!" She flew around the island, arms out. "That was so mean. I can see you're struggling, and I just reacted so selfishly. I'm sorry. I'm sorry!"

Beck wrapped her arms around Savannah, squeezing her through the next sob.

"It's okay, it's okay."

"No, it's not okay. That was not fair." She leaned back. "I'm such a brat!"

"You're hormonal."

"And of course you let me off the hook." She squeezed Beck harder. "I'm awful and you're so good and I'll never be half the mother or daughter you are and that's the truth."

Beck laughed at the dramatics, brushing Savannah's hair back and drying her tears.

"Do you think it will happen?" Savannah asked on a ragged whisper. "I mean, Eddie and Lovely? Is it real or are they just—"

"It's real."

They spun around at the sound of Eddie's voice to see him standing in the doorway.

"And I'm afraid I've crashed a mother-daughter moment."

"No, no, it's fine," Beck said, easing away from Savannah. "I just share everything with my girls—"

"As do I," he said, smiling at Beck. "Maybe too much, eh?"

"Where's your hair?" Savannah asked on a shocked laugh.

"Gone with the wind," he said. "Winds of change."

Beck rolled her eyes and he winked at her. But his expression grew serious as he stepped into the room.

"Listen," he said. "And I'll be straight, Beck, I promise. No lyrics." He let out a sigh. "I did not come here to wreck anyone's life. I don't even know if I would have come if I'd known Lovely was alive. I would have worried about dredging up her past and throwing some massive monkey-wrench into her life. And that's exactly what I've done. Forget the past, I've gone and ruined her present by asking for her future." He cringed and looked at Beck. "Too lyric-y?"

"Very honest," she replied.

Savannah crossed her arms and regarded him, her look unreadable, and Beck braced for whatever snarky joke might come out to slice him in half.

"Also awesome," she said, surprising Beck completely.

And Eddie, judging by his response.

"A rare man who puts others first and has a good heart."

His eyes flickered. "Thank you, Savannah."

"That's the kind of guy I married," she said. "And he, as you know, left a thriving Hollywood career, a hit show on Netflix, and fame and fortune to move to Coconut Key and marry me." She lifted her brows. "Just *sayin'*."

He chuckled. "I hear you."

"Do you, though?"

Beck took a step back, instinctively knowing that the morning was slipping away fast. If she didn't hurry down the beach, Lovely could walk in the door and she'd never get a chance to talk privately to her. She'd awakened this morning with that as her main goal.

Plus, this grandfather-granddaughter duo clearly needed some alone time.

"I'm going to be gone for a while," she said, pointing toward the door. "Are you two okay together?"

"I don't know," Eddie said.

"Guess we'll find out," Savannah countered. "Scone?"

"Don't mind if I do."

Smiling, Beck walked out, certain they would find

common ground and be just fine. For now, she had to talk to Lovely.

WHEN SHE CAME up the back stairs, the first thing Beck heard was music and Lovely's voice ringing out a little louder than Joni Mitchell's, the sound bringing her to a complete standstill.

"'*Help me! I think I'm fallin'...*'"

Beck closed her eyes and listened to her mother's slightly off-key warble, belting out the song about falling in love too fast. Ava had once called the tune a whiny cry for help, and Lovely had chastised her great-granddaughter mightily.

Whiny or not, it was a cry for...something.

A cry for Beck to let her mother wallow in the beautiful glory of her first love? Or for Beck to take a stand, insisting that *their* love—the one between a mother and daughter who'd been unfairly separated for decades—took precedence over what could amount to a crush?

She just didn't know, but had to find out.

Taking the last few steps, she listened to her mother—and Joni—sing about hoping for the future and worrying about the past. It sounded like echoes of Eddie's perfectly-paced pronouncements that could be real...or could be song lyrics meant only to rhyme and sound good.

"Good morning, songbird!" she called out to her mother when she reached the top of the stairs, her voice instantly getting the dogs to bark.

"Oh, Beckie!" She heard footsteps, then the music stopped. "Come in, honey. Hush, puppies!"

She pulled the screen door open, not surprised to find the sliders thrown wide to let in the glorious January air and sunshine. Inside, Lovely, wearing one of her favorite flowered dresses—

Beck gasped. "Lovely! Your *hair*! Eddie told me, but... wow. That is so different. And bangs!"

She fluffed the just-past-shoulder-length locks. "I like it," she said, a tad defensively. "Don't you?"

"I love it," Beck assured her, coming closer, staring. "You look..." She pressed her hands to her chest. "Aunt *Lovey*! That's how you looked when I was little. Before Olivia took me away."

She smiled, her eyes misty. "Yes, that's the last time I had bangs. But...here we are. Like...old Lovely."

"You said you'd never cut it!" Beck exclaimed. "Not for..."

"Love or money," Lovely finished, laughing at their inside joke. "Well, maybe for one of those things."

For...*love*? Was her mother really and truly in love?

She came closer, studying the actual cut. "It looks amazing," she said. "He did a great job. So did you, since his looks so much better."

"Doesn't it? I kind of hated that ponytail, which he told me several people have now admitted."

Several people...including Beck. But that conversation was in the middle of the night. "When did you talk to him?"

"He texted me good night when he went to bed sometime in the middle of the night."

Middle of the night texts? Oh, boy. This was serious. Of course, she only had to see the gleam in her mother's eyes to know that.

Could Beck demand that joy be wiped away? Hardly.

"Any news from Peyton?" Lovely asked.

"Nothing this morning." Beck gave her a hug and added an extra-strong squeeze. "You look positively glowing, dear mother of mine."

Lovely trilled her laugh. "Well, you know..."

"But I don't know." Beck lifted a brow. "As Savannah would say, spill some tea, please."

"Actually, I just brewed a fresh pot of coffee. Can I get you a cup?"

"Absolutely. Let's get comfy on the patio and talk." Beck stepped back out to the screened-in area, only now noticing the easel and partial painting, and the guitar resting on the sofa, with an open notebook on the table.

"Some new additions to your décor, I see," Beck called as she walked toward the easel and studied the particularly brilliant tones her mother had selected for this painting of the view. "This is great work, Lovely. You're inspired."

"I'm...worse than that," Lovely said as she stepped out holding two mugs. "I'm...in..."

Beck bit her lip and took the cup, studying her mother's face. "In what?" she finally asked.

"In something." Lovely gestured toward the table where they'd shared so many teas and coffees and lemonades and mimosas. They'd sat here for hours and planned Coquina House's remodeling, the room décor, the business strategy, and the joint venture they'd started together.

Beck's heart dipped at the thought of it being over already.

"In...what?" Beck pressed again.

"Insane?" Lovely laughed. "In deep? In over my head? In...somniac? At least I was last night."

"There's an epidemic of that going around," Beck said, still searching her mother's newly framed face. "But all those 'ins' are bad. Are you in anything good that doesn't have you feeling crazy, drowning, or sleepless?"

She smiled. "You want me to say it, don't you?"

"I wouldn't mind hearing it from your mouth," she agreed. "It's a big word and I have never heard you say it before."

She put her cup down and sighed, her gaze moving to the guitar. "Okay, fine. I know it's dumb and wrong and silly and—"

Beck put her hand on her mother's. "It's none of those things, Lovely."

She closed her eyes. "Beckie, darling, I think I'm in love."

For a moment, neither of them said a word, letting the full weight and impact of the confession just press on both of them.

Then Lovely opened her eyes and looked right at Beck. "What do you think of that?"

"I think that no one on the face of this Earth is more worthy of love than you."

She blinked and her eyes filled with tears. "Thank you. But what am I going to do?" she whispered the question, as if saying it out loud made the dilemma all too real.

"Well, first you're going to enjoy the ride," Beck said. "You've never been in love before."

"Never. And I guess I can say I totally understand the hype." She gave a soft giggle. "It's like a glorious sunrise, sweet dark chocolate, the perfect melody, and a warm breeze all at the same time. Also like free-falling from a cliff and hoping there's someone or something to catch you. And..." She made a face. "It makes me tingle all over."

Beck cracked up, her heart rising with each word. "It's all that and more," she agreed. "You just described how I feel when I see Oliver's name on my phone."

Lovely dropped her head back and sighed. "Whatever am I to do, Beck? I mean, yes, I'm enjoying the ride. But like any good rollercoaster, we're going to cruise to the end far too soon and then..."

Beck pressed her mother's hand. "If you want there to be more than just a rollercoaster ride, all you have to do is say so." The words hurt but they had to be said. "I will release you from any responsibility and...and...never, ever stand in your way of living your life how and where and with whom you want. You deserve every happiness, Lovely Ames."

Lovely straightened her head and gazed at Beck. "Why, sweet Beck, can I not have it all? Why do I have to choose between one beloved and another? Between home and heart? Between love and loneliness?"

Beck smashed her lower lip between her teeth to keep from crying. "I don't know why, Lovely, but are you sure you have to?"

"He's not moving here."

Beck stared at her, waiting for the rest. Waiting to hear, "And I'm not going there," but her mother didn't say another word.

After a few seconds that felt like an hour, Beck leaned closer. "We have options, you know. We could hire a manager to run the B&B."

Lovely's eyes flashed. "What would you do?"

"Oliver wants nothing more than for me to split my time between here and Australia. I'd live there with him, and come back to see my kids and grandchildren."

Lovely gave a humorless smile. "Do be sure to fly through San Francisco so I can see you, too."

Beck winced. "Yeah, I know how that sounds."

"Other options?" Lovely asked.

"I've had an offer on Coquina House, which I rejected outright."

Lovely stared at her, jaw loosened. "You...have?"

"If we sold, you and I would be set for life and...and..." Oh, the very thought was unspeakable.

"And our season would be over," Lovely finished for her. "Our glorious season of mother-daughter bonding, of hospitality and happiness, of mimosas and memories and..." She blinked, a tear rolling down her cheek. "I sound like Eddie writing a song."

"But we'd start a new season," Beck said. "One of deep, lasting, song-inspiring love."

Lovely considered that, holding Beck's gaze. "Is that what you want, honey? Do you want to split your time and be with Oliver? Because I will not stop you, either."

"I don't know what I want except for you to be deliriously happy," she countered, squeezing Lovely's hand. "You have never had this kind of love before, and I want you to revel in it."

"I've also never had *this* kind of love before, daughter of mine." She lifted their joined hands. "And I want to revel in it some more."

They stared into each other's matching green eyes, both of them agonizing over the same question: why couldn't they have both the things that they wanted? Why did it have to be an either-or situation?

"Hang on," Beck said when she heard her phone vibrate from her bag, somewhat relieved to break the tension that stretched over the patio. "Could be Peyton."

She stood and pulled out her phone, reading the text with a gasp.

"What is it? She's in labor?" Lovely was up in an instant.

"It's Marc," Beck said, pressing her hand to her chest as she read Kenny's text again and again. "He's missing. They have no idea where he is."

"Let's go," Lovely said, no other discussion necessary.

Wordlessly, they scrambled, gathering bags, locking doors, soothing barking dogs who somehow understood there was a crisis.

A crisis that demanded an entire family come together to support, pray, love, and search. An entire family that could be shattered by…love?

It didn't make sense. But right then, to Beck, nothing made sense. Nothing at all.

CHAPTER NINETEEN
HEATHER

"How far could he have gotten?" Kenny asked, pacing the living room in frustration. "How long has he been gone?"

Heather just whimpered. "He went to bed early and I didn't go into his room because he hates that."

Kenny nodded. "I know, but..." Then he shook his head and crouched down in front of her. "It's not your fault."

"It most certainly is," she fired back. "My own kid leaves the house—maybe in the middle of the night—and I don't know about it? Is he in a car? Flying? Taking a bus? I have no idea!"

She curled up on the corner of the sofa, reliving the moment that she realized her son had run away. What had started as a normal Saturday morning with no game, work, or event scheduled had rolled into nightmare status with no warning.

They'd actually been whispering out of respect for Marc and his teenage desperation to sleep as late as possible. Kenny had dropped Ava off so she and Maddie could spend the day working on a school project together, then left to visit one of his construction sites, fixing a problem that had cropped up. Heather had planned a day of readying her home for two more residents after the wedding.

She was giving up the spare room she rarely used so Ava would have her own room. It had never been an office or much of a guest room, but had sadly become a dumping ground for things they brought from Charleston but never really needed.

Heather completely lost track of time making piles for donation and trash. She'd gone through the hardest memories when they'd packed to move here, so she wasn't terribly emotional, even when she'd come across something that belonged to Drew.

But when her stomach growled and she realized she'd never had breakfast, she pushed up and headed into the kitchen in search of food. Passing Marc's bedroom door, she paused, feeling the inexplicable urge to check on him.

That, she knew now, had been the Holy Spirit.

When she opened his door and saw a neatly made bed, her heart fell. When she found a note on the bed, her hands shook. And when she read the words, she let out a blood-curdling scream that had Ava and Maddie running into the room.

She could still see his scratchy handwriting on a piece of paper torn from a school notebook.

Don't worry about me, Mom. I'm fine. I just can't stick around here for this wedding. I'm on my way home and I'll be okay, I promise.

Marc

Not only hadn't he texted, Marc had also turned off the tracker on his phone, so she had no idea where between here and Charleston—which she assumed he meant when he said "home"—her fifteen-year-old son could possibly be.

By the time she calmed down and they got Kenny here, she was fairly certain she knew what happened but still had no idea where her son was. Grandpa Andy seemed stunned by her call. None of Marc's friends had a clue. And Aunt Blanche conveniently didn't answer her phone.

Kenny stroked her arm every time her voice rose in panic.

"We can call the police," he said. "We can have every flight out of Miami checked."

"How would he get to Miami?"

"It's not hard," Ava said, leaning forward from where she and Maddie were tucked together on the loveseat, speaking gently. "I did the same thing when I was his age. Remember, Dad?"

He grunted at the unhappy memory. "Took ten years off my life when I found out you were down here and not at your aunt's in Fort Lauderdale."

"How did you do it again, Ava?" Heather asked, knowing she'd heard the story but forgetting the details.

"Dad shipped me off to my mom's ex-sister-in-law in Fort Lauderdale—"

"I didn't *ship you off*." He shot her a dark look. "I was... never mind. I was struggling."

"So I was already in Florida," Ava finished. "I wanted to meet Beck, since my grandma wrote a letter for her before she died. I took an Uber to Coconut Key to meet my 'real' grandmother."

"A very, very expensive Uber," Kenny added with a playful smile.

"Sorry I was a brat," she said. "But it should give you hope, Heather. Look how awesome I turned out."

She smiled because the exchange did give her hope. This difficult time would pass, but only if Marc was safe. Right now, that was all she cared about.

"Does he have money?" Kenny asked. "A credit card?"

"No credit card, but he has allowance money that I thought he'd spent on video games and such. He got a lot of gift cards and cash cards for Christmas from Blanche..." She closed her eyes and sniffed. "I know she's behind this."

"Let's call her again," Kenny said, pulling out his phone and sitting next to her. "She won't recognize my number. What's hers?"

Heather handed him her phone, too upset to go through the motions of sending the contact, but he did it, wonderfully calm in this crisis.

"I can't believe he's gone," she muttered, biting back more tears. "I just can't."

Instantly, Maddie was up, kneeling in front of her. Ava followed, the two of them with their hands on her legs, offering support.

"Do you want to pray?" Maddie asked softly. "I know that makes you feel better."

She felt the blood drain from her face. "I didn't even think of that. Some Christian I am. Some lousy mother and terrible widow and—"

"It's ringing," Kenny said, bringing her pity party to an end. "I'll put it on speaker. Girls, stay quiet."

They both nodded but kept their hands on Heather's knees. Ava's eyes were closed, and Heather knew she was praying, which folded her heart in half. What a wonderful stepdaughter she would be.

"Blanche Henderson, how can I help you?"

Only Blanche answered her personal cell like that. Obviously thinking the same thing, Maddie rolled her eyes.

"Blanche, this is Ken Gallagher."

For a moment, she was dead silent. "As in Kenny?" she asked, that cutting edge in her voice. "What do you want?"

"Marc. Is he with you?"

"Not yet, but his plane hasn't landed—"

"His *plane*?" Heather practically shrieked the question. Her son was on a plane, and she hadn't even known it? "How is that possible? How is it legal? He's fifteen years old and they let him fly alone?"

"Will you please calm down?" Blanche's voice cut through the room, getting matching eyerolls from Maddie and Ava.

Heather stood, ready to fire everything she had, but Kenny put his hand on her shoulder, oozing strength and sanity as he eased her back on the sofa. She let out a sigh instead.

"He's old enough to fly," Blanche said. "I sent him a ticket and he used his phone and legal ID. It's not a huge deal, for heaven's sake. I also Venmo'd him the money to get to Miami, which he did very easily without you even knowing he'd left your house. Good parenting, Heather."

"Oh, come on, Aunt Blanche!" Maddie exclaimed. "Stop being so mean to Mom. You know you shouldn't have done that."

"I know nothing of the sort," she replied. "That boy is miserable and wanted to come home. My father misses him. We all do. He doesn't want to be down there for that farce of a wedding, and who can blame him? Your father hasn't been gone that long, Maddie."

"Mom's happy," she said. "You're wrong about everything."

Heather squeezed her hand. "Don't fight with her," she mouthed.

"Listen to me, Blanche," Kenny said, his voice strong and authoritative. "I want to know what airline and flight he's on and we want to talk to him the minute—the very minute—you have him in your sights. And then plan on seeing me in about twelve hours, because that's how long it will take me to drive there. Enjoy your visit, because he's coming home with me tonight."

"I think you should let him decide that," Blanche said.

"He's fifteen years old and not an adult," Kenny replied. "And I don't think you want me to have you met at home by the police arresting you for kidnapping."

"He's not your son," she fired back. "*You* could be arrested for kidnapping."

"Do not test me, Blanche," he ground out.

"Oh, please!" She tried to sound dismissive, but for the first time, Heather heard a hitch of fear in the woman's voice. She *should* be afraid. This was wrong on so many levels. "Fine. I'll text the flight information and arrival time to this number. I'm on my way to the airport."

"Have him call us immediately," Kenny ordered.

"All right, all right." With that, she hung up, leaving them all a little stunned.

Heather pushed up, her whole body shaking from the conversation while the girls ranted about how awful Blanche was. On a shaky breath, she headed into the kitchen, not even sure why but needing to burn off nervous energy.

"We know where he is," Kenny said, following her.

"He's in the air," she replied. "Thirty thousand feet in the air and I didn't even know it."

"You know it now."

She swallowed hard and turned to him. "This is a..." She wet her lips, choosing her words carefully. "This could be a... a closed door."

"Do not give that woman so much power," he insisted. "No doors are closed. Marc is acting out, just like Ava did. You heard her. Same age, similar situation. They lost a parent, and it rocks their foundation. Add on to it that he's upset about his grandfather and probably really struggling with us getting..." His voice faded out as he realized what he was saying. "But he's not calling the shots."

"Isn't he?" she challenged. "It feels very much like he's in control right now."

"Well, I'm driving up there," he said. "I'll bring him home."

She studied him for a moment, thinking. "Wait until—"

"Mom?" Maddie came into the kitchen. "Beck and Lovely just pulled in. I think Savannah's on her way and Peyton, too. Probably Callie, some kids, and...more."

She groaned, not sure she wanted to face all of them right then.

"They want to support you," Kenny said, reaching to put his arm around her.

But she slipped out of his touch, hating herself for it, but way, way too upset for anything or anyone right then.

He let her go and didn't follow as she walked back to the living room. On the way, she finally stopped to pray, but could barely find the words to ask for help.

THERE WAS STRENGTH IN NUMBERS, Heather realized. Somehow, her soon-to-be in-laws who were already dear friends swooped into her crisis and made things better. No, they couldn't make the phone ring, but they circled her with love and support, humor and hugs, and just an appropriate amount of space when she needed it.

Which was right this minute, in fact.

With strict orders to get her if Marc called, Heather walked toward her room for a moment of quiet and prayer. On the way, she passed Maddie's room and heard the comforter rustling, which was weird because both the girls were in the living room.

Stepping inside, she found Peyton on the edge of the bed, leaning over.

"Are you okay?"

She shot up, her eyes wide. "More Braxton Hicks," she said. "I didn't want to make a big deal with all this going on."

"Do you want me to get Val?" Heather said, coming into the room. "I think he was about to leave to get everyone some food, but I'll stop him if—"

She waved her hand and shook her head. "No, no. It's fine. It's a false alarm. I should have stayed home, but I didn't want to be alone or miss all this."

"The family crisis?" Heather asked on a dry laugh, sitting next to Peyton.

"The family *together* in a crisis," Peyton corrected. "We come together. It's what we do. You know that."

"I do and I'm grateful." She put her hand on Peyton's back. "Are you scared?"

She sighed and sat straighter, one hand on her admittedly large belly, the other on her lower back.

"Just of the unknown," she confessed. "Everyone I talk to says giving birth is nothing like the books and videos—or movies—and that parenting is the same way. But we have this family"—she gestured toward the hall and sudden burst of laughter—"who seem to find Marc's antics hilarious."

"They find Savannah hilarious," Heather said. "Marc's going to be grounded for a month."

"What's going on in here?" Beck poked her head in the doorway, lifting her brows at Peyton. "You okay, honey?"

"I am, I just—*oof*!" She doubled over with a gasp.

"Peyton!" Beck launched into the room and Heather held her tighter.

"Ooh, is it baby time?" Savannah appeared out of nowhere, followed by Callie.

Peyton grunted and reached over to grab Heather's leg. "This...is...bad. And, to be honest, that was like the third one in about five minutes."

"I'll get Val," Callie said, rushing back into the hall.

"No, wait—"

Beck cut Peyton off with a swipe of her hand. "Get him, Cal. Savannah, start timing."

"Do you want to lay back, Peyton?" Heather asked, gently easing her toward Maddie's pillow.

"I want to...hang on. Okay." She exhaled with relief. "It's better now. I feel better. That was just a lot harder than..." She looked up, her gaze on Beck, but not really focused. "This might be it."

"Peyton!" Val came rushing in, his dark, good-looking features set in an expression of true concern. "Don't try to be Superwoman, okay? When it's time, it's time."

"I'm eight days early."

"Doc said you were ready, babe. It might be time to roll."

"Do you have her bag?" Savannah asked him.

"At home," he said. "I can get it. Or take her to the hospital and someone else can bring her bag." He sat on Peyton's other side, putting his arm around her gently. "Hey. You promised you wouldn't wait too long, remember?"

She nodded. "I just don't want to spend a day in the hospital."

"Better than delivering in a bedroom, like I did," Savannah said. "Of course, it was a hurricane."

Peyton looked up at her. "You scared the life out of us that night."

Savannah shrugged. "I like drama. Not you, though. You like things just so, Pey. Go to the—"

"Owww!" She blanched and buckled again.

"We'll get the bag," Savannah said. "And we'll meet you at the hospital. Mom, you go with Val in case he needs backup."

Everyone started moving at once, barking orders to each other, cooing support to Peyton, getting her out to the living room, where there was even more noise. So much that Heather didn't hear her phone ringing until Maddie handed it to her.

"It's Marc," she whispered. "Go in your room and talk to him. I'll send Kenny in."

As dazed as Peyton, Heather took the phone and stared at her son's name and a picture of him leaning on his baseball bat with a cocky grin after he hit a homerun.

He *ran away*. How was that even possible?

Slipping into her bedroom, she tapped the screen. "Honey—"

"It's me," Blanche said.

"Where's Marc?"

"He's right here and you can talk to him when you're calm."

A shiver of fury shot through her. "Let me talk to him, Blanche. I swear to—"

"Hold on, hold on. He's getting his bag. He does want to talk to you, so just relax."

Kenny walked in and he softly closed the bedroom door, blocking out the noise from the living room.

He reached for her hand and gave it a squeeze. "Put him on speaker," he whispered.

"Okay." She nodded and tapped the screen, the two of them sitting on her bed side by side.

"Hey, Mom."

She let out a grunt of pure adrenaline and relief. "Marc. What the heck were you thinking?"

He was silent for a beat, long enough that she could picture his face, the set of his jaw—the one he'd just started shaving.

"Sorry if I scared you."

"Out of my ever-loving mind," she said. "Why did you leave?"

She heard him huff out a breath. "I don't want to go to that wedding."

"So you run away to Charleston? You get to Miami... when? And then fly to Charleston?" She hated that her voice rose in panic, but she still couldn't wrap her head around what happened or how.

"It was Aunt Blanche's idea."

Why was she not surprised?

"Well, it was a bad idea."

"Maybe, but I knew if I was there, you'd make me go and do some dumb thing like walk you down the aisle."

She closed her eyes as the words hit their intended target and broke her heart. Kenny tightened his arm around her.

"You aren't old enough to just leave this house, Marc. It was wrong. It was inexcusable."

"Well, sorry, but I had to get out of there."

The words cut her. "Why? Is it so bad here? We have a good life with a big family and you like school and… Why? Why did you leave?"

Kenny rubbed her back and whispered, "Don't cry, babe."

But how could she not?

"'Cause I'm mad," he said, the words garbled but the message clear. "Dad died, like, you know, yesterday. At least it feels that way to me. I like Kenny. He's nice. I like Coconut Key and all, but I think it's too soon to have another dad."

This time his voice cracked with tears, and she had to bite her lip to keep from sobbing while Kenny sat stone still.

"I do, Mom. I miss Dad. I just want him to come back!"

"I know, honey," she said, her voice thick. "But that isn't going to happen."

"Then I want to be here where he was. With Grandpa. I'm going to stay with Grandpa. Please, Mom. Please let me stay. I'll catch up in school and I'll be okay, but I want to stay here."

She looked at Kenny, his expression as broken as she felt.

"What should we do?" she mouthed.

He lifted a shoulder. "Let him stay."

She swallowed hard. It felt like defeat. It felt like failure.

And it sure felt like a closed door, because she wasn't getting married without her son there.

"How long?" she managed to ask.

"Just until…after you get married."

"Okay," she whispered. "But I'm going to call Grandpa now. And every day. And you call me every day. Twice. More."

"'Kay. Thanks, Mom. I'm sorry."

"So am I. Bye, honey. I love you."

"You, too."

She hung up and practically fell into Kenny's arms.

"Shh." He stroked her shoulder. "It'll be fine."

Would it? "I *was* going to ask him to walk me down the aisle," she said on a sob. "He called it a dumb idea."

"Then he'll be busy, because I was going to ask him to be my best man."

"Oh!" Heather exclaimed. "That would have been…" She sniffled and wiped her face. "But now he won't even be there."

"We don't know that yet," he said.

But Heather knew. Marc was as stubborn as his father, and she knew that once he made his mind up, nothing could change it.

CHAPTER TWENTY
BECK

When they hit the twelve-hour mark, just about midnight, Beck nearly collapsed in the waiting area outside of Peyton's labor and delivery room. The Lower Keys Medical Center wasn't a massive facility, but it was the only hospital for miles that delivered babies. It was a blessing that L&D was slow for most of the night, so they didn't have to share the family waiting room with anyone else.

Which was good, because at one point around six o'clock, Eddie, Mel, and Jazz showed up with a mountain of food for everyone, so happy the baby would be born before they headed back to California the next day.

The group had filled every seat. Jessie was there with Chuck, and a shockingly well-behaved Beau. Nick had Dylan—who wasn't quite that well-behaved and had to be taken for long walks by Maddie and Ava.

The little ones went home with their fathers around eight, along with the teenagers, so the crowd got smaller, but the hum of anticipation had been palpable throughout the night.

Beck missed Oliver terribly, though. She'd texted him a few times, but it had been overnight for him. It was two in the afternoon now in Wollongong, where he said he'd be going for a few days, and they hadn't connected all day. But there were certainly enough loved ones around her to keep her mind occupied.

Kenny and Heather walked in after taking a break outside, both wearing the only real miserable expressions Beck had seen all day.

"Hey." She reached out her hands to them, gesturing for them to come closer to where she sat. "How are you two doing?"

Heather lifted a shoulder. "We just talked to Grandpa Andy," she said. "I feel better, since Marc is with him. Andy said he'd try to talk sense into him, and take him fishing."

Beck looked at Kenny. "You don't want to go get him?"

"More than anything, but we've decided to give him a chance to work it out. Talking to Andy definitely made me feel better. I'll get him when he's ready."

"I'll figure something out with school," Heather said. "And get his work."

She nodded, taking Heather's hands. "It's never easy, this motherhood thing, is it?"

Smiling, Heather sank into the chair with a sigh. "Not a bit. Any word from— Oh, there's Val!"

All the chatter and soft laughter stopped when Val came into the room, wearing the scrubs they'd put him in what felt like days ago.

"No news, no news," he said, holding up his hands.

"How is she?" Beck asked.

"Well, between contractions, she still laughs at my bad fish puns, so that's a good sign," he said with an exhausted smile. "Doc thinks we're getting late for an epidural and she's trying to hang in without one."

A mumble rolled through the crowd, the general

consensus being that she should do whatever could be done to stop the pain. But Beck knew how much Peyton didn't want drugs during labor, unless it was a life-saving situation. God willing, it was not.

Val took a few steps closer and beckoned her with a flick of his finger. "She needs a little Momma time, I think."

Beck practically knocked her chair over getting up. "Of course."

"And Foster sisters," he added, looking across the room to Savannah and Callie. "And Lovely."

"Oh! Yes!" Lovely stood and let go of Eddie's hand, a move that had a few looks sliding among them. "Let's go be her human pain relief."

The four of them gave a wave to the rest and followed Val into the dimly lit birthing suite where one very sweaty, pale Peyton leaned back on the raised bed.

"Hey," she said weakly.

"Oh, Peyton." Beck rushed to the bed, taking her daughter's hands. "You're going to be fine."

"I know. It's just...yikes."

"Get the epidural, Peyton," Callie said, her dark eyes shadowed with worry and exhaustion. "I've done all the research and it's safe."

"Maybe. I'm learning to get through them." She lifted her hand to the others. "C'mere, you guys."

They surrounded the bed, Beck and Savannah on one side, Lovely and Callie on the other.

"We picked a name," she said softly.

"Are you telling me she's not going to be Baldy McFat-Face?" Savannah joked, but her humor lost its bite when she gazed at her sister with love and sympathy.

"You can call her anything you want, Sav," she whispered. "As if I could stop you."

"Oh, Pey-Pey," Savannah crooned. "I love you and I hate that your labor is endless. What are they saying? How much longer?"

"Hours more. This whole dilation thing is slow. She's just not— Oh, boy. Here we go. It's...crunch...time." Her face contorted as she tried to breathe, one hand squeezing Beck's, the other clutching Lovely's. She groaned, arched her back, whipped her head a little from side to side, and puffed out air.

At the peak of the pain, she let out a long, hideous moan, then her grip eased as the contraction subsided.

"Oh. *Oh.*" She let go and wiped her forehead, but Callie produced a washcloth, and Beck used it on Peyton.

"Baby girl," Beck murmured, her heart torn for her daughter but knowing there really wasn't any other way out of this.

"Exactly. Oh, baby girl." Peyton smacked her dry lips.

"Ice chip?" Callie asked.

"Cold beer?" Savannah gently jabbed at Peyton's leg.

Her eyes shuttered, too wiped out to laugh or respond. "I want to tell you her name. Now, I just...want to."

"Of course," Beck said.

"And we'll love her name no matter what it is," Lovely said.

Peyton looked from Beck to Lovely and back to Beck again. "I wouldn't be here today, and I wouldn't be having this baby, if not for you two."

Beck sighed. "But *you* were the one who made me come

to Coconut Key," she reminded her daughter. "I almost threw 'Aunt' Lovely's invitation away."

Lovely tsked. "Thank you for talking sense into her, Peyton."

"I remember that day," Peyton said in a whisper, as if using her voice was too much effort. "I was miserable in my office, and you were so sad about Dad and selling the house and you called from a coffee shop and told me you had this weird invitation."

Beck smiled at the memory, which was crystal clear. She could still see the Old Navy T-shirt dress she'd worn after that officious Realtor had sent her out of the house. She remembered the hand-addressed envelope she'd stuffed into her bag, and how lost and confused she'd been after her husband dumped her for his law partner.

It had broken Beck to be forced out of the beloved home where she'd raised her children. She'd cracked that day— many days during that dark time—and called her go-to bestie, her oldest daughter.

"And look where we ended up," Beck said. "Best decision we ever made to get in the car and drive to Coconut Key."

Peyton nodded. "I was thinking that, and Val agrees."

"This is all sweet, girls," Savannah said. "But if you don't tell us the name soon, you're going to have another contraction. And then we'll just call her Crunch Time."

Peyton did smile then. "I wanted a little buildup."

"Take your time, Pey," Beck said.

She tried to sit up, grimacing in discomfort. After a moment, she took their hands again. "Her name will be... Rebecca Lovely Sanchez."

"Oh!" Beck and Lovely gasped in unison.

"Peyton!" Savannah exclaimed. "That's perfect!"

"Isn't it?"

"Best two names in the world," Callie chimed in.

"We won't call her Beck, obviously. Just Rebecca. Full name. Not shortened. And her middle name is all you, Lovely."

For a moment, no one spoke, but Beck leaned over, kissing Peyton lightly on the head, a tear falling from her eyes.

"I don't know what to say," she whispered.

"I'm so humbled," Lovely said, stroking Peyton's hand, tears flowing from her eyes, too. "I'm honored and delighted and shall shower her with every bit of love I have."

"I love you both so much," Peyton whispered, her voice ragged. "But...here...it...comes...again."

"Oh, boy," Lovely said. "I mean *girl*."

"Settle down there, Rebecca Lovely," Beck teased, placing a loving hand on Peyton's belly. "Just come on out and let us meet you."

"And hurry it up," Savannah pleaded, all of them tightening in a loving, supportive circle to get Peyton through what seemed like an endless contraction.

Tears stung all their eyes when it was done, especially Peyton's, who seemed wiped out.

"I need Val," she muttered.

"I'm right here, sweetheart."

They all turned, not even aware he'd come back in the room.

"What do you think?" he said, a wide smile brightening his handsome face. "Rebecca Lovely Sanchez?"

"I think she needs to get here already," Beck teased, hugging him.

"She's on Cuban time." He gave Beck a kiss on the forehead and stepped closer to Peyton, nothing but love and concern on his face as he reached for her hand. "That last one was *fin*-tastic." He tapped her nose playfully, but she only had the strength to roll her eyes.

The nurse came in then and the room got crowded, so Beck and the others left Peyton with Val.

"Come in every hour," Peyton called. "I want you here when I deliver her, Mom. Val will get you."

"I'll be wherever you want me, honey."

Outside in the hall, they gathered in a circle and hugged for a long time, emotional but so happy.

After a minute, Savannah got a call from Nick, so she stepped away and Callie started back to the waiting room, but Beck snagged Lovely's arm and shared a look.

"Wow," Beck whispered. "Rebecca Lovely. Can you believe that?"

Lovely's eyes were still damp, a storm of emotion brewing. "Beckie. What am I going to do?"

The fact that she was even asking the question nearly took Beck's breath away. Was she considering a move to California?

"You'll...follow your heart," Beck said, knowing it was a lame cliché that didn't give Lovely the answer she needed.

But the truth was, only Lovely knew where that heart was headed. And Beck was starting to get very scared that she was going to hate the ultimate destination.

Rebecca Lovely Sanchez was the tiniest, most perfect, most precious, most pink squirmy bundle of beautiful that Beck had ever held. And she'd had three baby girls, each more spectacular than the next.

But there was something indefinably wonderful about the one-hour-old infant Grandma Beck cradled in her arms, a few tendrils of espresso-colored hair poking out from the pink cap she wore.

"Hello, little button nose," she whispered. "Hello, Cupid's bow lips and...oh, I know there are blue eyes, but they are not going to be revealed."

"A day and a half of labor will do that," Peyton said groggily from the bed. "But Mom, you've been here as long as we have. Please, you can go home now."

Beck looked up from one beautiful baby to the one she gave birth to almost thirty-three years ago, a slow smile pulling at the sight of the woman who'd battled through childbirth and barely complained.

"I can't put her down," Beck confessed.

"You need sleep," Peyton said. "Did everyone leave?"

"They did, after they got a glimpse of our newest family member. Poor Lovely was half asleep on Eddie's shoulder, so he took her home. And I'll go...although...." She lifted her brows up as she realized she was stranded without her car. "I'm not sure how I'll get there."

Eyes closed, legs out, Val was conked out in the recliner. But he held up one hand. "I'll drive you, Beck. And stop at home for a shower and coffee. I'll be back before the sun's up, Pey."

"And you shall sleep, little one," Beck said, standing to

gently place the pink-blanketed baby in the basinet next to Peyton. "Good heavens, she's beautiful."

"All that dark hair." Peyton beamed at her. "She's definitely Val's little girl."

Beck leaned over Peyton to whisper, "That's a Foster nose, though." She kissed Peyton's head. "Great job, Mom. Welcome to the club."

"Oh." Peyton put her finger over her lips. "Can you believe it? I've never been so happy in my whole life."

"You deserve it," Beck said. "You earned this joy."

She sighed and looked up. "You earned your joy, too, Momma. I know what you're struggling with. If you want to split your time and go to Australia for six months a year to be with Oliver, it's okay."

Beck gave her an "are you serious?" look. "Now? When my namesake is an hour old?"

"I just don't want to hold you back from happiness. None of us do. He's perfect for you and makes you happy."

Beck studied her, thinking of how strange it was that she and Lovely were juggling the same challenge. They'd found great men...who wanted to take them from the place they were happiest.

"I think it's just a function of falling in love later in life," Beck mused. "We've built families and businesses and whole, wonderful lives in very separate places. You don't take that into consideration when you're young."

Peyton nodded, and sighed, fatigue etched on every feature.

"We'll figure it out." Beck gave her another kiss. "Sleep now, while she does. Because, trust me, you won't sleep much for the next eighteen years."

Peyton smiled and let her eyes close.

Val, standing over the baby and gazing down at her, angled his head to the door. "Let's go and let them both sleep." He blew a kiss to his snoozing wife then they left together, walking through the hushed hospital halls in the cool pre-dawn darkness.

Quiet when they first got into the car, Val finally turned to her as they neared home.

"You know, Beck, Peyton and I had the same issue, remember? I had this amazing job offer in New England."

"Oh, I remember," Beck said with a dry laugh. "I thought Peyton would be a single mom."

"And she would have been because she wasn't leaving Coconut Key."

Gnawing her lip, Beck looked out at the sky, the very first whisper of light lingering over the horizon.

"So, I did the only thing I could do," he said quietly. "I forced the company to let me work remote because love beat work, geography, and everything else."

She turned to him. "I know you did, and I so appreciated it." She reached for his arm. "You're a wonderful son-in-law and I love you."

He smiled at her. "You know the feeling's mutual, Beck."

"Thank you."

"The thing is," he said after a beat. "You women need each other. You and Lovely and Peyton and Savannah, and even Callie, although she doesn't know it yet, but she will. You are each other's life's blood and support system. Without you, Peyton would have had a hole in her heart. And without Peyton, I'd have had one in mine."

Her eyes filled for what felt like the fortieth time that day, tears springing easily after the sleepless night in the hospital. "That's...sweet."

"It's a fact," he said. "And I don't mean to stick my nose where it doesn't belong, but any man worth his salt will acknowledge that and respect it. Asking you—or Lovely—to leave or move or even do some fifty-fifty thing that takes you away from your foundation and family, your home and your heart?" He shook his head. "I don't think that's right. And, again, I don't mean to overstep—"

"It's fine," she assured him, the tears rolling now. "You're right. There's really nothing else to say about it. You're absolutely right."

And somehow, these men, wonderful as they were, would have to realize that.

As they passed Lovely's cottage, she noticed a dim light from the living room and wondered if her mother had ever gotten to sleep. She considered asking Val to drop her there, but thought better of it.

Lovely needed sleep, and so did she. And maybe Eddie was still with her, trying to persuade her to do some...*California Dreamin'*.

He pulled into the circular drive of Coquina House, which was completely dark.

"Thanks, Val," she said. "Oh, and congratulations." She laughed as the most important thing came out as an afterthought. "You made a beautiful baby."

"Another addition to the next generation of the most wonderful women I've ever met."

"You're sweet." She leaned over and kissed his cheek, then climbed out of the car, standing for a moment as he drove off.

When the taillights disappeared down Coquina Court, she turned to the house, pausing for a moment to look up at the sky and thank whoever created and ran this world for giving her another healthy, beautiful grandchild. And for—

"I don't want to frighten you, but I'm here waiting."

She gasped. "Oliver!" Squinting into the darkness of the veranda, she spied him standing by the railing. "What are you doing here?"

"I tried to make it to the hospital to surprise you, but I just pulled in about ten minutes ago. I texted Nick and he said you probably had left by now."

"Oh, my goodness!" She rushed to the steps, meeting him halfway as he wrapped his solid, strong arms around her and lifted her right off her feet. "I've missed you!"

"Not," he murmured into a kiss, "as much as I missed you."

She laughed into the kiss, giddy and delirious, feeling... light and thrilled and as ecstatic as she'd been the first minute she'd held baby Rebecca an hour or so ago.

"I can't believe you're here! How did you—"

"One stop, Sydney to Miami. Rented that thing. Broke a whole lot of laws driving down US 1 in the middle of the night."

She glanced into the shadows to see a compact car tucked away. "You made record time, even in that."

"I pushed the travel process to its limit, Beck, and it's still too far," he said. "Too long, too far, too much."

At his tone, which sounded a little defeated, she drew back, searching his face. "Is that news to you?"

"It was a realization." He tucked her under his arm and

walked her up the stairs, guiding her to the sofa to sit together. "A big, fat wake-up call, if you will."

"To...what?" she asked, not entirely sure where this was going.

"You were so far away, and I hated that," he said, pulling her closer. "The few times I've gone back since meeting you have always been hard, but this was..." He shook his head. "I don't want to be away from the woman I love."

"Aww. That's kind. I don't want to be away from you, either."

He looked hard at her, his expression serious. "And the distance—in the heart and around the globe—is mind-boggling."

"It's...far," she agreed, realizing that seemed like a silly understatement.

"The fact is, I don't want to take you that far away from the people and place you love, even for six months at a time. I love you too much to do that." He took her face in his hands, looking right into her eyes. "Beck, you are *you*—the woman I love—*because* of those people and this island. I just can't forget that."

She sucked in a soft breath, mostly at how eerily the sentiment echoed what Val had just said. "Oh, Oliver. What are you saying? No split time?"

"No split time," he confirmed. "Yes, we should take a vacation Down Under when the time is right and your girls stop having babies. I'm putting the beach house in property management to be rental income and I'm staying here. I can use my advertising experience to take a more active role in marketing Coquina House, and help you run this place. You're my life now, and this is where you belong."

For a long moment, she just stared at him, taking in every beautiful detail from his dark gold hair, thick brows, strong bones, and that beautiful mouth she loved to kiss. This was her man, her one true love, her fated mate, if she could use Lovely's silly term.

"What do you say?" he asked on a whisper, getting closer for a kiss.

"I say..." She kissed him lightly. "I could not love you more and you just proved you love me just as much. I don't know what the future holds, but—"

"I do," he said, with typical Oliver confidence.

"You do?"

"Yep." He folded her into his arms and leaned them both back. "It's bright. Now tell Olipop all about our beautiful new granddaughter with the perfect name. You better have pictures."

"Olipop." She laughed softly, but it caught in her throat, her heart filled with so much joy she honestly thought she would burst.

"I have a million pictures. How much time do you have?"

"The rest of my life," he whispered.

They cuddled on the couch and looked at every picture she had while the sun came up over Coconut Key, her forever home that she would share with this amazing man.

CHAPTER TWENTY-ONE
EDDIE

Sunrises just didn't get enough credit. Maybe that was because Eddie had lived most of his adult life in California, the land of endless sunsets. Here, on the East Coast, he'd really grown to appreciate the slow, lemon-yellow ripening of the sky that came with the first morning light. He'd never realized how different this was from the orange and violet drama of a sunset.

Sunrise was happier and hopeful, a dawn of possibilities and change.

But this morning, despite the fact that he'd just met his newborn great-grandchild, he didn't feel happy or hopeful. He'd brought Lovely home and brewed some coffee while she disappeared into the back to shower, leaving him on the screened patio to watch the sunrise and…brood.

There was no other way to describe his mood in these hours before he and his daughters were scheduled to fly home. How could he not feel disappointed? He'd lost the battle to win her heart.

Well, maybe he had her heart, but she wasn't moving, that was for sure.

And the baby who bore Lovely's name was just one more powerful tie to Coconut Key, so Eddie hadn't even bothered with the full-court press he'd planned for his last day here.

He knew better than to hope she would start to reorder her life and plan a move, or to think that somehow, in their mid-seventies, they could pull off long-distance. Not a chance.

This was the end of a beautiful romance, and it made him deeply sad.

He stepped back and caught sight of her unfinished canvas, the seascape she'd been slowly working on since he got there. She promised to send it to him when it was done, and he'd hang it right over the fireplace in his den.

It would look out of place there, he knew, but didn't care.

But would she send it?

He reached into his pocket and pulled out his phone, stepping back to capture the partial painting in the magnificent morning light. She'd painted the sand and water, the hammock and sea oats, and started the blue of the sky, which she'd told him was the most challenging.

He'd call the painting *Sea Change*...because that's what he'd been through these past few weeks. A sea change of transformation. And it could be a song, too. Maybe when it hung in his den, he could look at her finished painting and write that song.

Or bawl his stupid eyes out.

Something tickled his bare foot and he looked down, meeting the soulful gaze of little Sugar, who'd become quite attached to him. Smiling, he bent over and picked her up, nuzzling her silky fur against his neck and stroking her little head.

"Look at you, paying attention to someone who isn't Lovely," he whispered. "Do you want to go out? It's early."

She licked his ear.

"I'll take that as a yes. Come on." He glanced around. "Where are the other two?"

Basil lifted his head from a dog bed and Pepper bounded over from outside Lovely's bedroom door, where she'd been protecting her mistress from anyone who might enter. Still holding Sugar, Eddie quietly opened the screen door, letting out Basil, then Pepper, who gave up her post at the possibility of going out.

At the bottom of the stairs, the dogs found their favorite patch of grass while he dropped his head back and sucked in a deep, deep breath. Exhaustion slammed him, making him a little dizzy.

Well, sure. It had been a long time since he did an all-nighter, but he'd sleep on the plane.

At the thought of his pending departure, he let out a soft grunt of disappointment and defeat. Then he opened his eyes and looked at that bright and hopeful sunrise again.

Maybe he hadn't tried hard enough. Maybe he hadn't painted a clear enough picture of how beautiful California was. Maybe he hadn't given her enough options or possibilities. Maybe—

"You left me."

He turned and sucked in a soft breath at the sight of Lovely in the golden glow. Her hair fell over her shoulders in damp waves, her narrow frame covered in a long pink cotton nightgown that didn't look much different from her many maxi dresses, at least not to his untrained eye.

But there was something intimate and vulnerable and downright youthful about this look, fresh out of the shower, glowing from soap and a new great-granddaughter.

It made his miserable heart ache at the idea of leaving her.

"I didn't leave you," he said as Sugar trotted over to Lovely. "The dogs wanted to hit the grass."

"I thought...you left." She bent over and picked up Sugar, snuggling like they both needed a comforting sniff.

"You thought I just walked out without saying goodbye?" he asked on a dry laugh.

"We said goodbye when I went into my room."

He shook his head and took a few steps closer to her. "Not...*goodbye*-goodbye. That was more like, 'Have a nice shower, I'll make coffee.' Which I did but forgot about. Want a cup?"

"No, I'm going to try and get some sleep," she said. "But I know your flight..." She swallowed, and buried her face in Sugar's fur again.

"You okay?" he asked.

"I don't like goodbyes, Eddie," she admitted on a whisper, finally putting Sugar down. "Not since the day my sister drove off with Beckie. Ever since that, I just can't take them."

"I've had a few rough ones," he said softly. "But *not* saying goodbye? Well, that's the worst. Like this girl I met in Key West a lifetime ago." He took a few steps closer. "She never said goodbye."

She closed the space between them and wrapped her arms around his neck, looking up at him. Without makeup of any kind, he could see the fingerprints of time, sun, and one hellacious car accident on her face.

But he could also see the clarity in her green eyes. The wisdom and warmth and humor and heart. All of it in her beautiful green eyes.

"Now I have to write a song about your eyes. I have to remember the seafoam color that will always remind me of... of..."

"The two best weeks of your life?" she asked with a teasing smile.

"Our interlude," he finished.

"So poetic," she said.

"And like any good poem," he added, "that interlude was poignant, emotional, and way, way too short."

As she looked at him, those eyes grew misty. "I'm sorry I left without saying goodbye that morning. It could have changed the course of our lives."

"It would have," he said, no doubt at all. "I would have called you from payphones on my way to California. You would have told me you were pregnant. I would have come back and married you. We would have lived right here on Coconut Key, raised Beck, and—"

"Stop." She put her hands on his lips and bit back a sob. "Stop the would-haves that never happened. Don't torture me with what might have been. We don't know that 'would have' happened. It makes me feel like the road I took was all wrong. A waste of life. A huge mistake. A life without love—"

"Now *you* stop," he said, mimicking her move by putting his fingers on her lips. "None of that is true. None of it."

"The life without love part is," she said, her whole body feeling heavy in his arms. "I never had it," she added on a ragged breath. "I never had my soul mate or forever love. I never had that one person who woke with me and laughed with me and knew my every secret. I wanted it more than I ever let myself admit but I never, ever had it."

"You could have it right now." He wiped a tear from her cheek. "Maybe I'm the reason you were sent back after that accident, Lovely. Maybe God wanted you here to have these golden years with me. Have you thought of that?"

"A million times," she whispered. "But...the price is so high."

"Who cares?" He drew her closer, determined to get through and make her see. "Pay it and have everything you ever wanted. We'll wake up together and laugh together, Lovely. We'll write music and paint masterpieces and travel and laugh and sing and drink coffee and I'll never, ever let you go." He squeezed her tighter. "Let's make up for all those lost years by spending every single day we have left together. Please, Lovely, please. Who cares what it costs? Get on that plane with me and have the adventure of a lifetime. I love you so much and I will make you so happy."

She barely blinked as she listened to his impassioned speech, but when she did, tears meandered down her cheeks.

"I can't do that," she said softly. "The cost *is* too high. It's my people, my home, my very soul. I have my precious family, my beautiful beach, my comfortable home, and my whole world right here. I belong here, Eddie. I cannot and will not leave. I was born on Coconut Key, and I will die here."

"I know." He moaned the words, tasting defeat in the admission. "And to even expect you to is wrong."

"The same goes for you," she said, reaching up to cup his cheek in her smooth palm. "You, my darling Edward Sylvester, are a California boy, West Coast wild and free. And I will always love you and thank you not just for these two weeks but for the gift of Beck and all she brought into my life."

"She is indeed a blessing," he said. "We made a beautiful baby together. Just not a life."

"Oh, Eddie, darling. This is goodbye." She dropped her head against his shoulder with a sigh of resignation while a tune tickled the corners of his brain with lyrics now as familiar as his name.

He pressed his lips to her ear and whispered the lyrics he'd written during a different sunrise, not far from here.

Stars in the sky, stars in her eyes
girl in my arms, moon on the rise.
A secret kiss, I was never the same,
I can't forget her beautiful name.

He remembered that morning in Mallory Square, frantically climbing over sleeping teenagers, begging anyone awake if they'd seen the girl with green eyes and bangs. It had taken him fifty-seven years to find Lovely, and now...he'd lost her again.

HIS SUITCASE CLUNKED down the stairs of Coquina House and, as Eddie came around the corner, he heard Beck's easy laugh coming from the kitchen. And a man's voice with...an accent.

Had her Oliver come back?

Leaving the suitcase, he walked into the sunny room to find Mel and Jazz at the table with Beck and Oliver, laughing and chatting.

"Good morning, Pops," Jazz said, standing to greet him. "Even if it feels like afternoon."

"Long night for everyone." He walked to the table as Oliver stood. "You must be the elusive Aussie."

"G'day, mate," he replied with a grin, confirming the guess and proving he had exactly the wit and style that Beck deserved. "Sorry to meet you on departure day, Eddie. Good trip to Coconut Key?"

"Unforgettable," Eddie replied with a wistful smile. "And you're back sooner than expected."

"Couldn't stay away," the other man said, glancing at Beck. "In fact, I'm here for good. Officially one of the...what does Ava call them? Coconutters."

Melody laughed. "That sounds more like my girl Savannah than Ava."

As they all chuckled about Savannah's nicknames, Eddie tamped down the blues that threatened to strangle him.

"We just hope you'll all be back," Beck said, pushing up to come around the table to hug him. "Because a lot of us will miss you very much."

He held her, adding a squeeze, trying to memorize the feel and scent of his third—and oldest—daughter.

"Same." The word came out more gruffly than he wanted it to, making Beck regard him carefully.

"Tough goodbye?" she asked tenderly.

He gave a single nod.

"I'll go see her in a bit to cheer her up."

Swallowing against his tight throat, he stepped back and looked at Mel and Jazz. "Hate to break up the fun, but it's time to make the haul to Miami."

"If we must," Jazz said, reluctance in every syllable. "For

the record, all, I do not want to leave this place. I do not want to end vacation. And I do not want to wait years to come back. I have been cured of my workaholism and I don't even know what to do about it."

"Amen," Mel agreed. "On my next trip, I'm bringing my family. Lark and Kai will love this place."

"I like the sound of that," Beck said, turning to hug Jazz and Mel as they stood and brought the gathering to an end.

"Let's get our bags," Mel said.

"Nonsense," Oliver insisted. "I think I was officially promoted to Coquina House valet this morning, so I'll handle all the bags. You just hug and kiss and say your fond farewells."

They did all that, several times, between laughter and bittersweet embraces, eventually making their way out to the circular drive where Oliver had loaded the rented SUV for them.

With one more hug, the girls got in, with Jazz volunteering to drive.

Beck walked with Eddie to the open passenger door, both of them quiet for a moment.

"I do hope we'll see you soon, Ned," she said, a teasing smile in her eyes.

"I don't know about that, Beck."

Her smile disappeared. "You're not coming back?"

"I'm not sure my heart can take it," he confessed. "Goodbyes are too hard."

"Then come back and don't say goodbye," she said softly, reaching to hug him. "You are always welcome here."

"Thank you." He drew back and touched her cheek. "I'm as proud of you as my other daughters, you know.

You're a strong woman, a loving mother, a great hostess, and the image of your own mother, and I can't give you a greater compliment than that."

"Oh." She bit her lip. "I don't know what to say... except...thank you. For coming here, for giving us a chance, and for being so kind to Lovely."

"I left her in tears, so I don't know how kind I was."

She grimaced. "I'll take care of her."

"I know you will." He looked out to the horizon, his gaze snagged by the now infamous Beach Table where he'd revealed his identity to Lovely. "Just remember this, Beck. I didn't come here to wreak havoc, break hearts, or...fall in love. I honestly just wanted to meet you."

"I know," she said. "And who knows? Maybe one of you will change your mind. I mean, you both cut your hair, proving people do change!"

He laughed, but he knew no one was moving. He gave her a fatherly kiss on the top of her head, waved to Oliver, who stood on the veranda, and slid into the seat.

As they rolled down Coquina Court, he watched the little yellow cottage on the right come into view...and disappear when they turned the corner.

And though it's late, she won't forget
Maybe love was waiting...yet.

He was going to record *Yet* when he got home, he thought. And a whole lot of other songs he'd written. He'd make a whole album, press it in vinyl, and he would never forget this romantic, perfect interlude.

CHAPTER TWENTY-TWO
HEATHER

Kenny and Heather walked out of Pastor Allen's office holding hands, his closing words echoing.

Trust in the Lord with all your hearts...and marry each other on Saturday.

The pastor did not feel that Marc's decision not to attend should put the wedding on hold, although he was prepared to honor whatever they decided. Kenny didn't even think there was a decision to make—except whether or not he should get in his truck and bring Marc back.

With the wedding date just a few days away, Kenny would have to go...today.

Heather was torn. She'd talked to Marc almost every day since he left almost ten days ago, and frequently spoke to Andy. Those conversations, surprisingly, gave her the most peace and hope, since her father-in-law assured her Marc was doing well. She wished he was homesick for Coconut Key, but was relieved the time was healing him.

But that just hadn't happened quickly enough for them to keep this wedding day—unless they married without her son present. That didn't feel right at all.

"Let's stop in here," Kenny said, slowing at the door that led to the worship hall. "We always make our best decisions here."

He guided her into the cool and silent sanctuary that came to life every Sunday. Late-afternoon sun streamed in through the simple stained-glass windows, highlighting the wooden pews angled toward a small pulpit and the stage for the band.

He led her to the row where they'd once sat side by side and had their first kiss, which was now their favorite place to sit on Sundays.

Sliding in, they both leaned back and stared ahead, silent. She didn't know if Kenny was praying, and she couldn't quite bring herself to launch into yet another plea for God to give her what she wanted. Surely He'd heard her by now.

"It's hard to trust Him," Kenny finally said in a reverent whisper. "I mean, we use the word a lot. Pastor Allen just did. Trust Him. Let God show you the way."

She nodded. "I wish He would do that. Real clear, too. With no doubt."

Kenny sighed. "Plus, sometimes it's such a difficult path. We've both lost a spouse, and I've lost a son. There were times when I couldn't bear to look at that..." He jutted his chin toward the simple metal cross on a stacked stone wall. "But those losses led me to you. And on the darkest days after Elise and Adam died, I never dreamed He had you in mind for me."

The words warmed her. "I know. But what should we do, Kenny? Go after Marc and drag him here? Or just get married and show him the pictures, which will make all of us cry—including him, because that child is making a huge mistake."

"He is and I feel like it's my job to go get him," Kenny said. "Please let me go."

She sighed. "Let's call Andy when we get home. I haven't talked to him since yesterday morning. He said Marc was making progress and spending a lot of time talking about Drew. He's letting go of the last vestiges of the worst grief, something I guess he hadn't done in the last eighteen months."

"He's a deep kid," Kenny said. "He holds things in—I see it on the baseball field and in everyday life. But he needs to come home."

She exhaled and took his hand. "Will you pray?"

"Of course." He closed her hand in both of his, the strong grip as soothing as his deep voice as he addressed the Lord with reverence, awe, and love. He asked for wisdom, patience, and peace, and surprised her when he fervently thanked their Father for Grandpa Andy as a strong presence in Marc's life.

When he finished, she smiled at him. "Nice of you to see Andy as a blessing," she said. "He's such a strong tie to Drew and, in some sense, the very reason we're in this situation. I know it was Blanche who was the enabler, but it was Andy's age and health that Marc has been worried about."

"He's a good kid with a good heart," Kenny said, turning to the cross again. "I can't wait to call him my son."

Clinging to the beautiful words and the sense that the Holy Spirit was with them, they walked out and climbed into Kenny's truck.

"If Marc doesn't come back with you," Heather said when Kenny got in, "who's going to be your best man? We haven't talked about it."

"I was thinking about asking Josh," he said, referring to Heather's half-brother. "We've gotten pretty tight, but I assume with Marc not here, you'll want him to walk you down the aisle."

"I'm not a young girl being given away," she said. "I can walk myself down the aisle, and Josh can stand up for you. Have you asked him? It's getting late to spring that on a guy."

"We talked about it," he said. "But he agrees I should wait and see what happens with Marc. Josh'll step in at the last minute for our very small and kind of untraditional wedding."

She loved that their wedding was so intimate and informal. It was exactly what she wanted. Except she wanted Marc there, more than anything.

She tried not to think about the disappointment of him missing her wedding as Kenny drove the short distance home. She hated that anything clouded the day. There should be nothing but joy in her heart to join her life with this man's.

Smiling at him, she slipped her hand into his and looked out the window, her gaze sliding over her neighbors' houses, but still...all she could see was the one person who wouldn't be at her wedding. The one person—

"Um, Heather."

"Yeah?"

"Whose car is that?"

She squinted at the blue sedan in the driveway he'd turned into, not recognizing it...unless...wait a second.

"Oh! Oh, my goodness." She fumbled with the seatbelt even before he'd turned off the ignition. "Kenny! It's Andy's car!"

She barely waited for him to stop, flinging the heavy truck door wide and leaping down to the driveway, rushing to the front door that opened before she even got there.

"Marc!" Arms out, she ran to him, folding him in an embrace and covering his face with kisses. "You're home! You're here!"

He gave an awkward teenage boy laugh and returned the hug, then stepped back as Andy Monroe joined them.

"Surprise," he said. "I hope you don't mind that I drove him down without getting permission first."

"Mind?" Well, maybe she would have liked to have known, but it didn't matter. He was here—they both were.

Kenny hustled to join them, giving Marc a bear hug and shaking Andy's hand heartily.

"This is a wonderful surprise," he said, turning to Marc, who managed to look more than a little sheepish.

"Grandpa thought it was time I came home."

"Didn't you want to?" Heather asked, her heart squeezing.

He nodded. "I missed you, Mom. And..." He glanced at Andy, a loving look exchanged between them. "Grandpa and I have done a lot of...of..."

"Fishing," Andy said, making them all laugh. "And when you fish, you talk."

"I'm so glad," Heather said, pressing her fingers to her lips to keep from squealing with joy.

"Go ahead, Marc." Andy came a few steps closer to put a hand on his grandson's shoulder. "You promised me."

He shuffled from one sneakered foot to the other, letting out a sigh. "Mom, I'm really sorry I did that. I'm sorry I took off..." His voice grew thick from emotion. "It wasn't right, and I won't ever do anything that reckless again."

"Oh, honey." She threw her arms around him. "I forgive you. A thousand times, I forgive you."

"Really?" He drew back. "I'm not, like, grounded for life, off the baseball team, and no allowance?"

"I can't speak for the team," she said, glancing at Kenny. "Ask your coach. As far as being grounded, it's not my style. Plus, I need you to be somewhere on Saturday."

He took a deep breath. "The wedding?"

She nodded.

"Yeah, yeah, I'll be there. And, um..." He grunted and glanced at Andy, who gave him a classic "remember what we talked about" raised brow. "I'd like to do that...walk you down the aisle thing, if it's okay. I think it's what Dad would want."

Her heart soared, leaving her speechless. "Yes," she managed to say, reaching for him. "I would love that, Marc. I really would."

Over his shoulder, she caught Kenny taking a swipe under his eye. She clung to her son and closed her eyes, overwhelmed with love.

As they all walked inside, Andy hung back, putting his hand on Heather's arm to keep her outside a moment longer.

"You sure you're not mad I drove all the way down here without you knowing it?" he asked.

"I'm not," she promised him. "I wanted him here for the wedding so much, I simply can't thank you enough."

"And I know she can't say it or show it, but Blanche is really sorry. She knows she stepped out of bounds but doesn't have a clue how to issue an apology."

Heather closed her eyes, leaning on her faith to say the only thing someone who follows Christ could say. "She doesn't have to, Andy. She's forgiven."

He visibly relaxed. "I'm happy for you, Heather."

"You are?" She sighed. "Because I know it hasn't been that long..."

Taking her hand, he gave it a squeeze. "Marc and I *both* had to do a little soul-searching. I know the kind of woman you are—the kind of wife you were and mother you've been—and I want you to know that I think you deserve to be loved, protected, and taken care of. Ken's a good man and I don't think you're marrying him one minute too soon."

Suddenly, her heart felt light and whole, awash in peace and certainty. There it was—the very message she'd been waiting for, delivered loud and clear from the most unlikely source of Drew's own father.

"Thank you, Andy. You have no idea how much that means to me."

"He's gone far too young," he said, the grief clear in his voice, but no longer crippling. "But he'd want all of us to go on with life. And I think I persuaded Marc to realize that... and, to be honest, he did the same for me."

"I'm glad to hear that," she said.

"I guess we'll see how glad you are."

She looked at him, a frown pulling. "What do you mean?"

"I packed for a...long trip. I'd like to see what this Coconut Key deal is all about. I hear there's decent fishing."

"Yes, there is!" She felt her whole face light up with a smile. "That's wonderful news, Andy. Then you'll be at the wedding?"

"If there's a seat for me."

"Yes!" She put her arms around him and hugged him again, saying one of her future husband's favorite "three-worders."

Thank you, Lord.

CHAPTER TWENTY-THREE
BECK

"All my adult years, I thought I had three daughters and never dreamed I'd be the mother of the groom." Beck looked up at her handsome son, one hand on his broad shoulder, the other in his as they danced in the center of the Coquina Café. "Look how life surprises you, huh, Kenny?"

"We have Ava to thank for getting us together," he said, still unable to suppress the smile that he'd worn since the moment Heather had appeared at the back of the church a few hours earlier.

"And we can thank your mother, Janet," Beck said. "God bless that woman for keeping my name and sharing it with Ava. Otherwise…" She shook her head, slowing her feet a bit and maybe losing the rhythm to *You'll Be in My Heart*, the song the DJ told them was popular for mother-son dances. "We wouldn't be here right now."

He studied her for a long time, his smile finally waning. "We were both raised by women who weren't our biological mothers," he mused. "I guess you've thought about that before."

"Many times," she said. "Different circumstances but, yes, similar. And we turned out okay, huh?"

He didn't answer right away, still holding her gaze. "I think you know I loved my mom with my whole heart and soul," he said gruffly.

"Everything I've ever heard about Janet and Jim Gallagher was wonderful. Ava still talks about her grandmother with nothing but love."

He nodded. "Great woman, truly. But I want you to know something, Beck."

She held her breath, sensing she was about to get an emotional squeeze from whatever her son, a man of few words, was about to say. "Yes?"

"I love you as much as I loved my adoptive mother."

She bit her lip to stop the tears.

"I mean it," he said. "I know I got here with a bit of a chip on my shoulder—"

She laughed. "It didn't last long."

"How could it in the face of your unrelenting love?"

"Oh. Kenny. I loved you and Ava from the moment we met."

He gave her hand a squeeze. "I just want you to know that I may have had one mother for the first half of my life, but you have stepped in with grace and class for the second half. Thank you for that. And thank you for giving me Janet and Jim as parents. They were a brilliant choice."

She took in a deep breath and lifted her hand from his shoulder to wipe a tear as Phil Collins finished his ballad. "Well, we've hit every cliché here. The most popular cheesy song and you made me cry."

He leaned over and hugged her as applause broke out from the tables around the restaurant dining area that had filled as the guest list swelled from fifty to much closer to eighty. Beck hadn't even talked to everyone there yet.

Kenny gave her a sweet twirl and another hug.

"You're going to be a wonderful husband," she whispered into his ear.

"Only because I have a perfect wife," he countered.

They separated and Beck walked toward her table, seeing that Andy Monroe had taken her seat, chatting with Lovely.

"See? You see?"

She turned to find Maddie and Ava, both looking splendid in gorgeous dresses, doing their teenage girl quiet-clap like they did when they couldn't contain their excitement.

"See what?"

"Don't look!" Ava scooted two steps to the side, blocking Beck's view of the table.

She laughed and looked from one youthful and excited face to the other. "What am I not supposed to look at?"

"Lovely and Andy!" Maddie exclaimed in a breathy whisper. "Match made in heaven, thank you very much. My idea."

Ava shot her a look.

"It was," Maddie insisted.

"Maybe," Ava conceded. "But look how happy she is, Grandma Beck." She shifted her head an inch so Beck could see her mother smiling and nodding with Maddie's grandfather.

Was she happy? In the week or so since Eddie left, Lovely's laughter certainly seemed to be rare, and her smiles seemed forced. But only someone who knew her as well as Beck did would notice that.

"I'm telling you," Maddie said, taking another glance. "This will heal her broken heart."

Then again, maybe everyone could see that Lovely was hurting. "Oh, girls, I don't know if—"

"Ladies and gentlemen!" The DJ's voice broke into the conversation. They turned to look at him on the small platform in front of the dance floor Jessie had installed, turning the Coquina Café into a reception venue.

Heather and Kenny stood arm-in-arm next to the DJ. "After the mother of the groom dance, we traditionally have the bride and her father." As he took a breath, Beck's heart dropped. Didn't he know Heather's father wasn't here? That would be Jessie and Josh's father, too, who was notably absent and distant from that family. "And Heather has asked to have that dance with Andy Monroe."

At his name, Andy sat up straighter and everyone looked at him. He gave a soft laugh and said something to Lovely, slowly standing and making his way through the few tables to the dance floor.

Smiling, Heather walked out with her hand outstretched, the two of them lightly embracing for a poignant moment. How sweet of Heather to do that, Beck thought.

"Let's go talk to Lovely!" Ava said.

Beck glanced at her mother, seeing just enough pain in her eyes to know that a chatty fun "convo" with the matchmaking teenagers might not be what she needed most.

"Why don't you let me talk to her?" Beck said gently. "If there's any interest, I'll let you know."

"Of course," Ava said.

"But be sure to tell her he's really, really nice," Maddie said. "And he plays pickleball!"

Smiling at that, Beck threaded tables and chairs, taking the seat Andy had just left next to Lovely.

"You looked like you had fun with Kenny," Lovely said. "Good song choice."

Beck nodded. "He made me cry. And you looked like you were enjoying your conversation with Andy."

One brow flickered. "He's very nice. He did not make me cry, and after this week? That's a win."

"Oh, Lovely." Beck leaned in, hating the ache in her mother's voice.

"I'm fine, I'm fine," she insisted. "It's just weddings, Beck. They make a woman...long for things. Speaking of, Oliver just went to the men's room but he'll be—"

"Lovely." Beck put a hand over hers. "You don't have to do this. You don't have to miss him so much."

Her eyes shuttered. "I have no control over it, Beckie. It's like I've been...gutted."

"You should go see him," Beck said. "Go see what California is like. See the ranch, the winery. Meet his grandchildren. What's stopping you?"

She looked at Beck, a storm of emotions in her bottle-green eyes. "I'd love to say it's our business or this family or my desire or something as simple as the cost."

"What is it?" Beck pressed.

"Fear. I'm afraid I'll never come back. I'm afraid I won't be able to leave him."

"Lovely!" Beck crooned. "If you feel that way, then you have to go."

She closed her eyes and shook her head, turning to watch Heather and Andy share a warm dance to a slow country song.

Beck followed her gaze, her stomach tightening for how unhappy Lovely really was.

"I take it Maddie and Ava planning your wedding to Andy Monroe is a waste of time," she said, hoping to lighten the mood. "No chance?"

Lovely smiled, then released a heartfelt sigh. "I had no idea what chemistry was, Beckie. I didn't know it was fire and soul and as good as chocolate and better than a warm bath after a long day."

"Sounds like you're the one writing song lyrics now," Beck teased. "But I know what you're saying."

Just then, she spotted Oliver coming toward her with a woman a few steps behind him.

"Oh." Beck sat up straighter. "I didn't know Serena McFadden was here."

Before Lovely could respond, they reached the table and Beck rose to greet the other woman, who was resplendent in a fuchsia dress with a matching netted hat perched on her head.

"I had no idea you were coming," Beck said, giving her a hug.

"Neither did I, but I've been dating a firefighter who's friends with Kenny, and he asked me to be his plus one," she explained.

"And I convinced her it would be fine to come over here and talk to you," Oliver said, then leaned closer to Beck's ear. "But you'll still say no."

Beck frowned, gesturing for Serena to take one of the empty chairs at the table. "Why wouldn't you talk to me?"

"Because this is your son's wedding, and I don't want to discuss business. Plus, I know the answer already." She pointed at Lovely. "Did your daughter tell you she turned down a lot of money for Coquina House?"

"She did," Lovely said, smiling at Beck. "And I agree, you can't put a price on my childhood home or our booming business."

"And this buyer still won't let go?" Beck asked, smiling at Serena.

"Someone else has contacted me about buying the place, but no official offer."

"Our answer will never change."

Serena cocked a brow. "She threw around a number that was quite high. Like, stupid high. Do you want to know?"

For a moment, neither one of them spoke. Beck was about to give a resounding, "No!" but then she saw something in her mother's eyes. Pain mixed with...hope. Hope that could become a reality if they sold the place and freed her from all obligations.

"Sure," Beck said. "Doesn't hurt to hear a number."

"It'll hurt to hear this one," Serena joked. "'Cause it starts with a three and ends with a lot of zeros."

Beck's jaw dropped. Lovely's eyes widened. And Oliver smiled.

"I know the answer," he said. "But I thought you should know just how valuable the property is. If we want to take out a business loan and expand or put in a pool. There's a lot we could do with that kind of equity."

Or...buy out Lovely and free her to move to California? Beck glanced at her mother, who just gave a sweet smile.

"I don't care if the first number is a ten," Lovely said. "Or if there are more zeros than I can count. Coquina House is not for sale."

The words flooded Beck with an emotion she didn't quite understand. Not that she wanted to sell Coquina House, or use even that equity to make it bigger or better. She just knew that if Lovely were free...she might be happier.

And all Beck wanted in the world was for her mother to be happy.

"All right, family members!" The photographer cruised over to the table and gestured to them. "We're getting family dance photos. Let's make this fun!"

"That's my cue to leave," Serena said, standing and blowing them kisses. "Do the hokey pokey or something super cringe! And I'm sorry to barge into this event with business. Love ya!"

She headed off while they stood, something churning in Beck that she had to know. She had to.

"You go," she said to Lovely and Oliver. "I'll meet you in a minute." Snagging her evening bag, she hustled toward the fast-moving target of pink curves. "Serena!" she called. "Hang on."

The other woman turned and blinded Beck with a smile. "Second thoughts?" she asked with her dark brows high.

"No, no. I just..." She came closer and took Serena's hands. "I want to know the name of the buyer. Is it confidential?"

Serena let out a sigh. "Of course it is."

But Beck's gut was on fire. "Please. It would...help."

"Beck, I just—"

"Is the buyer in California?" she asked on a hunch.

Serena's reaction told her the hunch was right.

"Eddie?" Her voice rose as she thought of the only person who might have that kind of money.

"Jazz," Serena whispered. "And you did not hear that from me."

Jazz? Why? "Thanks, Serena."

As the other woman walked away, Beck turned to see her family—all her daughters, grandchildren, and the ever-growing clan gathering on the dance floor with much hilarity. Still acting on impulse, she slipped out the side door to the empty veranda, bathed in the moonlight that sparkled on the water.

Making sure she was alone out there, Beck pulled out her phone and scrolled for Jazz's number, pressing the talk button.

"Beck!" Jazz's voice filled her head. "Wait. Isn't tonight the wedding? What's up?"

"I'm at the wedding, Jazz, and you won't believe who's here."

"Not my father, I can tell you that. I just left his ranch and he's one unhappy camper. Who is it?"

"Serena. My Realtor. Apparently, she's dating a firefighter friend of Kenny's."

"Huh. That's... Oh, boy. I'm in trouble with my big sister, aren't I?"

Her heart shifted at being a big sister, reminding her that this woman was family—maybe not as close as the one dancing inside, but still family. And she had a good heart.

"I'm confused," Beck admitted. "Why would you throw a monkey-wrench into the works like that?"

"I didn't mean it to be," she said. "For one thing, I miss that heavenly little island. It was good for my soul."

"You can visit anytime. You could get a place here. But... mine? And Lovely's?"

"I just thought maybe you didn't want to sell to a stranger. But family? I knew Serena would tell you it was me if you pressed."

"She did," Beck confirmed.

"I thought it might interest you," Jazz said. "With that kind of cash, you're free. And so is Lovely, who might...come here and fix my poor Pops, because his heart is shattered."

Oh, she hated that both of them were so miserable. "I don't think this is the answer."

"No, probably not, but I'm a problem-solver by nature," she said. "I try everything until something works."

Beck stared at the silver streak of moonlight dancing on the water, inhaling the salty and familiar air.

"I don't think this problem can be solved," she finally said. "Not unless one of them is completely prepared to walk far, far away."

She heard Jazz's slow, sad sigh. "I know."

"Is he writing music?" Beck asked, thinking about her father's well-being almost as much as her mother's.

"He's writing, playing, singing, and producing," she said. "It's what he calls...a sea change. So, in that regard, Lovely brought him back to life."

"She's painting, too. But I don't—"

The sliding glass door opened, and Ava stuck her head out. "Everyone's waiting for you, Grandma Beck."

"I'll be right there, honey."

"You better go, Beck," Jazz said. "I hope you're not mad about me contacting Serena. It was a desperate attempt to make everyone happy. Including me."

"Come to Coconut Key anytime, Jazz," she said. "Bring Mel and her family and, of course, Eddie."

"Someday," she said. "Someday soon, I hope."

They said goodbye and Beck tucked the phone back into her bag and hustled toward the door.

The DJ had *We Are Family* blasting and the entire Foster-Sanchez-Frye-Ames-Bradshaw-Gallagher-Monroe clan was arm in arm, dancing and singing in the middle of the dance floor. Slightly apart from them, Lovely swayed with baby Rebecca in her arms, tears threatening as she watched the joy of her family.

Beck crossed the room, her own eyes misty, her arms outstretched as she hugged her daughters and kissed her grandkids and squeezed her son and sons-in-law and all the people she loved so very much.

Clapping her hands and singing the words, she sidled next to Lovely, who held a protective hand over the baby's head.

"You sure?" Beck mouthed.

"I'm not leaving," Lovely said simply. "Not for love or money, Beckie."

Or, in this case, *both*.

Lovely leaned over and kissed the baby, stepping away from the mayhem to let the younger people dance and sing.

Oliver slipped an arm around Beck, gave her a kiss, and brought her into the group photo as they all belted out the only words that mattered: *We are family!*

They sure were.

CHAPTER TWENTY-FOUR
LOVELY

The breeze floated through the screened patio, stronger now that it was springtime. Strong enough to flutter Lovely's growing bangs, tickling her forehead and blocking the phone screen angled at the bottom of her easel so she could see it while she painted.

Her two-month painting binge continued as she attempted to recreate yet another picture she had saved on her cell phone. She was usually a landscape and abstract kind of painter, but this new calendar year brought a different kind of inspiration: portraits. And memories.

She turned and looked at the new addition to her wall—a painting she'd just completed of Vesper the dolphin leaping in the air. Lovely had snapped the photo the day she and Eddie had gone swimming with the dolphins, then painted it in February. Last week, she'd finished a nightscape of fireworks and footsteps in the sand, and hung it in her bedroom.

Was Eddie writing songs about his interlude in Coconut Key, the way she was painting pictures? She didn't know. Their calls and texts had dwindled to next to nothing—it was too painful to try and love each other three thousand miles apart.

It was better, they both knew, to just let this end naturally.

Although, that wasn't easy, and she'd thrown herself into painting.

Today, she was tackling faces—something she didn't do too frequently. But this picture, of Beck with her arms draped over Jazz and Mel's shoulders, captured such a happy moment. An instant of sisterhood, she thought. And that would be a great title for this painting, which she planned to give to Beck.

She'd never completed the seascape she'd been working on when Eddie was here. She'd promised to mail it to him when she did, but now, it leaned against the wall out here on the patio, just the unfinished sky visible over the back of the sofa

She turned to look at it, to consider working on it today, but all she could see was the misty memory of a man who sat on those flowered cushions, strumming and singing.

He'd held that used guitar that now resided in her front closet, his fingers pausing mid-chord as he grabbed a pen and jotted something in a notebook. Then he'd warble new lyrics, testing them out for her...

It's the whisper of truth
Between you and me...
The quiet words
That set us free...

But had the truth *really* set Lovely free? Had knowing Beck's biological father and then falling in love with him given her freedom? Or had it transformed her precious, cozy cottage into a lonely prison?

She turned away, determined to finish that painting someday and send it to him. In fact, maybe she'd redecorate this whole screened patio so it no longer—

Pepper barked, jogging to the door. Over and over, she let out the steady bark that warned of an intruder.

On a Tuesday afternoon?

She waited for a knock or the bell but didn't hear a thing, and Pepper wouldn't stop. She dabbed the tip of her brush before laying it on her paint plate. Pushing those annoying bangs out of her eyes, she stood.

"Hush, Pepper! No one's out there."

She wouldn't stop. And Basil had joined in now. Sugar was on a chair in the sun, caring about nothing except that she had a view of Lovely.

She unlatched the door and inched it open so the dogs didn't shoot out, looking left and right, closing her eyes as disappointment punched.

What did she think? That one of these days she'd open her door...and Eddie would be standing there with roses and promises and a changed heart?

Yes, in her deepest, darkest dreams. That's exactly what she'd hoped. Surely those girlish fantasies would fade with time.

Looking down so she didn't catch a dog's nose in the door, she did a double-take at a brown box leaning against the door jamb. She hadn't heard UPS roll in, and that delivery man always knocked.

Bending over, she lifted the package, which was shaped like a pizza box but was sealed shut. She squinted at the label, handwritten and addressed to her, with no return address. What had she ordered?

Paint supplies? Wouldn't she remember that?

Taking it to the kitchen, she snagged her utility knife and sliced the box along the side, slowly lifting the lid to reveal a bed of teal tissue.

The paper rustled as she moved it to the side, surprised her hands were trembling. What was she expecting?

Oh. Oh. Certainly not this.

She stared at the flat, square image, instantly recognizing it as the yellow vinyl album cover, one she'd held in her hands a million times. Joni Mitchell's *Court and Spark*. But then she gasped at the scratch of black sharpie on the lower right corner.

For Lovely—
A forever fan!
Love, Joni

"Well, what do you know? A signed album from Joni Mitchell. What an incredible gift."

But instead of gratitude, guilt squeezed her chest. Eddie had the class and style to put the perfect ribbon on their romance, and she couldn't even bring herself to finish the painting she'd promised him.

Today, she swore. She'd put the portrait of the girls away and pull out the seascape and finish it. She had to. It would be closure, which surely was what this record represented.

She smiled at the autograph, and only then noticed a small, folded card attached to the top corner of the jacket. She picked it up, studying the embossed Sly Records logo, wondering for a moment if Mel had sent this for him.

She flipped open the card and read the handwritten words.

A little Joni in case you don't like the one underneath!
—E

In case... What was he talking about?

She lifted the album jacket and stared, speechless, as the blood drained from her face.

Another album jacket, totally unfamiliar. Well, not *totally*. The art was certainly familiar.

Setting Joni aside, she stared at the white background that somehow melted into a half-painted canvas. *Her* half-painted canvas. It was a replica of the unfinished version of the very seascape she'd just been staring at.

He'd used a picture of her work-in-progress as the cover of an album?

Gingerly, she lifted the jacket from the tissue, letting out a whimper when she read the words *Sea Change* embossed in classy capital letters across the middle. And at the bottom... Eddie Sly.

Tears blurred her vision as she pressed the vinyl jacket to her chest, dizzy for a moment. He'd recorded an album! And used her art for the cover!

She turned it over slowly, taking in the turquoise colors of water she knew so well, squinting at the song list on the back.

Whisper of Truth
Yet
Walk in the Moonlight
Sea Change (Title track)
Too Short
Seafoam Green
A Trip to Heaven

Was that one about his visit here, or hers to heaven, she wondered, blinking at tears as she read the rest.

Our Interlude
Her Name Was Lovely (Remix)
Vesper and Gilligan, A Love Story

"Oh! He made music about the dolphins, too!" For some

reason, that sent her over the edge, making her fight a sob she'd stifled for two months.

Grazing her fingertips over the embossed words, she carried the album to her record player.

With shaky hands and total reverence, she slid the disc from the jacket and saw the Sly Records logo on the label in the middle.

Not a CD, not a digital stream—a *vinyl* record. He'd told her that they were popular again and Sly Records pressed them all the time, but she never imagined *this*.

Oh, she'd never imagined *him*, let alone feeling this way about a man three thousand miles away. At her age. It was ridiculous...but it was real.

Swallowing and swiping a tear, she set the record down on the turntable, switched it on, and stepped back, not sure what this would do to her heart other than wreck it.

A rise of strings opened the first song, then a simple piano, then the guitar chords she recognized.

Hear the tremble in my voice,
I'm changing life with a choice...

But she didn't hear a tremble in his voice. The vocals were clear and crisp, bold and rich. The voice she'd heard sing "her" song for most of her life, and the voice she'd heard playing with lyrics over and over again.

The night is still, the stars align,
I tell the truth and your eyes shine.

His voice filled the room, backed up by a mix of instruments that melded together like the angels themselves played them.

She closed her eyes and just let the emotions and music wash over her, the beauty of hearing what had started as a single phrase turn into a glorious song that evoked emotion and dreams and memories.

It's the truth that sets us free,
Quiet words between you and me.

The chorus was familiar to her, even though she'd never heard it mixed and drenched in that haunting piano.

I never thought I'd let it show,
Never thought that you would know.

Of course he didn't. He came here thinking "Lovely" was "Olivia," who was long dead. But she'd surprised him, she thought with a wistful smile. And, wow. He sure had surprised her.

She listened to the last verse, to her favorite lines...

But love can live where shadows lie,
Tonight I'll let the silence die.
And whisper truth about our past,
And hope it brings love at last.

"But it didn't, Eddie," she sighed as the guitar and piano grew to a crescendo. "In the end, it didn't bring love. Not lasting love, anyway."

She pressed the album to her chest and closed her eyes, not surprised the tears flowed as she let his voice carry her through the final chorus.

It's the whisper of truth that sets us free...

But it hadn't set her free. It made her a prisoner!

The gentle breath that lets love be...

But there was no love!

She sang the last two lines, the words bubbling up from her memory.

"I thought I'd..." She stopped mid-word—because they

didn't match the song she heard and Pepper barked. What was Eddie singing?

It changed my heart and cleared the way,
And now, my love, I'm here to stay.

What? That wasn't the right line. He said—

"I changed the ending."

She gasped at the sound of Eddie's voice on the patio, close enough to make her heart soar, shock and disbelief freezing her in place.

"I didn't like it," he continued, the sound a little closer. "I don't like sad endings to a masterpiece of...anything. Music, painting, stories...romance. So I decided on a different ending."

Very, very slowly she turned to find him standing in the living room with three dogs in his arms, licking whatever they could get to in an effort to express their unspeakable joy at the sight of him.

And if Lovely could, she'd do just about the same thing.

For a moment, neither spoke. They just looked at each other as the last few notes faded out. Lovely could feel her heart hammering her ribs, the blood rushing in her head, and the echo of his words.

So I decided on a different ending.

"Eddie," she breathed his name.

Wordlessly, he lowered the dogs to the floor, giving them a chance to bark and circle him and run to Lovely as if to say, "Look who's here!"

He took a few steps closer, his sky-blue eyes leveled on her with nothing but love and humor and hope shining through.

"Do you like the new ending?"

"Eddie..." She pressed her hands to her lips, blinking at him.

"I mean, we could still change it. That's first-press vinyl and I own the studio, so change isn't an issue." He fought a smile as he came closer. "I could go back to the old ending, which, if you ask me, was sad and kind of...meaningless."

He was one foot in front of her—real and beautiful and close and perfect.

"That's the cool thing about art. And life and love. We have the power to change the notes, the words, and...the meaning. So I dropped that old line about knowing what has to be and now it's... 'It changed my heart and cleared the way, and now, my love, I'm here...*to stay*.' Did you get that or were the dogs barking? I tried to time it right, but Pepper, you know. She's a barker."

"I heard it."

"And do you like that better? Do you like this new ending to our song and story?"

She closed her eyes as he wrapped his arms around her and she slid her hands around his neck, looking up at this man who surprised and delighted and, oh, yes, loved her.

"I think I love this ending," she whispered. "I'm having a hard time believing it's real, but I love it."

"Oh, it's real." He cupped his hand on her cheek. "I'm here and I have no plans to leave."

She angled her head into his touch. His soft, sweet, loving touch. "How is that possible?"

"Anything is possible, Lovely. We were all touched by the magic of Coconut Key, so Jazz has decided to buy a house here."

"She has?"

"It's not big, but it's on that same beach as The Haven, and there's room for my California Contingent to visit frequently. She wants a permanent tenant, and you're looking at him."

"I am?"

He laughed softly at her incredulity. "Yes, I am. There's room for a small recording studio—because now that the bug has bitten, I can't stop—and lots and lots of outdoor space to paint and cook and listen to music and laugh and spend the rest of whatever time we have left...together."

She swayed in his arms. "You'll do that? For me?"

"For you, for me, and for my family. My grandson, Kai, is going to come out here for the summer, and who knows? We might start Sly Records East. Or we might just go kayaking and count stars at night. I don't really care, as long as I'm with you. They all agree."

"Eddie..." She wanted to cry, but had to laugh. "You're... too much."

"What I am," he said, adding pressure to his embrace, "is in love. And without you, I'm nothing. With you, I'm alive. Lovely, I don't know how many years we have left, but I do know that I want to spend every one of them with you."

"Oh, are you sure?" Because this really felt too good to be true. At least for Lovely, who'd never known that love could feel like this. "Your family and your ranch and the winery?"

"My family wants me to be happy again, and really encouraged me to make the move. Lark's moving into my ranch, and I have a manager who handles things. The winery is really my ex-wife's baby. I don't make wine. I make music." He kissed her on the forehead. "You need a trim, gorgeous."

She smiled. "Good thing my hairdresser is back."

"I am." He kissed her cheek and hugged her against him. "I can't do it, Lovely," he murmured into her ear. "I can't live on the other side of the country while the woman I love is here. I can't pretend to be happy without you. I can't spend the rest of my life anywhere but with you. So I changed the ending...to the song and to my life. And, hopefully, yours, if you'll let me."

"Yes," she whispered, then dropped her head back and let out a laugh. "I've never been so happy!"

"There's the minor chord I love." He drew her right back in and kissed her as the next song on the album started.

Without missing a beat, he wrapped his arm around her and took her right hand, dancing with her like the lover she once could only dream she would someday have.

"Is this real?" she whispered, dropping her head on his shoulder. "Is this happening to me?"

He gave a soft laugh as the lyrics to *Yet* filled the room.

And though the sea would pull her near,
The salt and sand erased her fear.

He added a soft kiss and Lovely hummed the last line with him.

She thought she'd drift with no regret,
But could love be waiting yet?

Held in his arms, they swayed in the afternoon sun. She lost herself in the tender words, the glorious future, and this dear, dear man who'd brought a sea change to her life.

Finally, it all made sense.

After seventy-five years of waiting, Lovely Ames had found her one true love.

Love Coconut Key? Looking for more from Hope Holloway? Visit www.hopeholloway.com for information on *all* her series. You can sign up for her newsletter and get the latest on new releases, excerpts, and more! Sign up today and you'll also receive a special surprise — Jessie's crab cake recipe! Straight from her kitchen to yours!

THE COCONUT KEY SERIES

Set in the heart of the Florida Keys, these delightful novels will make you laugh out loud, wipe a happy tear, and believe in all the hope and happiness of a second chance at life.

A Secret in the Keys – Book 1
A Reunion in the Keys – Book 2
A Season in the Keys – Book 3
A Haven in the Keys – Book 4
A Return to the Keys – Book 5
A Wedding in the Keys – Book 6
A Promise in the Keys – Book 7
A New Year in the Keys - Book 8

THE SHELLSEEKER BEACH SERIES

Meet a "found family" that will steal your heart and have you wishing you could move to Sanibel Island!

Sanibel Dreams - Book 1
Sanibel Treasures - Book 2
Sanibel Mornings – Book 3
Sanibel Sisters – Book 4
Sanibel Tides – Book 5
Sanibel Sunsets – Book 6
Sanibel Moonlight – Book 7

THE SEVEN SISTERS SERIES

Fall in love with these strong, hilarious, unforgettable sisters on Amelia Island who love each other unconditionally and face every crisis as a family!

The Beach House on Amelia Island - Book 1
The Café on Amelia Island - Book 2
The Bookstore on Amelia Island - Book 3
The Florist on Amelia Island - Book 4
The Chocolate Shop on Amelia Island - Book 5
The Dressmaker on Amelia Island - Book 6
The Inn on Amelia Island - Book 7

THE CAROLINA CHRISTMAS SERIES

Enjoy a charming, heartwarming mountain Christmas co-authored by Hope Holloway and Cecelia Scott.

The Asheville Christmas Cabin – Book 1
The Asheville Christmas Gift – Book 2
The Asheville Christmas Wedding – Book 3
The Asheville Tradition - Book 4

ABOUT THE AUTHOR

Hope Holloway is the author of charming, heartwarming women's fiction featuring unforgettable families and friends and the emotional challenges they conquer. After a long career in marketing, she gave up writing ad copy to launch a writing career with her first series, Coconut Key, set on the sun-washed beaches of the Florida Keys. Since then, she's written nearly thirty novels in multiple series and has become a beloved bestselling author.

A mother of two adult children, Hope and her husband of thirty years live in Florida. When not writing, she can be found walking the beach with her two rescue dogs, who beg her to include animals in every book. Visit her site at www.hopeholloway.com.

Made in the USA
Columbia, SC
22 December 2024

50484082R00188